"You went out t

She hesitated, looking away. "Sure did."

"I thought I made it clear it wasn't safe—"

"Yes, you made everything crystal clear, Red."

He blinked at the sharpness in her voice.

"You didn't tell me about the vandalism, and you never gave me any reason for why you think Dad was killed. What else didn't you tell me about?"

He couldn't hold her gaze.

She shrugged. "That's what I thought." Her voice softened. "Anyway, I'll get some comfrey for your leg."

Something inside him relaxed, some burning pain eased, and he hadn't even realized it was there. She'd been thrown for a loop, seeing him with his injured leg yesterday without any warning, but now her healing instincts were kicking in. She did still care about him.

As soon as the thought came into his mind, he dashed it away. He had no right to her healing touch. He had no rights at all.

Books by Hannah Alexander

Love Inspired Historical	Steeple Hill Single Title
Hideaway Home #3	*Hideaway*
	Safe Haven
Love Inspired Suspense	*Last Resort*
Note of Peril #1	*Fair Warning*
Under Suspicion #25	*Grave Risk*
Death Benefits #60	*Double Blind*

HANNAH ALEXANDER

is the pseudonym of husband-and-wife writing team Cheryl and Mel Hodde (pronounced Hoddee). When they first met, Mel had just begun his new job as an ER doctor in Cheryl's hometown, and Cheryl was working on a novel. Cheryl's matchmaking pastor set them up on an unexpected blind date at a local restaurant. Surprised by the sneak attack, Cheryl blurted the first thing that occurred to her: "You're a doctor? Could you help me paralyze someone?" Mel was shocked. "Only temporarily, of course," she explained when she saw his expression. "And only fictitiously. I'm writing a novel."

They began brainstorming immediately. Eighteen months later they were married, and the novels they set in imaginary Ozark towns began to sell. The first novel in the Hideaway series, published in the Steeple Hill Single Title program, won the prestigious Christy Award for Best Romance in 2004.

HANNAH ALEXANDER

Hideaway Home

Steeple
Hill®

Published by Steeple Hill Books™

STEEPLE HILL BOOKS

Steeple
Hill®

ISBN-13: 978-0-373-82783-1
ISBN-10:   0-373-82783-0

HIDEAWAY HOME

www.SteepleHill.com

Printed in U.S.A.

And the God of all grace, who called you
to his eternal glory in Christ, after you have
suffered a little while, will himself restore you
and make you strong, firm and steadfast.
—1 *Peter* 5:10

We wish to honor our loved ones who risked
everything for our country's freedom
in World War II: Ralph Hodde, Larry Baugher,
Irwin Baugher, Loy Baugher, Cecil James,
Leonard Wesson and Glen Jones.

Acknowledgments

We're so grateful for our editor, Joan Marlow Golan,
her exceptional staff and for our agent,
Karen Solem, who help us make our books
the best they can be.

We thank Lorene Cook, who helped us
establish the authenticity of our story and patiently
answered late-night calls with questions about
"the way it was back then."

Ray Brown, Barbara Warren, Lee McCormick,
Soni Copeland, Mike Hemphill and Jackie Bolton
shared their memories, their knowledge, their
expertise and their historical material for this story.
We will always be grateful for their generosity.

Chapter One

Something was wrong. The news hadn't reached California yet, but Bertie Moennig knew something had happened. She couldn't pinpoint when she'd decided she wasn't jumping to conclusions, but her instincts had never failed her. She would have to wait and see.

It frustrated her no end, because she didn't like to wait for anything. Still…in the midst of this wretched war, she'd grown accustomed to it.

Bertie paused in the noisy workroom of Hughes Aircraft to untie the blue bandana from her head. Her hairnet had ripped this morning, too late for her to get a replacement, and there were strict regulations about keeping long hair restrained.

Now, half of her bun had fallen down over her neck and shoulders. As if this plant wasn't already hot enough! Folks liked to chatter on and on about the wonderful weather in Southern California; those folks must've never worked in a busy, noisy aircraft plant on a sunny day.

Another trickle of perspiration dripped along the side of Bertie's face, and she rubbed her cheek against her shoulder while fiddling with the bandana. She'd take a summer after-noon on the farm in the Missouri Ozarks over working in the heat of this plant any day.

Not that she disliked California. She loved it most of the time—the weather, the ocean, the mountains—but it could be a challenge for a country girl to get used to the crush of people and traffic, even after living here for eight months.

In Hideaway, Missouri, Bertie would've ridden her bicycle the three miles to work, but here she saw more cars passing by the apartment than she would see in a year back home. The crazy pace of Southern California had shocked her upon arrival and—

"Hey, hillbilly!"

She winced at the sound of the barrel voice approaching from behind her. Looking around, then up at the department supervisor, Franklin Parrish, she braced herself for yet another earful of complaining.

"Yessir?"

"Get back to work. And get that hair up," he snapped, looming too close, as he always did. He eyed the blond hair that fell around her shoulders, then his gaze wandered.

Even though he mocked her Ozark accent and figures of speech, he made no secret of the fact he liked her figure well enough.

She tied her hair back on top of her head. "A man in your position should mind his manners, Mr. Parrish," she said quietly, wishing Edith Frost, her roommate, was here. She'd have an extra hairnet.

Franklin leaned closer to Bertie, his face flushed like that of a child who'd been caught snooping in his mother's purse. "And you'd better mind who you're talking to, hillbilly. I can turn you out of here by signing the bottom line of a little sheet of paper."

Bertie met his gaze, trying hard not to show her irritation. After three hundred hours of instruction in St. Louis, she'd been sent here as a trained machinist at the company's expense. If he fired her for no good reason, he'd have to answer for his actions.

"You want these parts to pass inspection, don't you?" she asked. "We still have a war to win against the Japanese, and I aim to help win it." She knew she should smile to take the bite out of her words, but she held his gaze, straight-faced.

Franklin glowered. Bertie nipped on her tongue to keep it from getting her into deeper trouble. Franklin grunted and walked away.

Bertie sighed. Someday, she'd go too far, but she didn't think that day had come yet. Years ago, her mother had tried to tell her that a woman could get more accomplished with honey than with vinegar, but Bertie had found that the two mixed well together. That was especially true for a woman working in a man's world.

Besides, Mom never had depended strictly on honey to get what she wanted. When she was alive, Dad used to brag to the other farmers down at the coffee shop that his wife was full of more sass and vinegar than any plow mule in the county. Just recently, he'd accused Bertie of taking after her mother a little too much.

Those words had made Bertie proud, and it had given her courage to know that she had some of the same strength of character as Marty Moennig.

She felt a pang of homesickness. She missed her father and couldn't stop worrying about him. She'd tried to place this dread in God's hands several times last night and this morning, but her mind kept grabbing it back again. *Where was he?*

She also missed Red Meyer like crazy, and thinking about him raised her anxiety even more. Though Red was some-where in Italy, cleaning up after the surrender of the Germans last month, she knew she would feel closer to him if he was back home in Hideaway.

Of course, if Red was back in Hideaway, she'd be there, too. So many memories…so much she missed. She wanted to be able to step out of the house and stroll around the victory garden in the backyard. Had Dad even been able to plant one this year? He was all alone on the farm, with so much work to keep him busy.

Fact was, she worried about both the men in her life. News of Red hadn't come often enough to suit her lately. He'd stopped writing to her. Just like that, the letters had quit coming. She was pretty sure the Army hadn't suddenly stopped sending soldiers' mail home.

Charles Frederick Meyer didn't like being called anything but Red. With a head of brick-colored hair and a blue gaze that looked straight into the soul, he was strong and kind, and quick with a smile or a joke.

Bertie could usually spend much of her workday think-ing about him, dreaming of the time they would be back together again. That was easier to do now that the war with Germany was over.

But if he was out of danger, why wasn't he writing?

Red Meyer stared out the train window at the lush Mis-souri Ozark landscape, nearly lulled to sleep by the gentle rocking of the passenger railcar. The train took a curve, and he got a better look at the cars ahead of him. Four cars forward, one lone figure with the straight, stiff posture of the military, made his way to the rear exit.

Looked like at least one other person on this train was as restless as Red, but he didn't have the luxury of pacing along the aisles from railcar to railcar.

Instead, he tugged one of the envelopes from his left front pocket and pulled two folded pages from the raggedly slit top. Gently, he unfolded the sheets and looked at the handwriting.

He didn't read the words right off. He didn't need to. He practically had this letter memorized—maybe not every single fancy swirl and dotted *i*, but he could see an image in his mind of Bertie Moennig leaning over her stationery, chewing on the end of her pencil, eyes narrowed. It had been her first letter to him, and it was well nigh three years old. The smudges and worn corners of the pages showed how often he'd handled them.

Dear Red,

I'm sitting here at the station in Hollister, watching your train pull away, trying hard not to get the paper wet with my tears. If you ever show this letter to anybody, I'll make you pay when you get back home.

He'd laughed at that when he first read it, but he'd not been able to see the page very well for a few lines, himself.

I already miss you so much I want to run after the caboose and hop on, the way we did ten years ago. Remember how much trouble we got into when the train didn't stop until it reached Springfield?

Red nodded to himself. He remembered. Gerald Potts had had to drive up to get them, and then all the way home he'd lectured them about the stupidity of risking their lives for a lark. Neither of them had ever told Gerald that his own son,

Ivan, was the one who'd dared them to hop that train in the first place.

We've been friends for so long, Red, I can't imagine going on without you. You can make me feel better no matter how bad things are, even with Mom's funeral only weeks past. I don't know how I'd have gotten through it without you.

He squeezed the pages between his fingers and stared out at the passing countryside. He couldn't remember a time when Bertie wasn't in his life, whether she was socking him in the mouth for picking on her in their Sunday school class, or kissing him goodbye twelve years later at the train station, chin wobbling, eyes promising more than he'd ever dared ask of her. A future.

He looked back down at the letter, swallowing hard as he recalled her face, her voice, the love he'd held on to for so many long, hellacious months.

Red, you remember that talk we had on our first real date? You should, since it's only been a couple of months. You told me you'd always thought you'd end up a bachelor, because you never thought you had anything special to offer a woman in marriage. But you are somebody special, and don't let anybody ever tell you different.

His eyes squeezed shut. He'd never loved her more than he did right now. She'd been so true to him all this time. Her letters…they'd been his lifeline. Her love was what kept him going and kept his determination strong to do the right thing by her, though it was the hardest thing he'd ever have to do.

I've heard they treat soldiers rough in the Army, but you're strong enough to take whatever they throw at you. Don't you forget you're more of a man than most men ever even dream of being. You've got more heart in you than anybody I've ever known, and you'd make a fine husband. The woman who marries you will never be sorry. Just make sure you get home alive to get married.

I'll be waiting here for you, and I'll be writing so much you'll probably get tired of reading my letters. If anything happens to you, it'll be happening to me, too, so you'd better take care. You have both our lives in your hands.

If he'd smiled at all during these past three years, it had only been because of her. Oh, sure, he'd let himself joke with the guys, or at least chuckle at their jokes, but it was because thoughts of home kept him going—thoughts of Bertie.

He didn't pay any attention to the man in Marine uniform coming down the aisle, until that man plunked himself down in the empty seat next to Red.

"On your way home, soldier?" came an awfully familiar voice.

Red's head jerked up. He looked with surprise into the face of his good friend Ivan Potts, in the flesh.

Before Red could say anything, Ivan had him in a bear hug and was thumping him on the back so hard it felt like Red's spine might snap in two. The man had the muscles of a plow horse.

"I didn't know you were on this train 'til I caught sight of your face in the window when we went around that last curve." Ivan's grin showed the contrast of his white teeth against dark-tanned skin. "Thought it was you, anyway." He rubbed his knuckles over Red's scalp. "Can't miss this color, Charles Frederick."

"Well, if this don't beat all." Red tucked the letter back into his pocket, trying not to let it catch Ivan's attention. He shoved the cane out of sight beneath his seat with his foot. Happy as he was to see one of his closest friends alive and whole, he wasn't ready to do any explaining. Not yet.

Chapter Two

Red grinned at his old buddy—the first time his face had felt a smile in days. He almost expected to feel his lips crack, but they held firm. It was good to see Ivan all decked out in his uniform, with medals aplenty, some as golden as the hair on his head.

"Man, oh, man, I've missed you," Red said.

"Same here. Heard you won the war on your side of the world," Ivan said, clapping Red on the shoulder. "Now come and help us with ours. The Pacific's still hot."

Red felt his smile slip. "You're not home for good?"

"How I wish!"

Red's stomach clenched with fresh worry. He'd been relieved when he first saw Ivan, alive and well. "You're home on leave, then?" That wasn't what he wanted to hear.

Ivan nodded. Something seemed to darken in the deep brown of his eyes. "One week, then I'm back in the trenches."

"Maybe we'll have won the Pacific by then."

The grin returned. "Isn't going to happen without my

help. I want to make sure the blue star my folks have in the window at home doesn't get exchanged for a gold one."

"I think you're too ornery to die," Red said. "But you'd best take care, anyways." It might destroy Gerald and Arielle Potts if anything happened to their only child. They'd always doted on him.

Ivan had been the most rambunctious of Red's friends throughout their school years, leading the gang when it came to childish pranks, overnight hunting parties and outhouse tipping. He'd given his poor parents a lot of grief. Red recalled one night when Ivan had sneaked a cow from the barn of a local farmer into a high-school classroom. It wasn't discovered until the morning—along with a big mess.

"I've made it this far." Ivan's voice snapped Red from his memories. "I plan to make it through this war alive."

Once more, Red eyed the decorations on his friend's chest. Ivan Potts had a right to be proud of the medals he'd earned. He'd proven himself to be a man in this war, and his parents would be more than proud.

Red's medals were packed away in the duffle under his feet. He wore his regular uniform instead of military dress, and he had kept his head down most times on the trip home, hoping nobody'd notice him and start asking questions. The last thing he wanted to do was talk about the war. Or talk about anything, for that matter.

War sure changed people.

All his life, Red had started conversations easily with strangers, never running out of something to talk about. But that had been a different Charles Frederick Meyer.

Ivan glanced out the window. "We're getting close."

Red nodded, rubbing sweat from his forehead as the sunlight beat down through the window. "It's nice to be nearing home, sure enough." The hills got a little taller, the valleys deeper in the southwest part of Missouri.

"I can't wait to be back for good," Ivan said. "How about you, Red? Are you coming home to stay, or do they have plans for you over on our side of the world? To hear Bertie tell it, the Army can't do without you."

Red warmed at that but he didn't know what to say now. "War's over for me, probably." He couldn't bring himself to explain why.

It'd be easy for a man in his shape to think he wasn't worth much of anything anymore, since he probably wouldn't even be able to do the work that needed doing at home now, much less help tidy things up after the ruin of a whole continent. He'd wanted to be there still, liberating the prisoners and helping set things in order again.

He squeezed his eyes shut against the June morning sun, but he opened them again quickly, and caught Ivan watching him.

"I don't think the war will ever be over for us," Ivan said, his voice suddenly soft. "It follows a guy wherever he goes."

Red nodded. The nightmares...

"Thanks to Bertie and her friends, I've kept up with your whereabouts most of the year," Ivan said. "How's Italy?"

"Hardly anything there anymore," Red said. "Except the mud and rubble of wrecked buildings. Always the mud. Heard you took Iwo Jima."

Pain crossed Ivan's features, and Red knew he'd said the wrong thing. Would life ever get back to the way it had been, when everyone didn't have to tiptoe around minefields of conversation?

"You don't have to answer that," Red told him.

Ivan nodded slowly. He swallowed and met Red's gaze with a fierce stare. Then he looked down and swallowed again.

"We were landing on the beach," he said, his voice so soft Red had to strain to hear. "Next thing I knew, the night sky seemed to explode all around us."

Red winced. He knew what that meant.

"Five of my best buddies were killed before I could move." The words seemed to spring from Ivan—fast, hard, his voice low—as if he'd been bottling them up inside.

Red studied his friend, but didn't see any signs of damage, no Purple Heart. "But they didn't get you."

Ivan shook his head. "Sometimes I think it would've been better if I'd gotten a bullet, too."

"No, it wouldn't." But Red understood.

Ivan glanced at Red, eyes narrowing. "What's your worst memory?"

Red couldn't tell him. He could probably never tell anybody. So he pulled out another recollection. "German soldiers surrounding our fire support team."

The surprise didn't show in Ivan's eyes as much as it did in the sudden jutting of his strong chin—as if bracing himself for details. "You were captured."

"It's been a couple of months." Even now, Red could picture in his mind the grim, white faces of his captors. He could feel the fear licking at his insides, almost feel the rough hands shoving him and Conner and Beall through fields of mud.

"When?" Ivan asked. "Why didn't I hear about it? Bertie would have told me about it in a letter." He looked at Red's uniform for the first time. "Where are your medals?"

Red shrugged. "It don't matter. I'm alive. Before word could be carried back home that we were prisoners of war, we escaped in the middle of the night."

Ivan gave a low whistle. "If that doesn't beat all."

"Just in time, too. I got the impression, picking up on some of their words, that they'd planned to kill us soon."

"You speak German?"

Red nodded. "I learned some words from my pa years ago. I hadn't even realized I remembered them until I listened to our captors talking to one another. There were five of them and only three of us. I thought we were goners."

"How'd you get away?"

Red shrugged. He couldn't talk about the whole thing. "The fifth night, after a long day's march, we got loose from our bonds." He couldn't go into more detail without explaining more than he wanted to.

Ivan waited, eyes slightly narrowed in confusion. "Just like that?"

Red nodded. He'd never thought much about the humanity of the enemy. That wasn't something they talked about in the foxholes or on the scoutin' trail. All they did in the foxholes was curse the enemy, and do everything they could to make sure he died.

The rattle-clack-rattle-clack of the train filled the silence for a few long moments as the two men sat steeping in the ugliness they'd seen.

"Don't mention that bit about the massacre to my parents," Ivan said softly. "Why worry them about something that's already happened? They've worried enough about me in the past three years."

"Reckon there's lots our families are never gonna know about."

"Sometimes it seems the farther I get from the war, the more I remember," Ivan said.

Red knew what he meant. All that loud commotion clattered around in his mind, along with pictures of mangled or dead friends. He still felt the pain of his own wounds—both in his flesh and in his heart.

"Maybe we have to remember," Ivan said. "A man's got to stay on the alert."

Red agreed, but he couldn't help wondering if he was already going soft. Since he was a German by blood, he couldn't hate his former countrymen.

It was hard not to hate them when he heard about all those concentration camps, the awful things they did to other human beings. Torture? Gas chambers? Trying to stamp out a whole race of people? Genocide, it was called. Devilish. Straight out of the pits of hell.

As the thoughts started tormenting him once again, Red did what he always did to take his mind from them. He patted his shirt pocket, thick with letters.

Ivan, of course, knew without asking what was in Red's pocket. "You still writing to Bertie?"

Red grimaced. "She's been doin' most of the writing." Especially the past few weeks.

His sweet Bertie had a heart as tender and beautiful as spring violets, a face to keep a man alive through the worst of war, and a voice as warm and spicy as hot apple cider.

But he couldn't keep thinking like that…not about her bein' *his*.

"That little gal had a regular letter campaign going, you know," Ivan told him. "She had all her friends writing to me, and any time I'd mention a buddy who hadn't received mail in a while, sure enough, in a week or so he'd get a note from some stranger out of Culver City, California. Our Bertie's all spunk. If she was president, this whole war would already be won."

Red felt a quick rush of pride. "She's kept me going, that's for sure."

"How's Miss Lilly been getting on without you?"

"You know Ma," Red said. "She says she's doin' fine, but it's hard to tell 'cause she never complains."

Ivan chuckled. "Strong as a Missouri mule and the best cook in Hideaway."

Red returned his attention to the scenery sliding past the window. Now that Ivan had brought up the subject, Red remembered that he had someone else to fret about.

Until he was called up, he'd helped his mother run the Meyer Guesthouse in Hideaway. It had been a family operation since his pa's death.

Lilly Meyer never let on about how hard it was to keep the place going without Red's help—but he knew business must've gone slack without him to serve as fishing guide, hunting guide and storyteller, along with all the other chores he'd done for her every day.

Fishing along the James River had been a popular sport among their best and wealthiest customers, many of whom returned to Lilly's guesthouse year after year for the fishing. These guests had gotten the Meyers through the depression.

But how much of the work could Red do now?

Ma's letters were mostly filled with the goings-on in town, until this last one. Even the handwriting seemed to lack her usual pizzazz. Kind of shrunk in on itself, hard to read.

Red couldn't quite figure it. Seemed like Ma was trying to avoid the subject of Hideaway altogether. Maybe Drusilla Short was telling tales again. That woman was the orneriest old so-and-so in the county, exceptin' for her husband, Gramercy. Last time Red had been home on leave, Mrs. Short had the nerve to spread the rumor that Red was AWOL.

Ma, of course, had nearly come to blows with the old gossip about it—and Ma wasn't a fighter, unless someone tried to hurt one of her kids. Then, she could whup a mad bull, and she was big enough to do it.

Red glanced out at the peaceful countryside, at the cattle grazing in a valley. Pa had actually taken on a mad bull twelve years ago—and lost. That ol' bull had been raised on the farm as a pet, but then had turned mean, and caught Pa in the middle of the field where he couldn't get away in time.

Ma had been left to raise Red and his brother and sister alone.

What was up with Ma now?

And how was Red going to break his news to Bertie?

Chapter Three

Bertie thought about her father as she held the fine sandpaper to the gear shaft turning in the lathe. She moved the paper back and forth to wear the metal of the shaft to smooth, even perfection—to ten thousandths of an inch of the final recommendations.

She couldn't help feeling, again, that something wasn't right back home. At seven o'clock, on the second Sunday night of every month since she'd come out here, she'd telephoned Dad. If she couldn't reach him right away, he would phone her, and every time except once, he had been sitting beside the phone, waiting for her call. By the time their short talks were over—long distance cost too much to talk more than a few minutes—half of Hideaway knew what was happening in her life.

Everyone on their telephone party line got in on the call. It aggravated Dad half to death, and he wasn't always polite to the neighbors. But that didn't stop the townsfolk from picking up their phones, even when they knew the specific ring was for Dad and not for them. They were always "accidentally" interrupting the conversation.

Last night Bertie had tried four times, with no answer from Dad. He never called back. She'd talked to the Morrows, the Fishers and the Jarvises, but not to Dad. Nobody seemed to know where he was. Mrs. Fisher did tell Bertie that a couple of Dad's best cows and five of his pigs had gone missing two weeks ago. Bertie had heard Mr. Fisher in the background, telling his wife that if Joseph Moennig wanted his daughter to know about the lost animals, he'd tell her himself.

Mr. Fisher was one of the few people in their Hideaway neighborhood who believed in minding his own business. His wife, poor thing, held a dim view of her husband's anti-social behavior.

Why hadn't Dad mentioned the animals in his letters?

Mr. Morrow didn't have much to say about the matter, which struck Bertie as unusual. He'd never lacked for opinions before.

If Bertie didn't know better, she'd start getting a complex. First, no letters from Red Meyer for six weeks, and now even her father wasn't answering her calls.

She'd written Red's mother, but though Lilly Meyer's reply had been chatty and filled with news, she hadn't given Bertie any useful information about Red, except that he was "takin' a few weeks of rest from the battle."

But where was he doin' his resting? And if he was getting rest, why couldn't he write to her? Was he having so much fun on his rest that he didn't want to waste time on her?

Bertie heard news about the war from everyone but Red.

Until VE Day last month—Victory over Europe, May 8, 1945—which would always be a day of celebration, Bertie and Edith had kept up with the news from the European front through their favorite magazine, *Stars and Stripes*. They had especially loved war correspondent Ernie Pyle, who'd informed readers about all the things Red never wrote about—such as the living conditions of the men who were fighting so desperately for freedom.

How she missed those articles now that Ernie was dead. How the whole country missed him!

"Roberta Moennig, you know the boss is tough on daydreamers." Emma, the utility girl, came by with more parts to work on the lathe.

Bertie's hand slipped, fingers rapping against the shaft, and she yelped when she accidentally did a quick sanding job on her fingertips.

"Hey, you all right?" Emma asked.

"Yes, I'm fine." Bertie had too much on her mind right now. She'd developed too much of a worry habit.

Emma hefted the parts onto Bertie's table. "What's got your goat? Keep this up and Franklin Parrish'll be chucking you out the door."

Bertie grimaced and picked up a shaft. She placed it in the lathe, tightened it in, and started polishing it. Today her concentration was about as sharp as a possum hanging from a tree limb.

"Got another letter from my soldier last night," Emma said, leaning her elbows on Bertie's worktable, obviously of a mind to gab a while, in spite of the whine of the lathe's motor, and her own just-issued warning about Franklin.

Bertie nodded, wishing Emma would leave it at that, hoping the noise of the lathe would keep the conversation short.

"You heard from that man of yours lately?" Emma asked, raising her voice.

Bertie frowned. "Not for a few weeks. You know how the mail gets bundled up for days at a time, then a bunch of letters comes at once." Even to her own ears, the excuse sounded overly bright.

Emma gave Bertie a narrow-eyed look. "Red's never gone this long without writing to you, has he? He still a scout with the Army?"

Bertie suppressed a sigh and turned off the lathe. "He's called a fire support specialist."

"I thought it was a forward observer."

Bertie released her pent-up breath. How many times had she corrected Emma about Red's title? She didn't want to sound boastful, but she *was* proud of Red and what he did. He'd received several commendations for his skills—and his bravery. It was the bravery that worried her something awful.

Emma stepped closer, her pinched face and mouse-brown eyes sharpening with concern. "You don't think he's…I mean…you think he's—"

"Hush, now." Bertie gently patted Emma's thin arm. "Honey, you know we can't start thinking that way. Gotta have some faith that God's in charge. Our men are helping to win this war. Besides, bad news always seems to travel faster than good these days. If something had happened to him, we'd know by now. I got a letter from his mother a few days ago."

Emma's eyes narrowed even more as she nibbled on her chapped lower lip. "That man that got killed? You know, that reporter out in the Pacific? He wasn't even a solider, Bert! It's dangerous all over, and men are being killed every day, and what with our own president dying, it feels like everything's out of control."

"Nothing is out of control," Bertie assured her. "President Truman knows what he's doing. He's a Missourian, born not too far from my hometown. He'll see things through. We Missourians are made of tough stock."

Emma didn't seem to hear her. "Lives can be cut short

just like that," she said, snapping her fingers. "It could happen to anybody."

Bertie shook her head. She didn't need to hear this kind of talk right now. "It could even happen to you or me if Franklin catches us chatting instead of working," she said with a wink to keep her words from sounding too harsh. "He's already threatened to fire me once today."

To Bertie's relief, Emma nodded, sighed and returned to her cart. Bertie turned on the lathe again, which she shouldn't have turned off in the first place; there was no standing around talking except at break time.

At least once a week, poor Emma got all perturbed about her soldier. Every time, Bertie prayed for them both. She'd offered to pray *with* Emma, but that seemed to be going too far.

As it was, Bertie often felt overwhelmed with the amount of work she and Edith Frost had volunteered for these past months. During her free time, Bertie signed people up for war bonds, and she and Edith helped with the blood drive, which included giving their own blood as often as they could.

So many of her hometown friends had left for the war as boys and had returned as men. Three men from her hometown had returned in caskets.

She switched her attention back to the shaft in her lathe, trying her hardest to shake off the worry that Emma had helped stoke like the cinders of a woodstove.

Red sat with his feet planted firmly on the floor in the swaying railcar, growing more and more conscious of the cane he'd shoved beneath the seat and the attention of his friend, Ivan Potts.

It would be easy to reach down and pull out the cane and

show it to Ivan. Everyone in Hideaway would know about it by tomorrow, anyway, so why not show it first to someone he knew he could trust?

But something kept him from it. It was almost like another bad dream—if he kept pretending the problem wasn't there, maybe it would disappear.

Like the war?

Ivan peered out the window, then stood and gestured to Red. "Why don't you come up to my car with me? I've got to collect my things before we get off. Dad said he'd be waiting for me at the station, and I bet Mom will be with him. You can catch a ride with us."

Red hesitated for a few seconds, then declined. Ma would want to pick up Red herself, so they could spend the long ride back home catching up, just the two of them.

"Thanks, but I've got a ride," Red said. "Ma told me she'd see to it I got picked up."

Ivan nodded, then grinned. "Lilly probably cooked your favorite meal, knowing you were coming back today."

"If she had time. She's been awful busy."

"But if I know your mother, she'll have her famous chicken and dumplings waiting at the table for you as soon as you walk in the door." Ivan licked his lips. "And blackberry cobbler with enough butter in the crust to make a grown man cry."

Red couldn't help grinning at his friend. "Could be." Ivan loved a good meal, and though his mother was brilliant and kind and an excellent hostess, her finger pastries and cucumber sandwiches didn't exactly stick to the ribs.

"Think Lilly could be persuaded to set an extra place at the table for me?" Ivan leaned toward Red, looking like a hound about to tree a coon. "My mom has a party planned for my homecoming tonight, but man, oh, man, Lilly's chicken and dumplings for lunch would make the whole ordeal worth enduring."

Red sometimes kidded Ivan that he was not his mother's son. Arielle Potts was a cultured lady—an accomplished hostess, who loved to entertain. She was a savvy political wife who enjoyed helping her husband campaign for mayor of Hideaway—not that there'd been much campaigning to do. Gerald Potts's only opponent had been Gramercy Short, who likely didn't get more than a total of ten votes, all from his relatives, and there were probably at least two dozen Shorts in Hideaway.

Ivan, on the other hand, would rather go huntin' with Red and his coon dogs any night than socialize with the town's high and mighty.

"Sure," Red said, "come on over. Even if Ma hasn't made chicken and dumplings, the meal's bound to be good."

Ivan nodded. "I'll do it."

Ivan had the kind of face that revealed his thoughts several seconds before he spoke them. And he always spoke them. He didn't believe in keeping things to himself. As long as Red had known him, there was most often a hint of humor in Ivan's eyes, not quite mischief, but almost.

As Red watched, all humor left Ivan's face, and the darkness entered his expression again. Red didn't have any trouble knowing what was going through his friend's mind.

"Red, the war's taken something from us that we might never get back." He glanced up and down the aisle at the other passengers.

Red waited without speaking. This wasn't the time to talk about it. Not now. Not on this train with other people listening. Besides, he couldn't help thinking that if he spoke aloud what had been on his mind the past few weeks, it would make everything that happened over on those deadly fields too real.

"I think it's hit you harder," Ivan said at last. "Hasn't it?"

Red swallowed. "Not sure what makes you think that. We've all been through a lot."

Ivan leaned closer and waited until Red met his gaze. "Because I know you, buddy. You bury things down deep inside. Me, I sit by myself and write my poetry and get it out of my system. You should see the stack of poetry in my duffle bag. I've probably sent poems to half of Hideaway, and several of Bertie's friends in California."

"You oughta try to get them published. You'll be rich."

Ivan laughed out loud at that. "You think there's money in poetry? My Daddy taught me how to make a living, don't you worry. And don't change the subject."

"Thought the subject was poetry."

Ivan sobered. "You've lost something, Red." His words were soft and gentle, but they felt like broken strands of chicken wire digging into Red's heart. Ivan didn't know the half of it. "It's like all the laughter's dried up inside of you."

Red didn't know what to say. He'd not seen much to laugh about.

"Find some way to get this war out of your system," Ivan told him. "Don't let it keep you down."

Red nodded toward the window. "We're getting close. Better get your things. I'll see you for dinner."

Ivan frowned. "Lunch, Red. Noon meal is lunch."

"Not where I come from."

"You come from here, same as me."

"Your mother comes from Baltimore."

Ivan chuckled and gave Red a playful sock in the arm. It was one of their favorite arguments.

To Red's shame, he felt only relief when Ivan shook his head and walked back up the aisle toward the door that led to the forward car.

Chapter Four

Thoughts of Red once more filled Bertie's mind as she struggled with a misshapen part. She tossed it to the side so Emma could pick it up to send back for repair.

Time to switch the lathe to a higher gear and get some of these parts finished. Hurriedly, she turned off the machine, released the tension on the v-belt, and reached down to move it to a larger v-pulley. Her hand slipped. The belt which hadn't come to a complete stop, grabbed her forefinger. Before she could react, her finger was snatched into the pulley.

Pain streaked up her arm. She gritted her teeth to keep from crying out as she jerked her hand back.

Blood spread over and down her fingers, and for a moment, because of the pain, she thought all her fingers had been mangled. She closed her eyes and breathed deeply to keep from passing out, then turned to look around and see if anyone had noticed what had happened.

No one looked her way.

She reached for the bandana on her head. Her hot hair once again fell over her shoulders as she tore off a strip of the cloth and dabbed away the blood. To her relief, only her index finger was torn.

Maybe she could take care of this herself, without going to First Aid.

But she discovered she would have no choice. The blood kept flowing from a fair-sized cut over her knuckle. There was no way to deal with it on her own.

She used what was left of the bandana to tie her hair back into a ponytail, her movements awkward.

Reluctantly, she went to find her supervisor for permission to go to First Aid. She'd catch an earful this time.

Red peered out the window at the passenger cars curving along the track in front of him. He thought he saw Ivan's blond head in one square of window, but it was too far away to know for sure.

He couldn't say why he was relieved that Ivan had gone back to his seat. It'd been good to see his friend, to know there was someone else, someone he knew, who could understand what he'd gone through.

But then, looking into Ivan's face, Red had been able to recall the war that much clearer, when what he really wanted to do was forget it, not be reminded of every detail, every death. There were too many.

Rubbing his fingertip across the corner of one of the envelopes in his pocket, Red resisted the urge to pull them out again. He knew what the letters said. He had most every word memorized. He could see Bertie Moennig's face against his closed eyelids—her sweet, saucy smile, her thick, fair hair, and turned-up nose.

The letters he'd gotten from her were nearly falling apart, he'd read them so often. The latest ones, of course, were full of questions, full of worry and wondering why he hadn't written. Those were the ones that ate at him.

He remembered one letter he'd gotten last year, soon after he returned from leave. It had been even harder than leaving the first time, and it'd apparently been hard for Bertie, too.

I've made a decision, the letter had said. *I'm going to learn how to be good at waiting, because I know there are some things—some people—worth waiting for. Dad and Uncle Sam are urging me to take some training and work in one of the defense plants, and I think I'll do it. I want to do all I can to help win this war, and get our men home again. Write me soon, Red, and let me know you're okay.*

He'd written to her then, telling her how much he already missed her, how proud he was of her. He'd written more during just one week of war than he'd done all through school. Bertie had always been so good for him.

Problem was, he didn't know what to write now. Whatever he told her, it wouldn't be something she'd want to read. And she didn't *need* to know. Not yet.

He'd even told Ma not to let Bertie know about his injury. What good would it have done? Ma, of course, had argued, but he knew she'd done what he'd asked.

Thing was, he'd seen too many hearts broken already in this war. Too many of his buddies had died, leaving wives alone to grieve as widows, leaving mothers brokenhearted over their dead sons.

He'd also seen too many friends going back home as damaged goods, to wives who'd have to take care of them the rest of their lives. He couldn't do that to Bertie.

Nosiree, Joseph Moennig had a good farm that needed running, and what with his son, Lloyd, off in Kansas with a wife and family, his only daughter Bertie would be the one to take over the farm someday. She'd need a husband who was whole to help with that. A woman like her wouldn't have any trouble finding someone.

Red closed his eyes and tried to think of something else, because the thought of Bertie loving another man almost made him sick to his stomach.

Bertie watched the suture needle prick the skin of her knuckle in the first stitch. She jerked, in spite of her determination not to. How embarrassing! All this time she'd followed all the safety rules, been so careful about every single movement. And now this.

That was what happened when a person got in a hurry. She'd known better.

"That hurt?" asked Dr. Cox as he tied the stitch.

"Not at all. You do what you have to do."

"Are you left-handed?" He started the next stitch.

"No, sir."

"Good, because I would have to warn you against using your finger any more than necessary. Flexing that knuckle will make the healing time longer."

"I'm glad it didn't come to that. I have letters to write."

He worked quickly, his fingers moving with precision. He was the company doctor, and had probably done this a lot. "You have a beau in the war?"

Bertie hesitated. Was Red her beau? She nodded. It was how she thought of him, even if he couldn't seem to write now that he was on leave.

"Is he from Missouri, too?" Dr. Cox asked.

Bertie blinked up at him, her attention distracted from the needle. "How'd you know I was—"

"I pride myself in my ability to pick up on an accent within seconds of meeting someone. Southern?"

Bertie stared into his kind eyes. "You mean Southern Missouri? Yes, Southwest, almost into Arkansas."

"Ozarks, then. Your beau is from the Ozarks, too?"

"He sure is." Bertie felt herself relaxing. "We grew up in the same town along the James River." How she wished for those times again. "We went to school together and were close friends for as long as either of us can remember."

The doctor smiled. "Think you'll get married once this war is over?"

Bertie felt herself flushing at the thought. She'd considered it a lot. In fact, the thought of marrying and settling with Red was one of the things that had gotten her through her homesickness, her worry, her fretting. Until now.

"My father wouldn't mind," she told the doctor. "Red comes from a good, solid family. Dad knows Red real well." There were times Bertie had felt as if Dad preferred Red's company to her own. "He's already like a son to Dad." She grimaced. "Why am I telling you all this? You don't want to hear my life story."

Dr. Cox chuckled. "Sure I do. It keeps your mind off what I'm doing, and when you're relaxed, I can work better."

"Do you see many more patients now that so many doctors are helping in the war?"

"I sure do. Two of the other doctors with offices in this building are on hospital ships somewhere in the Pacific." He looked at her. "I love hearing stories from my patients, especially those involved in the war effort. Now," he said, fixing her with a pointed stare, "you were telling me about Red?"

She smiled at him, relaxing further, enjoying the chance to talk about her favorite subject. "Before Red's father died, the Meyers had two hundred acres of prime farmland along the James River. After her husband's death, Mrs. Meyers sold off a parcel of land every couple of years to the town, which was expanding and needed more room."

"To help get her family through the depression?" the doctor asked.

"Yes, even though Red warned her not to sell. He feels they could've gotten by without selling. It would've been worth more with the James River becoming part of a new lake, with a dam south of a tiny burg called Branson. That would've made her property lakefront. Now I guess it doesn't matter, though, since they had to put the plans on hold for the dam when war struck."

"Sounds as if Red is a smart man."

"Yes, but he comes by it honest. Lilly, his mother, opened their big house to paying guests. She did so well with it she was able to help send her two older kids to university in Kansas City."

"What about Red's education?" Dr. Cox asked.

Bertie shrugged. "He didn't go to college."

"Why not?"

"He knew his mother needed help with the guesthouse. He loves working with livestock, and he's won blue ribbons at the state fair for the cheese he cultured from their cows' milk."

"So he gave up his opportunity to go to college to help with the family business," the doctor said. "He sounds like quite a man. It looks to me as if you and your young man are a perfect match."

She shrugged, studying the neat work the doctor was doing on her hand.

Dr. Cox paused for a moment, frowning at her. "Am I detecting some hesitation about him?"

She shrugged. "We only started dating a few weeks before he went off to war."

"Maybe it took the war to show him how much he cared about you."

Then why had Red stopped writing now that the war with the Germans was over? "I know why everyone suddenly wants to see stardust," she said. "Life's too scary right now. When all this began, a body didn't want to think he might go off to some strange land and die without ever knowing if someone besides his folks could love him. Later, when he comes back alive and whole, he might change his mind. He might find someone he likes better."

Dr. Cox placed salve over the sutured wound, then gently wrapped gauze around her finger. "I like my theory better."

Bertie looked into the doctor's sincere gray eyes. "I hope you're right." But he didn't know enough about Red to judge.

"There you go, Roberta," he told her as he finished bandaging her finger. He gave her final instructions for sutures to be removed in ten days.

She thanked him and walked back out to the waiting room, where she found Connie, the company nurse, reading a magazine and chuckling at a "Joe and Willie" war cartoon.

Connie looked up at Bertie and grimaced at the bandage on her finger. "Guess you'll be put on special duty."

"No need," Bertie said. "I'm right-handed."

Connie got up, shaking her head. "You don't know Franklin Parrish, kiddo. Last gal who cut herself was transferred out of his department. He's about as easy to work with as a porcupine. You may find that out soon enough."

Chapter Five

The train slowed at a long uphill curve, and Red saw Lake Taneycomo gleaming in the sunshine out his window. Not much farther now. He started watching for familiar landmarks: the big cedar that'd been hit twice by lightning and lost most of its branches, but kept on thriving; the rocky cliff that looked like half a huge teacup—one of the area's bald knobs, where it was rumored that the old vigilante gang, the Bald Knobbers, sometimes met when preparing to raid a farmer's land.

He remembered riding the train to Springfield with his mother and listening to stories from old-timers about the places along the tracks that had been raided by that gang, the owners forced from their land with threats of beatings or burned homes—or death.

That had happened just before the railroad came in. It had become evident later that the vigilante gang had had inside knowledge about its course. Many men became rich when they later sold their ill-gotten land to the railroad.

Red closed his eyes, wondering when his mind would

stop wandering to brutality and the ugliness of humankind. When he looked again, the first buildings of the tiny burg of Branson came into view.

The train continued toward the Hollister station, a short jaunt south. He wasn't sure what kind of a ride his mother would've arranged, what with the gasoline rationing and so few cars in town, anyway. Could be she'd come for him with the horse and buggy, unless she was in a hurry to get back to the house, and was able to convince one of the neighbors to take a car out of hibernation long enough to drive her.

Lilly Meyer always said one of the big draws of the Meyer Guesthouse was her horse and buggy. In this new world of modern cars with all their speed and fancy buttons and gadgets, Ma believed her guests returned to Hideaway year after year because they wanted to be taken back to a time when life wasn't so hectic.

Red knew how it felt to be lulled into a sense of peace by the clopping of horse hooves instead of a smoking tailpipe.

Many who did have automobiles in Hideaway had followed Lilly Meyer's lead and parked their cars for the rest of the war. They rode their horses or bicycles to town when they needed to shop or have a haircut or deliver goods. The gasoline was left to the farmers in the rest of the country, who needed to supply food to the troops.

Most farmers around Hideaway still used mules as their power source for plowing and wagon pulling, cutting hay and reaping corn. This way they didn't have to fret about the shortages as much. They could save for other things.

Red had discovered just how well-off he and his neighbors had been in Hideaway by talking to other soldiers who'd come from farms across the Midwest. His hometown had five hundred and fifteen of the best people he'd ever known. That was why the population had doubled in the past ten years, smack dab in the middle of the depression, and that was why it would keep growing long after the war ended. Why, he could even see it doubling again in time, maybe to a thousand or more.

The train stopped at the Hollister station. He looked out the window for signs of his ma. Other men in uniform left the train, including Ivan, who glanced back in Red's direction and waved. They'd see each other soon enough. Ivan could never resist Ma's cooking.

Red waited, watching happy reunions taking place on the train ramp. Two soldiers and an airman stepped off, uniforms proudly decorated, as Ivan's was. Many were probably home for good after the victory in Europe.

Home. It was the one thing everyone in the field dreamed about and talked about most.

Until now, Red hadn't been any different. He slid his left hand down the side of his thigh to his knee, where shrapnel had ripped into the muscle and bone. He'd been held in the stateside hospital for three weeks, with daily injections of some new drug called penicillin that was supposed to kill the infection.

He didn't know how well it had worked. The surgeon had told him the bone looked good, the infection gone, but for some reason his brain didn't seem to be getting the message he was healed. He couldn't put all his weight on his left leg yet. Smart as the surgeon was, he wasn't God.

Red still didn't see his mother or anyone he recognized who might be here to pick him up. And so he stayed put, the darkness of the past few weeks haunting his thoughts.

Dark and heavy. Dark and hopeless.

Here he'd been thinkin' that Bertie would be better off without him, but wouldn't that be the same for everybody else, as well? Nobody needed a lame soldier taking up space, Ma least of all, with all the work she needed done.

The last of the passengers disembarked, and the crowd on the platform began to thin. Red looked on glumly as Ivan greeted his parents in the parking lot.

Ivan's father, Gerald, broad-shouldered and smiling— teeth gleaming so brightly Red could see them from where he sat—gave his son a bear hug. Both men towered over the fair Arielle Potts, whose Swedish coloring Ivan had inherited.

Ivan gestured toward the train, and they all glanced toward where Red sat watching them from the shadows. He didn't think they could see him, looking from the bright sunshine into the darkness of the railcar, but he waved back.

The three of them climbed into a shiny black Chevrolet.

After most others had left the train, Red hefted his duffle over one shoulder and reluctantly grabbed the cane, forcing away his brooding thoughts. He dreaded seeing the look on his mother's face when she saw him with his cane for the first time.

Sure, Ma knew about the injury, but to see her youngest hobbling on a cane like an old man? No mother should have to witness that.

Finally, out of the window, he saw Lilly Meyer come riding up in a buggy pulled by the big bay gelding Seymour, and Red felt a rush of relief.

Ma's broad, sun-reddened face showed him she'd spent a lot of time outside in the vegetable garden—one of Red's jobs when he was home. She guided Seymour carefully through the crowd in the parking area, waving to several acquaintances along the way.

Even before the gasoline rationing of the war, Lilly Meyer had held with her horse. She wasn't afraid of cars. She wasn't afraid of anything. She just always loved her horses. Pa had tried to teach her how to drive when he was alive, but she would have nothing to do with it. She didn't mind people thinking of her as a little backward.

In fact, Ma was the envy of the town with a business that had thrived through the depression and kept going during the war.

Hay and oats weren't rationed here because the farmers raised their own. Neither were garden vegetables or milk from their own cows, or meat and eggs from their own stock. In his travels, Red saw what the rest of the country had had to do without. He couldn't believe how blessed he'd been all those years.

Red grabbed the metal soffit over the door and tried his hardest not to grimace. As he stepped down, he saw his mother look at his cane, then his leg. The pain in his leg was nothing compared to what he felt when he saw the look in her eyes.

"Now, Ma, don't you go worrying about me," he greeted as he rushed to hug her. Ordinarily, he'd pick her up and twirl her around—well, maybe that would be called lumbering her around. Lilly Meyer was, after all, nigh on three-hundred pounds. He couldn't lift her now, but he wrapped his arms around her bulky form and was grateful for her strength.

She clung to him for a long few seconds, and this surprised Red. Their family'd not been much for shows of emotion.

She drew back at last, and he saw tears on her cheeks. She patted the moistness on his uniform collar with alarm.

"Now, look what I did," she said.

"It'll dry, Ma." His mother didn't cry. Even at Pa's funeral, she'd been as strong as a man, setting the example for Red and his older sister and brother, Agnes and Howard, not to show a trembling lip or damp eye. The Meyers wore brave faces for the rest of the world, no matter what.

Her double chins wobbled as she looked up into his eyes and brushed her fingers across his cheek, like he was a little boy again. "It's going to be okay now. My hero's home." She glanced around them. "And none too soon, either, from the looks of things," she muttered.

"What're you talking about?" he asked. "The war's half over."

"Germans aren't exactly the best-liked people in Hideaway right now, especially since we're hearing about all those death camps."

"But we're not German, we're American, Ma."

"We're German enough for somebody to hate us."

"Who's been snubbing you?"

She sniffed once more, then composed herself. "That ol' Drusilla Short says I'm a Nazi sympathizer. Thinks I oughta surrender and be locked up and my guesthouse shut down."

"Since when did anyone ever listen to that woman's opinion?" Red patted Seymour on the nose and received a welcoming nudge that knocked him off his stride.

"Since two nights ago when someone threw a brick through our window that nearly conked poor John Martin on the head when he was reading the paper," Ma said.

"John!" Red paused before he climbed in beside his mother. "He okay?"

"Fightin' mad, but other than that he's just got a mark on his noggin from some flying glass. Tough young buck."

Red clenched his hands into fists as anger streaked

through him. "Who do you think did it?" If he found out, he'd hobble out and bang some heads. They'd never try to hurt his mother again.

"You know bullies are cowards," she said. "They don't show themselves. And our house ain't the only target for mischief. It's been going on a couple of months. Mildred went missing last month."

Red stared at his mother. The loss of one of Ma's two milk cows would've been a huge blow to her. "You never told me that. You never found her?"

"Nope, but Joseph Moennig loaned me one of his. Said he's got his hands full with all the farm work now that Bertie's in California." She nodded. "That Joseph is a good man. But he paid for his goodness two weeks ago. Some of his own stock went missing."

"His cattle?"

"A couple of cows and some pigs, and you can bet they were taken off to market and sold. He'll never see them again, and they were the best of his stock." She shook her head. "I'm tellin' you, Red, this place is in for troubled times. Want to know why I was late gettin' here?"

"I figured you had a good reason."

"Somebody decided Seymour needed to be let out of his corral sometime last night. If he wasn't such a homebody, no tellin' where he'd be by now. As it was, I found him washing his feet down by the river. I saw a chalk mark on the side of the shed. It was that broken cross the Nazis use."

"A swastika?"

"That's the sign."

"Anything else?"

"Nope. Don't you think it's too much of a coincidence that

ol' Dru Short's been hurling lies about us, and now we've got bricks through our window and Nazi signs on our stable?"

"Is the sheriff doing anything about the thefts?"

"Not that I've seen. Mayor Gerald says he'll not let 'em get away with this, but he can't stop it if he don't catch nobody." She patted Red's arm. "Not to worry now. You'll take care of it. You'll find out who's doing this, if anybody can."

Red climbed into the buggy, glad for the sturdy handles he grasped to pull himself up. He felt more helpless than ever. What was happening in Hideaway?

Chapter Six

On the short ride back to the plant with Connie, Bertie slid Red's last letter out of her purse. She'd studied it over and over when she'd received no new letters, thinking maybe it held a hidden reason why he hadn't written again.

Sometimes she nearly convinced herself he'd met someone else—not that there was much chance of meeting a woman in the muddy trenches where he'd been stuck for so many months. Still, she'd heard there were women aplenty in the towns where the men went when they were on leave.

In all his letters, Red had never made any promises to her about the future. What if he'd met some Italian beauty off in that foreign world? From what she'd read in letters from other soldiers, a man could get mighty lonely, mighty desperate in the midst of war.

She carefully unfolded the letter written nearly six weeks ago. It was two pages of awkward words that had gripped her heart and convinced her for sure that she loved him and he was the only one for her.

Bertie, you keep asking me if I've gotten a chance to see

Italy. I've seen more of this place than I've ever wanted to see of any country, anywhere, anytime. I've seen whole orchards battered to kindling wood. I've seen people living in bombed buildings, starving, begging us for food.

I see your face every time I close my eyes, and can almost hear your voice every time I pull your picture out of my pocket.

Funny, ain't it? I always thought of all Italians as dark haired, dark eyed. That's not true. Some are as blond as you are, with skin like yours. I've been into some towns a few times, and I can't tell you how often I thought I'd seen you in the crowd on the street, and I'd run toward you and call your name, and when I got there, I'd find a stranger watching me like they thought I was about to shoot them.

She looked up from the words, as the warmth of them flowed through her. Instead of the California highway, she saw the lines of Red's smiling face—he was most always smiling or laughing at something—never at someone else, most times at himself.

She wanted to cry over his loneliness for her. And yet she felt reassured. A woman couldn't read such heartfelt words and doubt a man's love for her.

Straightening the fold in the page, she read on.

These people aren't the enemy. They were dumb, maybe, and weak when they should have been strong, but how can I say what I'd have done in their place? They're defeated now, you can see it in their eyes, and especially in their land.

There's times I can hear your laughter or your voice in the middle of the night when the shells are whizzing through the sky, and that voice keeps me from going plumb out of my mind.

Bertie, if I get home alive, it's because of you. I feel like I have somebody waiting for me. I feel like I have a future. So many of my buddies've gotten their Dear John letters— their women didn't want to wait around. All this time, I keep on getting letters from you. I never expected different, but I want you to know something. If I don't make it home, it's not because you didn't pray hard enough, it's because the evil caught up with us, after all, and the old devil won a battle. Like you keep reminding me, he won't win the real war.

You take care out there in California. You never know what could happen in a place like that, so close to the ocean. The enemy can reach you better there than he can in Missouri. Don't let that happen.

If anything happens to me, I want you to be happy. Marry somebody you know I'd approve of, settle and have that passel of kids you've always wanted. And know that there was one soldier who went to his reward fighting for the best gal in the best country in the world.

I kinda like you.

Your Red

She folded the page and slid it back into her purse, and felt the sting of tears in her eyes. No promises, for sure, but he never "kinda liked" anybody else. He'd always been good at understatement. But she knew Red Meyer better than most anyone except his mother. He never made a promise until he knew for sure he'd be able to keep it. And then he kept it.

Just because he hadn't written in the past few weeks didn't mean he'd forgotten about her.

This letter was filled with his affection for her, his abiding friendship. She'd read love letters received by her friends at work that didn't show as much love as this letter did.

Could the man who'd placed his life in her hands stop writing because he'd met another woman he liked better?

She knew things were different now, and she couldn't help worrying about how lonely a man could get. But Red wasn't the type to lead one woman on with letters while courtin' another. It wasn't his nature. He was constant, steadfast, not a ladies' man at all. He was a man any lady would be proud to marry, who would put a lot of joy and laughter into her life—as he had always done in Bertie's.

She couldn't help smiling when she remembered how Red had changed after he'd first asked her out on a bona fide date more than three years ago. Always before, he'd seemed as comfortable with her as he was with his old bluetick hunting dog. Then, suddenly, when he came to pick her up with the horse and buggy for a drive down to the lake, or when he and Ivan double-dated with her and Dixie Martin, John's sister, and went to the cinema in Hollister in John's tan Pontiac, Red got all tongue-tied. He didn't know how to talk to Bertie.

He opened doors for her, paid for her meals and movie, treated her like she was someone special, but he stumbled over his words and his face flushed more easily.

His awkwardness touched her. She felt honored that he thought that much of her.

"We're here," Connie said, interrupting Bertie's thoughts. "You want me to walk back to the department with you in case Franklin decides to strangle you?" She grinned. "That way I can administer first aid quicker."

"I can handle him," Bertie assured the nurse.

She wasn't so sure of herself once Connie left, but if Red could depend on thoughts of her to get him through the horrors of the battles he'd fought, she could keep him in her heart as she tried to deal with Franklin.

* * *

Red took the reins from his mother and guided Seymour toward the road that followed the course of the White River back to Hideaway. It would be a long ride.

"Let's check on Joseph on our way home," Lilly said.

Red looked at his ma. "He sick or something?"

"Nope, I'm worried about him, is all. I didn't see him outside anywhere on my way here, and Erma Lee Jarvis called out to me from the garden as I passed their house. Joseph didn't answer Bertie's calls last night."

"Calls?"

"Four times, according to Erma Lee."

"He never misses her calls."

"That's what I'm saying. Something could be up."

Red flicked the reins to urge Seymour forward at a quicker walk. "Why didn't the Jarvises check on him last night?"

"You know how tetchy Joseph can be when a body tries to coddle him. Besides, he gets tired of the neighbors always listening in on his calls with Bertie. He can be sharp at times, you know."

Red nodded. Yep, Joseph could be that. Bertie called him grumpy, but she knew better. Joseph tried hard to be a tough ol' farmer, but he was a man with a soft spot for those he was closest to.

Red remembered when one of Joseph's prize milk cows took out after Bertie for petting her new calf. That poor ol' cow got sold so fast, she never saw it coming.

"It'll be good to see Joseph again." Red cast his mother a quick glance. She looked worried. "He been around in the past day or two?"

"I saw him at church. He was lookin' forward to his daughter's call." She shook her head. "That's another reason it's so strange he never answered. Hope he's not had any more trouble with cattle rustling."

Red flicked the reins again, and Seymour broke into a trot. Red tried not to worry, but worry seemed to've become a part of him since going off to war.

Joseph had always seemed partial to Red, and taught him a lot about being the man of the house, looking out for his mother, taking on a lot of the workload. He'd shown Red everything from stacking firewood the right way to handling newborn calves to plantin' a garden.

Joseph had also written to Red at least twice a month all the time he was in Europe. Nobody would take Pa's place, of course, but Joseph Moennig came the closest. He had to be lonely with Bertie out in California.

Red cast another curious glance at his mother. Well, maybe Joseph wasn't always lonely. Ma would see to that. And it didn't seem she'd mind all that much.

"I can't do much right now to help him on the farm," Red warned her.

"He won't care none about that, he'll be worried about you." She sighed and shook her head. "Can't deny it'll be a relief to share the load a little."

"What load's that?" Red asked.

She jerked her head toward his leg. "Since you didn't want Bertie to know about your injury, I couldn't tell nobody about it. Somebody'd have blabbed for sure. You're gonna be a shock to all our Hideaway friends, Red. Nobody even knows you got shot."

He nearly groaned aloud. Why had he done that to his poor mother? "I didn't get shot. I got hit by shrapnel. They'll know soon enough."

"Guess that means you need to have a talk with Bertie

before long, because you're sure not going to keep this thing a secret now. You're back in the States, you can pick up a phone and call her. She's really gonna be hurt you didn't tell her about this right off."

"I couldn't, Ma. I didn't know how it'd all work out, and you know how she worries."

"You can tell her now."

Red nodded. "Guess I could."

"You know, I never did like keepin' this thing a secret from her, especially when she asked about you time and time again."

"I know, and I'm sorry."

"I've never been a liar, and keeping this from her felt like I was lyin'."

He sighed. "I know, Ma. I know."

"And you never did tell me why you did it."

"She's gone through a lot, Ma. Her brother moved away, then the war hit, then her mother died. And now she's all alone in California without any kin nearby."

"And now her beau's stopped writing to her," his mother said, giving him a pointed look.

"I'd rather have her wonder about a few missed letters than know about this." He tapped his leg.

"It's gonna heal fine," Ma said.

Red didn't argue, but he couldn't agree, either. That'd be lying. For the past few weeks, he hadn't believed anything would be fine again. But no reason to try to tell his mother that.

Still, she was right. He had to tell Bertie about this leg. He dreaded doin' it, because it would change everything. Could be that was why he hadn't said anything about it yet—pure selfishness. As long as Bertie didn't know there was anything wrong, in her mind, at least, they were still together at heart.

But when he told her about the leg, he'd also have to tell her his decision about the two of them. He still didn't know how he could bear it.

"So you might as well get it over with," Ma said. "She's hurtin' out there in no-man's-land, all alone, thinkin' her man's done dropped her like a hot biscuit."

Red started to speak, and he couldn't. He swallowed hard, feeling his mother's sharp gaze. "I will, Ma. Soon as she's had time to get home from work tonight, I'll call her and tell her all about it."

From the corner of his eye, he saw his mother nod, saw her mouth open to speak, and he cut her off.

"I heard tell you've cooked Joseph a meal or two lately." He hoped she would let him change the subject.

When he glanced at her, his eyebrows nearly met his hairline at the sight of the blush that tinted her face.

"Bertie tell you that?" she asked.

Red nodded. Bertie had written a lot of things in her letters that he'd never realized before—about her dreams of living on a farm and having kids, of maybe someday having her own guesthouse like his mother's.

He'd also learned how much Bertie admired Lilly—and Red. It was a funny thing about Bertie—when they were growing up, Red had treated her about the same way he treated all his buddies. Like a guy. Never took much notice of her any other way until they were nearin' high school. Then he'd struggled for years to come to terms with his feelings.

Even when the war hit, spurring him to finally ask her out on a real date, they'd never talked about feelings and such, not the way she wrote about them now. They'd talked baseball scores and fishing, and, of course, they'd talked about the war.

"Joseph never says anything about how he's doin' alone out

on the farm," Lilly said. "Used to be he wouldn't even let me bake him a pie, but lately, he's helped me out with a few things—like when Mildred got lost—and he hasn't minded when I cooked a few things up. He's still as stubborn as a mule."

"His daughter has some of his stubbornness," Red said, unable to keep his thoughts from settling on Bertie, same as they'd done throughout the war—same as they'd done for nigh on twelve years or so.

"Soon as he heard about the brick in the window, he came to town and helped shore up the hole," Ma said. "Then he went looking for signs of the scoundrels."

"Maybe he's figured something out by now," Red said.

"Could be the two of you need to put your heads together." She nudged him. "Seeing as how he's practically your father-in-law."

Red noticed that his mother's teasing grin didn't reach her eyes. She was worried about that, he could tell, and he could almost hear her unasked question.

Joseph Moennig and his daughter weren't the only stubborn ones. Ma could be hard to live with when she wanted something she couldn't get. Like a certain young lady for a daughter-in-law.

Also, that brick and the missing cow had scared Ma worse than she would let on, but Red knew if he pushed, she'd clam up. Best to talk about other things for a while. And so they did, throughout the hour-long ride back to Hideaway.

Chapter Seven

The dirt road to Hideaway from Hollister skirted the southern ridge of hills that formed bluffs above the James River. Simply named the Hideaway Road, it continued on from Hideaway to Cape Fair, where it was called the Cape Fair Road. The Moennig farm was barely a quarter mile from Hideaway.

Being near town was the reason the Moennig place had electricity, while most of the farms in rural Missouri didn't. For the last few years, the Moennigs also had indoor plumbing and hot and cold running water, another rarity around these parts. Before that, they'd pumped their water out back of the house, heated it on the wood cookstove in the kitchen, and bathed in a tin washtub, like most other folks out in the country.

As Seymour kept up a steady trot down the road, Ma chattered about the young men coming back home from the war, about who'd been discharged early, and hinting that some of the discharges hadn't been honorable.

"You mean like Hector Short?" Red asked. No wonder Drusilla was so mean. Her own son was a scoundrel, bringing embarrassment to the family.

"I've seen neither hide nor hair of him around here," Ma said. "If I had, I'd've suspected him of throwing that brick through the—" Her voice broke off. "Would you listen to me? I'm getting as bad as Drusilla. I need to wash my mouth out with lye soap."

Red turned Seymour in at the Moennig driveway and kept going until they reached the corral gate. Then he stopped the horse and frowned.

"The gate's open. Did you notice that when you came by earlier?" he asked.

"Nope, you can't see this gate from the road." She gestured back toward the tall hedge around the front of the yard. "That isn't like Joseph, even if he didn't have cattle in the corral."

"Hello!" Red called as he reached for his cane. This time of day, Joseph would usually be out in the field, working the hay, or in the garden.

Ma gasped, then put a hand on Red's arm, gripping him hard. "Charles Frederick."

He turned to her, startled at her use of his full name. She was staring at something out in the cattle lot behind the barn. Red saw a patch of blue. A human shape, red-checked shirt and blue overalls.

Red tossed the reins to his mother and scrambled from the buggy, then reached back for his cane. Without a word, Ma pulled it from beside her on the wagon's running board, passed it to him, then gripped the railing beside her to get out.

"You stay right here," he said.

For once, she did as he told her.

As he hobbled along the rutted driveway toward the back fence, he felt chilled to the bone. If only this was just another nightmare he'd wake up from any minute.

But it was real. He'd seen too many images like this.

He felt sick as he stepped into the cattle lot and got a close look of Joseph Moennig. The side of Joseph's face was so white it seemed to reflect the hot, late-morning sun.

Red dropped awkwardly to his good knee next to his friend and gently rolled him to his back. Joseph stared without sight toward Heaven—his new home.

"Roberta Moennig."

Bertie caught her breath, and looked up at Franklin.

"Yessir," she said, taking care to turn off the lathe and keep her hands away from the moving parts. Her wound was beginning to ache as the pain killer wore off.

Franklin's broad face didn't have the usual scowl she'd come to know and dislike. When she met his eyes, he looked away. Then she realized he'd called her by her real name instead of hillbilly.

"You want something?" she asked.

"Your injury doing okay?" he asked, his voice still gruff, but sounding almost sincere.

"I'm fine."

She started to return to her work, but then he spoke again. "You need to report to the front office. Talk to Charlotte."

She stared at him as a chill traveled across her shoulders and down her arms. "What's she want to see me for?"

He avoided her look. "You've…got a call."

"What kind of a call?" Had he actually followed through with this morning's threat to dismiss her?

It couldn't be. Franklin enjoyed firing people, didn't he? Right now, he didn't look as if he was enjoying himself too much.

"Just get to the office," he muttered, turning away.

She nodded and left her worktable. She refused to beg.

If she got fired, she'd find another job easily enough. Hughes Aircraft wasn't the only place in town that could use a trained machinist.

Still, she wished she'd watched her mouth a little closer with Franklin this morning. Sass and vinegar weren't always a good thing.

Minutes later, she stepped into the business office, abuzz with so many typewriters clattering and telephones ringing. Most folks in the plant wanted an office job, but not Bertie. Give her a machine over a typewriter any day. Machine work made more sense to her, and she loved operating a lathe, forming the parts that would be used to build the airplanes that would help win the war. She felt she was doing something useful. Of course, the people working in the office were useful, too.

If she couldn't work with machines in the shop, give her a barn full of milking cows rather than a typewriter in a stifling office. In fact, she'd pretty much prefer anything over being cooped up in an office all day.

A woman with dark hair tied severely away from her face was the first person Bertie encountered when she walked through the door. The woman didn't stop typing, didn't even look up, when Bertie approached her desk.

"Help you?" the woman asked.

Bertie paused, waiting for eye contact.

When the woman finally looked up, her fingers continued their clattering across the typewriter keys. "What do you need?" she snapped.

"I'm Roberta Moennig, and I was told to report to Charlotte. You care to point her out to me?"

The woman's eyes widened, and she stopped typing. The sharpness vanished. "I'm Charlotte," she said in a voice suddenly gone soft. She paused, eyeing Bertie. "Why don't you have a seat, Roberta." She pointed toward the chair in front of her desk, then picked up a telephone receiver from the desktop and handed it to her.

"I'm so sorry," she whispered, placing a hand on Bertie's shoulder before rising from her chair and walking away.

Bertie stared after her in confusion, aware that others in the office had stopped their work and shot glances toward her. Something wasn't right.

She closed her eyes and took a deep breath. "Hello?" she said into the telephone receiver. "Who is this?"

"Bertie? It's me. It's Red."

Her mouth dropped open, and she gasped. It was him! Here she'd been thinking about him and…"Red! Where are you? I've not heard from you in so long I was beginning to wonder if you were okay. What's…why are you…" She frowned. "*Are* you okay? Why are you calling me in the middle of the—"

"I'm…home." His voice was gentle, uncommonly soft. "I'm back home in Hideaway."

"For good? You've been released?"

"I've been discharged."

"I wondered if they'd send you home after Germany's surrender, but since I never heard a word from you in six full weeks, I couldn't help wonderin'—"

"Bertie, we'll have a long talk about that later, but I didn't call to talk about me right now." He paused. "Ma picked me up at the train station, and we stopped by your Pa's place to check on him." Another pause.

Bertie leaned forward. She hated the solemn sound of Red's voice. "What is it? Is Dad all right? Is he sick?"

"Bertie, I'm sorry. I…" He cleared his throat. "I found him…he's gone."

Chapter Eight

For a moment, Bertie didn't grasp what Red meant. She was dreaming—or this wasn't really Red. It was some kind of practical joke.

"I don't understand," she said, hearing the tremor in her own voice. "H-how can you find him if he's gone?"

"I found his body."

She shook her head, unable to let the words sink in. It couldn't be… She'd been worried about him last night when he didn't answer her call, but this?

"Bertie? You there? You okay?"

She closed her eyes and swallowed hard. "I'm sorry, Red, I didn't—"

"Your father's—he's dead," Red said. "I found him myself, out in the cattle lot behind the barn."

She gasped, and her vision went dark for a moment. She became aware of someone standing beside her with a hand on her shoulder, placing a glass of water on the desk in front of her. She looked up to see her friend and roommate, Edith

Frost, looking down at her, dark hair mussed, dark eyes narrowed in concern.

"What's the water for? And what're you doing here?" Edith should be home asleep. Her shift wouldn't begin for a few more hours.

"Charlotte called me," Edith whispered. "She wanted me to be here for you."

"Bertie?" Red said, his voice growing gruffer. "You okay?"

"Yes, I'm...I'll..."

"What's happening out there?" he asked.

"Would you just...give me a minute?" She closed her eyes. "Oh, Dad," she whispered.

It was true. It must be. But reality clashed hard against denial. "No, this can't be," she whispered. "Not Dad. He wasn't fighting in the war."

"He's been fighting a war, all right," Red said.

"How?" she asked. "What happened to him?"

"I wish I knew for sure."

"What do you mean? Was he sick? What happened?"

"There looks to be a...an injury to the side of his head."

She frowned. "And he was in the cattle lot? Could be the bull got him, but ol' Fester's never been a mean—"

"Not Fester. Not an animal...not a four-legged one, anyway. It looks like...like something small hit him in the side of the head, Bertie."

Bertie nearly dropped the phone. "Something like what?"

"I'm not sure yet. The sheriff's out there now, along with the mayor."

She heard something in his voice, some thread of doubt, as if he was hiding something from her, unwilling to say what was on his mind.

"You're saying somebody killed my father?" she heard her

own voice, loud with shock, saw the surprised faces of the people standing around her, and felt as if the floor was buckling beneath her.

"I'm not saying anything yet."

"Oh, yes you are. That's what you're thinking, I can tell."

"Now, don't go putting words in my mouth. I'm gonna find out what happened," Red promised. "You hang on out there, you hear?"

Bertie took a few deep breaths and managed to keep her hands from trembling. "What are you thinking, Red? Talk to me!"

Edith slid a handkerchief into Bertie's hands and placed an arm around her shoulders, but Bertie wouldn't let tears fall.

"Don't you worry, Bertie," Red said. "We'll see to it your father has a good, Christian funeral."

She took a few more breaths. "Red Meyer, what aren't you telling me?"

"I don't know, yet, okay? I don't know what happened. Give us time to figure things out on this end, and I'll call you. You stay put, though. You don't need to be traipsing back here. We'll take good care of your pa's body."

"Don't make any plans until you know how soon Lloyd and I will be able to get there. I'll have to call him right away." Her brother would be working on his in-laws' family farm in Kansas this time of day, but someone should be able to get to him.

There was a short silence, then Red cleared his throat. "Bertie?"

Again, the tone of his voice alerted her. "What?"

"I don't think you oughta come to Hideaway right now. Lloyd neither."

"Of course I'm coming. You can't call and tell me my

father is dead, then think I'm not coming home as soon as I can get there."

"I'm not saying you shouldn't grieve, Bertie, I just think you need to do it out there in California. It's safer there."

Her grip tightened on the telephone receiver. "What do you mean, safer?"

"I already told you, I can't say for sure what happened to your father, but it might not be safe here right now for you or Lloyd, not until we know for sure what happened."

She waited for him to continue.

"Could just be my own reaction to the war," he said, "expectin' trouble when there isn't any, but I can't help thinking the war's brought out some enemies we didn't know anything about, even here in Hideaway."

She felt a chill down her spine. She wasn't sure she wanted him to explain more, wasn't sure she could take much more information today. *Oh, Lord, someone might've killed my father?*

"You hear what I'm saying?" Red asked. "You stay put and stay out of trouble right where you are."

"I can stay out of trouble, but I'll be in Hideaway while I'm doing it," she said. "That's where I'm going to be as soon as I can get there, and don't you try telling me different. I'm not some helpless little thing who can't take care of herself."

There was a quick grunt of irritation over the line, then, "Bertie Moennig, you might cause more trouble than I can handle if you come traipsing into town right now. I never said you was helpless, but don't be daft, either. Stay put!"

The sharpness of his words pierced her anger. But even though part of her could see the wisdom of his words from his point of view, she wasn't him. She couldn't do what he wanted her to.

"Don't you worry about a thing, Red Meyer. I won't be a burden to you."

"Now, Bert, you know that isn't what I meant, I was only trying to—"

"You'd better give me some space *when* I get there, because I'm comin'. Don't you dare treat me like I don't belong." She returned the phone receiver to its base, and pressed her forehead to the cool desktop for a few seconds.

A hand touched her shoulder. "Are you okay, sweetie?"

Edith's voice was soothing, but it also cautioned her. Sorrow and self pity too often formed a partnership, but it wasn't going to happen this time. Not with Bertie Moennig. She couldn't afford that weakness.

The door opened, and she looked up to see Franklin walk in, his beefy shoulders grazing the sides of the door frame. For once, his presence didn't threaten her.

"I won't be back to work today," she told him, bracing herself for an argument.

"I know. I've already got someone on your job." He glanced around at the office workers who hovered near. Though he wasn't their supervisor, they scattered back to their desks.

He crossed the room and leaned over Bertie. "I'm sorry about your father. Are you going to be okay, hillbilly?"

The sudden, unfamiliar note of gentleness in his voice surprised her. "Thank you. I'll be fine, but I have to catch a train to Missouri."

He nodded. "Any idea how long you'll be gone?"

She hesitated. She may not be back. Yes, she was needed here, but she would be needed on the farm at Hideaway with Dad gone. Cows would have to be fed and milked, the crops gathered, and she couldn't expect Lloyd to leave his in-laws in the lurch so he could tend to everything.

"Hillbilly?" Franklin said sharply. "When do you think you'll be back?"

"I'm not sure. I've got a farm to run now, and the troops need food as badly as they need airplanes."

"Not sure I can keep your job open for you."

"I'm not askin' you to."

He ran a thick palm across his forehead. "I'll tell you what, you give me a call when you decide."

She gave him a wry look. "I thought I was about to get fired today."

A hint of a smile touched his mouth, and his eyes wandered downward. "That's what I wanted you to think. You work better that way." He gave her a wink, then turned and left, his thick shoulders grazing the sides of the door frame once more.

Edith stepped up beside Bertie. "Well, what do you know? That slave driver might have a heart, after all."

Bertie allowed herself to be distracted. "Don't count on it. He just knows good help when he mistreats it."

"Are you sure you're going to be okay?"

A quick swallow, a deep breath, and Bertie regained control of her emotions. There were things to do. "All I need is a train ticket to Missouri."

Edith nodded. "We'll make that two tickets. I'm not letting you go by yourself."

"You have a job to do," Bertie said.

"I have a friend to sustain, and that is more important to me than my job right now."

"You have a war effort to support," Bertie repeated. "I'm going alone. Don't you argue with me, Edith Frost."

She had to make arrangements to get home to Hideaway.

Chapter Nine

Red stared at the telephone receiver, then replaced it in its holder on the wall of the dining room. Curious paying guests returned their attention to their noontime meals at the long table. He'd tried to keep his voice down, but it hadn't worked very well.

Most of the guests were lodgers for a day or two, maybe a week at most. Two he recognized from years past, four of them he'd never seen.

Then there was John Martin, a good friend who'd been lodging at the Meyer Guesthouse for years, ever since he'd started teaching school in town. On weekends he went to the family farm several miles out, to help his father and fifteen-year-old brother work the fields while his older brother, Cecil, fought in the Pacific Theater. With school out, John continued to work in town during the week, helping build new classrooms.

Ivan Potts was also at the table. He and John had both been so shocked to see Red's cane and his limp, their reactions would have been almost comical if Red was in the mood to laugh. He wasn't.

After a couple of short words from him, both John and Ivan knew better than to ask about his injury in front of the guests.

It was awkward trying to take care of business with strangers hearing everything he'd said to Bertie over the telephone.

Ma was working in the kitchen, pulling dessert out of the oven. She hardly ever sat and ate with the lodgers and other customers. No time. No help. As soon as she got all the food on the table, it was time to start cleaning up.

The guests showed a sudden interest in their chicken and dumplings. They were almost convincing. This meal was Ma's specialty, with thick chunks of chicken in the creamiest gravy and lightest dumplings this world had ever tasted.

These people didn't fool Red, though. They were hungry for more details of his conversation with Bertie, in spite of the fact that their meal was late in coming because of all the awful activity after finding Joseph's body.

"Bertie's coming back home, isn't she?" asked John from his seat halfway down the table.

Red nodded. "I don't know how I could've made it more clear that she needs to stay away."

"Me, neither," John said. "But you know Bertie. She's going to do what she wants to do, and you'd better not get in her way. I bet you made her cry, didn't you?"

Red cast his friend a glare. "No."

"You aren't that great with women, are you, Charles Frederick?" asked Ivan, who sat at the far end of the table.

Red glowered at him. "You're not making this any easier." Ivan never hesitated to speak his mind, but he might be in danger of a tongue lashing if he didn't mind his manners, war hero or not.

The six other lodgers kept their heads down and ate in

silence. Red might've been gone a long time, but he sure didn't remember ever having a quiet dining table before.

Ma bustled out through the kitchen door and gave Red a warning look. She never liked airing private matters in front of paying guests, and though his call to Bertie within hearing of everyone had been unavoidable, further talk was not.

Red got the message. He took a few bites of his food, but could barely swallow. He didn't have much of an appetite, even though his ma's chicken and dumplings were his favorite food, and she had prepared it special, just for him.

He couldn't get his mind off Joseph. Who could have done something like this to him? Those lifeless eyes… Bertie had her father's eyes.

A widower, all alone on the farm. Everybody knew there was no truer man in Hideaway. Joseph had helped his neighbors when they needed help, and he worked hard to keep his farm going.

He had been the first person in the county to learn that this soil was ideal for raising tomatoes, and so he had planted fields of tomatoes, and encouraged others to do the same. Could be his wisdom had saved the community from a lot more loss during the depression.

His death didn't make sense, and Red felt especially helpless—particularly since he'd been told by the sheriff to stay out from underfoot.

Underfoot! Old Butch Coggins was the one underfoot. He wouldn't know a crime scene if he stumbled over a murder weapon and saw the victim bleeding to death in front of him.

Red grabbed his plate in one hand, his cane in the other, and left the table. If he stayed, he'd for sure shoot off his mouth about something he shouldn't. Ma would forgive him for his rudeness in leaving the table. Eventually.

Right now he couldn't force a smile, couldn't make friendly conversation.

He hobbled through the large living room, past the fireplace, and turned into the front parlor. He used the cane to close the door behind him, then stood for a moment, still holding his plate of dumplings as he stared out the big picture window toward the river. He had a bad feeling that life in Hideaway was about to change even more drastically than it already had. He hated the thought.

A fella was bound to expect the worst after seeing the things he'd seen in Italy.

He'd heard too many tales about the way Japanese Americans had been treated here in America during the past few years. They'd been driven from their homes and forced into detention centers, often losing their property, their friends, their jobs. Men had been separated from their wives and children, and sometimes had been forced to return to their native country—where they were now considered the enemy.

He'd also heard rumors about Germans being treated the same way, though he wasn't sure if there was any truth to it. Wild stories flew through the Army as fast as bullets.

"Wasn't this war enough, God?" he whispered, half angry, half pleading. "Does it have to be brought right here to our own doorstep?"

Edith Frost turned from the telephone ten minutes after she'd picked up the receiver, her dark gaze lingering on Bertie's face, concern evident. "Well, sweetie, we've got tickets for early tomorrow morning unless we get bumped by servicemen coming home or being called out for duty."

Bertie nodded her thanks. "I could've made the arrangements myself."

"Hush, now, and let me pamper you a little. It's not much, considering how much you've done for me the past months. I told the clerk this was a funeral trip, but she wouldn't budge. We'll still have to wait to know for sure until the last minute."

Bertie put her hands on her hips. "You mean she wouldn't let both of us travel for bereavement. I bet *she'd* let me go by myself, *unlike* a certain person who doesn't think I'm capable of traveling alone across five states."

"Six."

"Missouri doesn't count. We're barely inside the state line by fifty miles."

"Seventy."

"Not in a straight line."

"From what I hear tell, there aren't any straight roads in your part of Missouri."

"Edith, you need to stay here. How long have you waited to work on this new project?"

Edith waved her hand. "The Spruce Goose project won't get off the ground, and no pun intended." She shook her head. "Wood and glue? Howard Hughes must have lost his mind when he decided to fund that contraption."

Bertie shot a glance around at the secretaries, who had returned to their typing. "You shouldn't talk about him that way. He's dedicated to the war effort."

"This war effort is making him plenty of money."

"Edith, what's changed your mind? Last I heard, you were gung ho for that project. You begged for weeks to be transferred, and now that you are, you—"

Edith took Bertie's arm and glanced at the others, then the two of them walked out the front door. The bright Southern California sunlight touched their faces and seemed to settle beneath the surface of Bertie's skin. She closed her eyes, wondering if she would ever feel this west coast warmth again, smell the air, enjoy this clearness that she had only experienced in California.

It was like honey to the soul.

Edith waited until they were out of earshot of the office, then said, "What's changed my mind is you, Roberta Moennig. You don't need to be alone right now."

"What makes you think I'll ever be alone? The trains will be packed with servicemen coming home, and Hideaway is filled with friends. I know I'll be in your daily prayers."

"How will I know how to pray for you if I don't know what kind of mischief you're into?" Edith asked.

"I don't get into mischief, and if I ever do, I'll be sure to call you," Bertie said dryly.

Edith shook her head, resolute. "I spent too much time alone after Harper got killed at Pearl Harbor. I don't want that to happen to you."

In spite of herself, Bertie was touched by the admission. Edith hadn't spoken much about losing her husband, and at times it seemed she stayed especially busy for the sole purpose of avoiding thoughts of her loss.

"You heard what I told Franklin," Bertie said softly. "I may not be back. In fact, the more I think about it, I know I probably won't be, not with Red back home." Hearing the tremor in her own voice, she realized again how much she'd come to love this place in such a few months.

And yet…Hideaway was home.

"It's too early to know what you're going to do," Edith said. "So don't go making plans."

"Don't lecture me," Bertie said. "My brother, Lloyd, is working for his in-laws on a huge ranch in Kansas. He can't leave them and move back home to take care of things. There's no one but me."

"Farming's no life for a single woman," Edith said.

"But the farm's still there, and it can't be left to manage itself."

"You aren't the only person in the world who can run a farm."

"I can't sell off what Dad worked so hard to build."

Edith shook her head. "Nobody's asking you to. Look, I'm sorry, I shouldn't have brought this up. You're already over-whelmed. Give yourself a chance to grieve your father's passing. I had a pastor tell me not to make any big decisions for at least six months after Harper died." She shrugged. "Thing is, it's been three and a half years, and I still don't have any plans."

Bertie closed her eyes. "If I'd only known, when I came out here, that I'd never see Dad alive again…I wouldn't've left Hideaway."

Edith put her arms around Bertie and drew her close. Bertie hugged her back, but still she refused to cry. If she did—if she started thinking about how much she'd lost—she'd be stuck in despair.

Chapter Ten

The parlor door swung open and Red turned to find Ivan Potts and John Martin filing in, both solemn, heads bowed.

Ivan sank into the wingback chair beside Red and gazed outside. John sat on the sofa. None of the men spoke for a few moments. They didn't need to. The three of them had known each other well-nigh all their lives.

"I can't believe Joseph's gone," John said.

"Me neither," Ivan agreed. "Bertie's got to be hurting bad."

"Especially after Red yelled at her," John said.

Red scowled out the window. "I might as well have called from the coffee shop, so's half the town could've gotten into the conversation."

"For pity's sake, Red, she's just lost her father," John said. "You're not going to keep that little gal long if you can't learn to treat her any better than that."

Ivan frowned at John. "In case you hadn't noticed, my friend, Bertie's been loyal to Red for three years. I was in the service for barely six months when your sister decided she wanted to up and marry Eugene Arthur."

John scowled. "Dixie never promised to wait for you."

"I never asked her to." Ivan turned to Red. "Did you ask Bertie to wait for you while you were off fighting for our freedom?"

Red shook his head, suddenly uncomfortable. They needed to change the subject.

Ivan nodded to John, as if Red's answer had proved a point. "There you go. Right now Red's the only man here who's even got a girlfriend."

"That could be due to his not being around to run her off," John shot back.

John Martin had a full head of dark brown hair and the tanned skin of a farmer, deep now with summer's glow. He'd tried three times to enlist in any branch of the service that would have him, but he had flat feet and a partial deafness in one ear. He'd been told to help out on the home front.

John was an elementary school teacher in Hideaway. His brother, Cecil, had been a high-school science teacher before joining the Marines.

"How'd Bertie seem to be holding up when you talked to her?" Ivan asked Red.

"Good as can be, I s'pose." Red had never been sorrier for the way he'd spoken. Bertie'd lost her father, and, like John said, he'd practically yelled at her, and for sure scared her half out of her wits, hinting about ugly deeds afoot in Hideaway.

What had gotten into him?

Of course, he knew. It was the same thing that had gotten into everybody—this awful war.

But he'd needed to make Bertie listen, and what he'd said hadn't been a lie. Joseph's death looked suspicious to him. Bertie didn't need to worry about that on top of everything that'd happened to her.

Red had been surprised by the depth of his own grief for Joseph, so he could imagine how Bertie was faring right now.

"Something's wrong," Red said. "It's just wrong. I don't think this was any accident."

"The sheriff's checking things out," John said.

"Dad's out there with him," Ivan reminded him. "As mayor he'll make sure everything's done right. They're looking over the house to see if they can come up with any clues. Maybe they'll find something."

Red gave him a sideways glance. "Butch is not going to get by with brushing this death under the rug just because he doesn't know how to investigate it, or because Joseph had a German heritage."

"Might not have anything to do with Joseph's heritage," John said. "The whole town's filled with Germans and even a few Italians somewhere in the mix, I'd suspect."

"But Joseph hailed from the old country," Red said. "He wasn't born here. You know about the brick through Ma's window."

"I'd say I do." John brushed his hair back, demonstrating how close the brick had come to his head. There was a small gash on his forehead from the flying glass.

"And Ma's German," Red said. "To me, that smacks of prejudice."

"Old Butch has never had a murder in these parts," John said. "He doesn't know what one looks like."

"That's because he turns a blind eye to most meanness," Ivan said.

Red thought about that a minute, then looked at his friends, leaning forward, glancing toward the door. He kept his voice low. "Think this time Butch might be part of the meanness?"

Ivan and John looked at each other, and the silence in the room filled Red's ears before talk and laughter reached him from the dining room. Chairs scraped across the wooden floor, and voices drifted into the living room.

"I know you've never been too crazy about the sheriff," Ivan told Red. "But do you really think he could be behind this?"

"Well, now, just wait a minute," John said. "Butch and Joseph never have seen eye to eye about anything. And I overheard Butch a few weeks ago telling a bunch of the men down at the coffee shop that there weren't enough detention centers in this country to place all the folks who don't belong here."

Red sighed. "I don't mean to accuse the sheriff of something like that, but it seems to me Butch has always been less interested in keeping the peace than in using his position to con favors from the citizens." Hideaway didn't have a police force. The town wasn't big enough. He'd heard tell that some churches in big cities were larger than Hideaway.

That was hard to imagine.

"Well," Ivan said, "at best we have to say the sheriff doesn't know what he's doing. He could use some help, whether he asks for it or not."

"Red, you're the tracker," John said. "What your daddy didn't teach you, the Army did."

"You saying a crippled man oughta run for sheriff?" Red asked.

"You oughta take the lead on this investigation," John said.

"*We* ought to take the lead," Ivan said. "We've been in Hideaway longer than Butch has. We know the people. Red and I know how to hunt for the enemy."

"I can do my share," John said.

Lilly Meyer bustled through the French doors, deftly holding a tray with three dishes of blackberry cobbler straight from the oven. "Pardon me for eavesdropping, fellas, but you can start right out there in our backyard, Charles Frederick. Whoever threw that brick at John might well be the criminal we're looking for."

"That's where I aim to start," Red told her. "You got a room for Bertie? I guess you heard she's comin' to town, and she sure oughtn't be staying out on the farm."

"There's always room for our Bertie, even if I have to give her my own bedroom," Lilly said. "You boys just be sure to find out what happened to Joseph."

Red didn't plan to stop until he had the job complete.

Bertie pulled her best skirts and blouses from the tiny closet on her side of the bedroom. If only she had some idea about how long she'd be in Missouri—or if she was even coming back here. She was tempted to pack light, but then she reached beneath her narrow bed and pulled out a box of letters from Red. Just thumbing through them, she discovered many tiny, pressed blooms of some of her favorite flowers—picked by Red for her when they were dating just before he left for boot camp.

The memories suddenly cascaded over her, and her eyes blurred with tears. She pulled another letter from the pile.

Dear Bertie,

I won't tell anyone you cried, if you won't tell everyone I sleep with your picture in my pocket, close as I can get it to my heart.

Did I tell you that the guys here don't believe in baths? Some kind of superstition, I guess. One soldier—didn't get his name—said I washed too much. It erases the mud that gives me some camouflage. All I got to say about that is I'd rather be shot than stink like these folks do.

A fella doesn't have to live like an animal over here, most of them just want to.

Another buddy of mine got a Dear John letter yesterday. I'll send you his name and address, and maybe you have another pretty friend who could write to him, make him feel not so alone.

Don't know what I'd do without these letters, Bertie. It's so easy for a man to give up hope altogether, seeing the pain and death that stalks these fields.

When we both get back home to Hideaway, I don't ever want to leave the state again. I just want to settle and stay. Give it some thought.

I kinda like you.

Your Red

She'd reread this one two or three times a week, and had pressed a lilac between its pages, because that was Red's favorite flower, and this letter was the closest he'd ever come to proposing to her. He'd skirted all around the issue, making hints, letting her know he might be interested, but never committing.

To tease him, she'd ignored the subject altogether in her reply to him, hoping he might write something a little more romantic the next time.

The next time, there was nothing about settling. Months passed, and nothing even close to that subject came up again.

What was she expected to do, ask *him* for his hand in marriage? She smiled at that thought. Maybe she could ask Red's mother for permission to ask him. What a laugh that would give Lilly.

On a whim, Bertie packed all the letters, placing them neatly in the bottom of her heavy old carryall. On top of them, she folded her work jeans and boots, and then her dressier clothes for the funeral, church, and entertaining company after the funeral.

In spite of all that had happened, she wanted to look her best when she saw Red for the first time in a year. Dad would have understood.

Chapter Eleven

Late Monday afternoon, Red felt the burn of the sun on the back of his neck, tellin' him the summer heat had already begun to rule the season. Humidity was just as uncomfortable as the heat, settling back in after a short relief from the rain the area had gotten yesterday evening.

He didn't look up when he heard the squeak of the back door, but continued to study the grass and packed mud along the back fence. Someone had been this way recently, taking care to stay on the grass for the most part—but not taking care enough.

He watched where he stepped, as well, not only to avoid possible tracks, but to keep his shoes free from goose and chicken poop. Ma hated when that got tracked into the house.

"I wouldn't let nobody but Joseph Moennig out in the backyard since the brick shot through the window," Lilly Meyer called across the half-acre yard she'd planted with roses and irises, along with cabbages, lettuce, okra, tomatoes, green beans, carrots and potatoes, and a half dozen other vegetables.

Red glanced at her over his shoulder. His mother had once been almost as good at tracking as his father. In fact, back in their younger days, she'd been better at following the coon dogs.

It hadn't set well with Pa.

"You check for any prints before the rain?" Red asked.

She nodded. "Found a few. Looked to be a couple different people, but a couple of the prints matched shoes belonging to our boarders." She pointed toward one set farther along the fence line. "See that gash in the heel of the left shoe?"

Red nodded.

"That one don't belong to any boarder."

Taking care not to step on the tracks he'd found, Red followed the line of the white picket fence, and soon discovered where someone had climbed the old hawthorn tree.

"See this?" he called to his mother. "The grass must've been pressed into the mud here where somebody stepped. It's straightened since, but the mud dried on it."

She pointed to the lowest limb of the tree. "Some of the mud got smeared onto the wood, here. Young hoodlums, maybe?"

"Could be." He wasn't convinced.

"Kids climb trees," she said, obviously reading his mind.

"They're not the only ones. I've seen soldiers on both sides of the war climb trees when they had to."

"You think this has something to do with the war, then," she said.

"I'm not saying that. Did he mention anything about someone causing him trouble?"

"Only the missing livestock. His neighbors lost some, too. But I'll tell you one thing—if someone was causin' Joseph grief, he'd have fought back."

Red agreed. Joseph was never one to back down from a fight.

"Why don't you ask Bertie when she gets here?" Lilly asked. "He might've said something to her about a problem."

Red gave his mother a sharp look. "She call you back after lunch today?"

"Sure did. She's on her way, if she can catch the train tomorrow. Should be here by Thursday, in plenty of time for the funeral on Friday."

Red sighed, leaning against the tree limb. "Ma, you don't need to be encouraging her about anything. We can't stop her from coming, but she oughta get back on that train as soon as the funeral's over and head on back to California."

Lilly gave him a look that expressed her opinion of his advice. "You're sure in a hurry to get rid of her."

"I already said it ain't safe here. Why won't anybody listen to me?"

"Could be 'cause I happen to think she's as safe here as she is anywhere in the world. She's got friends and neighbors to protect her. There might be some villains in this town, but the good folks outnumber 'em." Ma's eyes narrowed. "I think there's some other reason you want her gone from here."

Red looked away. "I don't know that you two oughta be getting so close."

"Don't you go tellin' me who I can and can't be friends with. Bertie and I have always been friends, long before the two of you started your romance. Why are you suddenly so worried about it?"

"Because you've got plans in mind that won't ever come to pass now."

"Why don't you let me mind my own plans? I'll be

friends with Bertie no matter what happens between the two of you, though I'd for sure love to have her as my daughter-in-law."

He sighed, a heavy sigh that he knew his mother would probably read well. "Ain't gonna happen, Ma." He turned and held her gaze.

Her thick red eyebrows lowered over large blue eyes. "You two have a fallin' out besides the one on the phone today?"

He shook his head.

She nodded at his leg. "That got something to do with it?"

He didn't answer, but returned his attention to the tracks again.

"You can't let something like that change your life, Charles Frederick," she said. "You can't let it ruin what you got goin' with Bertie. That's too special."

He glanced at the garden. "I might not make such a good husband like this, but at least I can help you with the gardening." It was once his job to keep the vegetables in good supply, keep the chickens fed, the cows milked, and till and harvest the plot of rich farmland between the house and the riverside.

Sure, with the war on, the boarders—especially those who knew Lilly Meyer's circumstances—sometimes helped with household chores. Havin' a little help now and then wasn't anything like having her own healthy, strong son at home.

"You know anything about that G.I. bill they voted into law last year?" she asked.

"I might."

"It means the people who served our country in the war can have their college schoolin' paid for by their country."

"Yep."

She placed her hands on her broad hips. "So why don't

you tell me which college you plan to attend? I don't need you here underfoot all the time when you could be gettin' a good education, learnin' a good trade that'll keep you going through your whole life."

"I don't need to learn farmin', Ma. Nor fishin', nor huntin'. Don't fix what ain't broke."

She sighed. "You can't have it both ways. You don't seem to think you can farm with that leg like it is, so you'd better start planning for something else. You're smart, you can learn something new. Accounting, maybe, or teaching, or even doctoring." She grinned, sighing theatrically. "My son, the doctor. Wouldn't ol' Drusilla Short turn green over that? What this town really needs is a good—"

"Think you could give me a day or two before you ship me off to school?" He kneaded his aching thigh.

She watched him in silence for a moment. "The doc say it was your muscle causing you the most trouble?"

"That's what seems to be the problem now."

"Bertie might be able to help you with that."

"Think we could get off that subject for a while?" He didn't want to keep being reminded about what he needed to give up. His own thoughts of Bertie were enough to keep him awake at night.

"Her ma taught her all she could about those medicinal herbs she used on folks who didn't like to leave Hideaway to go to the doctor."

Red sighed. As usual, his mother had ignored his request. Some things the war didn't change. "Bertie's got enough to worry about," he said sharply.

His mother gave him a wise look. She let the silence fall between them, just as she always used to when he sassed her, giving him plenty of time to think about what he'd said.

"Don't treat me like a little kid now, Ma."

"You didn't say anything to her about your leg when you called her."

"How was I gonna do that? Tell her, 'Sorry, Bertie, I found your father dead out in the cattle lot. Oh, by the way, I've got a war injury that's changed everything?'"

"I'm not saying that, but you can't let her come all the way here and see you without warning her first."

"I don't know what else I can do about it now."

"You should've told her weeks ago," Ma muttered. "I should've told her and gotten it over with."

"She'll know soon enough, I guess," he snapped again, then leaned hard on his cane on the way back to the house.

"Still got some of your pa in you," she said loudly enough for him to hear. "Stubborn old cuss had a little too much o' that male pride. It wasn't pretty on him, either."

"Don't talk ill of the dead, Ma. It's bad luck," he called over his shoulder.

"Yep, and it's not respectful, but you're not dead," she called after him. "Leastways, you're still up and movin' around. Don't give up on life until it gives up on you."

He kept walking. He hadn't given up on life, had he? Maybe life had given up on him. Or maybe God had.

Could be God had given up on the whole world, not just him? Everybody who'd seen the mass of war scars on Europe had reason to wonder. Now everybody was counting the loss of lives. They weren't done counting yet, but it was many millions, that much they knew.

And still people trusted in God?

Lately, he'd been wondering a lot about whether God had turned His back on the whole lot of the earth. Maybe they had disgusted Him to the point that He had finally decided to leave them to their own orneriness. They would be allowed to destroy one another without His interference.

Judging by the death and killing Red had seen on the front lines, he couldn't say he'd blame God.

Chapter Twelve

Late Thursday morning, Bertie slowly stood from her seat on the train, stretching her arms and rubbing achy back muscles. Worn to a bare nubbin from the constant movement of the railcar in which she and Edith had ridden for the past two days, she yawned as she reached for her carryall and turned to look at her friend.

Edith looked fresh and pretty and well rested. Bertie's head ached, her legs were stiff, and no matter how much she stretched, she couldn't work out the kinks.

"After sleeping on these hard, rocking beds for two nights, I have a feeling it'll be a while before I can walk without wobbling," she muttered.

Edith grinned at Bertie, her dark brown eyes filled with a little too much wide-awake cheer. "You'll be fine in fifteen minutes."

"Sure, you can say that. You slept last night."

"I knew you were having trouble. That's why I didn't wake you first thing this morning. Didn't you get any sleep at all?" Edith asked.

"Not until the wee morning hours."

Edith frowned as she studied Bertie's face. "You've been fretting more and more the closer you've gotten to home. I'd have thought you'd be relieved to get here."

Bertie shrugged. What kind of welcome would they find here? Or would they even get a welcome? "Lilly promised she'd make sure we had a ride home from Hollister, but I can't help wondering what's going to happen when we get to Hideaway."

"It's going to be fine," Edith assured her.

Bertie wasn't so confident about that. She'd had two long days to think about Red's words, to compare them to what the sheriff told her about the case when she called him from a stop in Albuquerque. According to Red, danger was afoot. According to Butch Coggins, the town was fine, nothing was wrong and Dad had been in a little farming accident. It happened.

She wanted to believe Butch so badly that, until about the middle of last night, she'd been reassured. But the more she thought about it, the less likely it seemed that Dad had been that careless. Joseph Moennig was one of the most careful men Bertie had ever known. To have the sheriff—who wasn't even a citizen of Hideaway—say such a thing about her father had begun to gall her.

And then she'd begun to wonder if Red hadn't reacted the same way. Red loved Dad almost as much as he'd loved his own father. Maybe he'd simply resented Butch's casual dismissal of Dad's death. Or maybe, being among men from all over the country, he knew something more about what was happening to German Americans in this country. Suspicions ran high at times like these.

Edith looped her arm through Bertie's. "Care to tell me what's working through that mind of yours?"

"I think I know what Red's worried about."

Edith raised her eyebrows as other passengers bustled past them to the exit. "Care to share?"

"You've heard about the internment camps, same as I have," Bertie said.

"What does that have to do with you and me arriving in Hideaway?"

Bertie lowered her voice. "The Meyers and the Moennigs are German Americans. Red and I are both children of German immigrants. It isn't just the Japanese who've been forced into those camps."

"The Meyers and the Moennigs didn't qualify for those camps any more than most other Americans of German descent," Edith said. "Besides, the camps here in America are nothing like the concentration camps we've heard about in Germany, or even the detention camps in Japan."

"I still don't have a hankerin' to go there." Though Bertie knew Edith was probably right, it didn't stop her from worrying. Folks did all manner of hideous things to one another during times of stress. Though the war could bring out the best in some, it could bring out the worst in others. Hideaway was no different than any other town in America.

Of course, her government had taken men—even whole families—to internment camps. That was a long way from stealing cattle and then killing the owners.

A very long way.

Bertie allowed the porter to help her down the steps of the passenger car, then moved aside for the rest of the passengers disembarking. The moist warmth of mid-June surrounded her as the brightness of the sunlight hurt her eyes. The faint smell of smoke from the train engines permeated the air.

She knew she probably looked as tired and gritty as she felt.

She glanced around the crowded station, saw no familiar faces, and slid her tiny hand mirror from her purse.

Ugh. Puffy eyes. Limp, stringy hair. A streak of black on the collar of her blouse—dirt? Grease? She didn't know. All she knew was that she didn't want Red to see her this way after being apart a year—and especially since the last time she'd spoken with him on the telephone, she'd hung up on him.

She'd felt badly about that ever since. Red was just worried about her, and here she'd lashed out at him as if he was the enemy.

By this time, she was so tired of travel that she shouldn't care how she looked, as long as she didn't have to climb back onto that train.

She tugged at the sleeve of her red-checked blouse, knowing it wouldn't help with the wrinkles or the dirt, but glad she wasn't wearing something in a solid color. Prints didn't show stains or wrinkles as badly. She wished she'd thought to pack more than two dresses. Her denims were practical—and a lot more comfortable than the formfitting skirt she had on—but according to Lilly, there would be quite a few townsfolk wanting to see her as soon as she arrived in Hideaway.

Still, she'd be busy on the farm. She would need the work clothes more than dresses.

Foremost on her mind, however, was her father and the questions that she couldn't stop from churning in her head.

Why had she lost so much in three years? First Mom, now Dad. And her brother? She'd discovered, after calling Lloyd on Monday night, that he was too sick to travel home for the funeral. He had been taken to the sanitarium in Mt. Vernon, Missouri, with a possible diagnosis of tuberculosis. The test results wouldn't be final for several weeks, and until then, he would be kept isolated from his family. Typical of Lloyd, he had decided not to call Bertie or Dad about it until he had the results.

Instead of coming to Dad's funeral, Lloyd was being forced to grieve alone.

Bertie could only pray the final diagnosis was negative. If it was positive, her prayers would be that her sister-in-law, Mary, and her little niece and nephew, Joann and Steven, hadn't contracted the horrible disease from him.

How much was one family supposed to take?

She felt Edith's arm around her shoulders. Edith was such a comfort, always knowing when Bertie needed to have her mind distracted from painful thoughts.

But even Edith's presence didn't cheer Bertie when she caught sight of two familiar faces in the small crowd waiting to board. She should be glad to see people she hadn't seen in nearly ten months. Instead, she avoided their gazes.

She couldn't bear to see the sympathy in their eyes. Even worse, what if those gazes held accusation of her German heritage?

The thought stunned her, and she swung away quickly. Where had *that* come from? Was she really that consumed by the fear that her own country could turn against her, dragging her, the daughter of a German immigrant, off to some internment camp? What nonsense!

There was something else going on here. Her government wouldn't have murdered Dad.

If that was even what had happened to him. How was she supposed to know for sure?

A wave of loss smacked her hard yet again, as it had numerous times since she'd left California. Home would never be the same, because she wasn't coming home. Family was home. How could Hideaway be home without her loved ones there?

She turned and scanned the crowd for Red's brick-colored hair and broad shoulders, but instead she caught sight of someone hailing her from the parking area in front of the rail station.

Heavy arms flapped in the air as Lilly Meyer waved to her from the open window of a shiny black Chevrolet pulling into the lot.

Bertie stood on tiptoe and waved back, relief washing through her.

"You know that woman?" Edith asked.

"Red's mother." Bertie looked at the driver. He was bent over, and all Bertie could see was a head of short blond hair. Not red. She looked into the backseat of the car, but it was empty.

The enormity of her disappointment surprised her. Red hadn't come. All those letters about how he'd missed her, and yet when it came right down to the moment of truth, he didn't show up to meet her.

Why not?

She picked up her suitcase and carried it toward the car. "Looks like Red decided he didn't have time to meet us." The bitterness in her voice surprised her. What an ugly trait in a lady. But what an ugly act for a man not to appear when the woman he'd sworn to be missing all these years was finally arriving.

He'd had the chance to see her get off the train, to greet her and let her know how glad he was to be with her again, to hold her in his arms. But he hadn't found the time for that.

"Don't you let a man get you down," Edith said. "You've got more important things to…" her voice trailed away and her steps slowed.

Bertie looked up to see what had distracted her friend's attention, and saw her staring at the car's driver, who was rushing around the front toward the passenger door to help Lilly out. Lilly, however, was already making her own way out.

"If that isn't Red, who is it?" Edith asked.

"Lilly's obviously gotten someone else to drive her." As they drew closer, Bertie recognized that muscular frame and that characteristic grin, and felt another rush of relief. Ivan Potts was home from the war. When had he arrived?

"How long ago did you say Red's father died?" Edith asked.

"Twelve years."

"And his mother still doesn't know how to drive?"

Bertie shook her head. "She always said that if she needed to get anywhere farther than her horse could take her, she'd better get her head examined."

Edith chuckled. "Sounds like quite a homebody."

"She is," Bertie said, admiring the car. So Gerald and Arielle Potts had followed through with their promise to buy Ivan a new car when he arrived home from the war. From the looks of it, they'd gone all out. Of course, that couldn't be a brand new car, since no new cars had been manufactured since 1942. Still, a three-year-old Chevrolet was the newest thing out there.

Nothing had ever been too good for Ivan, according to his parents.

"Remember I've told you that we folks in Hideaway live at a little slower pace than you've been used to in California," Bertie said.

"Sounds good to me." Edith's gaze remained on Ivan as they approached the car. "That's a friend of yours?"

In spite of all, Bertie felt a grin spread across her face. How good it was to see Ivan again! Her old friend seemed to have matured. With his broad shoulders, short, golden hair and dark brown eyes, he could pass for a star of cinema.

"You've already been introduced, silly," she told Edith. "You've even written to him a few times. I've known Ivan Potts since first grade. His father, Gerald, is the mayor of Hideaway."

"So that's the eloquent Marine with the neat handwriting and the heart of a poet."

Bertie grinned. "I'd've never thought that about Ivan. I'm surprised he didn't tell me he was coming home." She glanced at Edith. "In fact, I'm surprised he didn't tell you, if he's writing you poetry. Come and let me introduce you to Ivan and Lilly."

Edith linked her arm through Bertie's once more. "That's my girl. Now you're talking."

Chapter Thirteen

The ripe odor of the Moennig's barnyard filtered around Red in the warm sun as he knelt beside the closed gate. Curious cows and calves snuffled at his head. He paid them no mind. He'd found what he was after—footprints that matched those in the backyard at home. Leastways, he was pretty sure of it.

He'd discovered quickly that he'd get no help from the sheriff on Joseph's case. There was no case, according to Butch Coggins. As it had turned out, the hole in the side of Joseph's head wasn't made by a bullet, but a nail in a piece of wood. Butch decided Joseph had simply had an unfortunate accident and fallen on it.

Red knew Joseph would never have kept anything like that in the cattle lot, because it could have injured one of the animals. No farmer in his right mind would be so careless, and certainly not Joseph. Cattle were a precious stock, always had been, but especially now, when most of the beef was being sent to the armed forces to help keep their fighting men well fed.

The lot itself, where Joseph had fallen, was useless to

show tracks. The animals had destroyed anything Red might've found there. But he did pick up on some dried mud on the wooden gate, where someone had climbed over. From there he had followed tracks through the grass and into the woods south of the house. They led him downhill to the James River and then disappeared.

Had whoever it was left by boat or swum across?

Red knelt again in the mud at the edge of the woods, and reached for a layer of bark he'd peeled from a tree. With another piece of thin bark, he gently dug and lifted the dried mud around the shoe impression, until he placed the whole, unbroken print into the makeshift holder.

Back at home, he could make a plaster impression of the print, trace it on paper, and quietly make some comparisons.

He didn't doubt someone in this town was up to no good. He'd find out who the dirty rascal was before anybody else was hurt, or his name wasn't Charles Frederick Meyer.

He might not be able to return to the war, but he could still fight in his own special way. The war had come to his home turf. He'd have to turn it away as best he could.

Bertie sat in the backseat of the car behind Lilly Meyer on the drive back to Hideaway. The backseat wasn't as comfortable as the front seat, and though Lilly had tried to convince Bertie to take the front, Bertie wouldn't hear of it.

"I've been reading about how busy you girls have been out in California," Lilly said. "Makes me almost wish I was the kind of gal to go out there, myself, helping with the blood drive, working on the very airplanes that might win us a war. I'm so proud of what you've done."

"You're doing plenty," Bertie said. "You've kept up the business with everyone gone. And a son in the Army."

"Yes, but you know how backward we are out here in our own corner of the world. Never catching up with the news of the war until a day or so after the rest of the country already knows about it."

Lilly seemed to have put on some weight since Bertie left for California, but she was as kind as ever, and as pretty. Her red hair was more golden than her youngest son's, and her clear blue eyes often shone with the same good humor that characterized Red. Lilly's eyes also frequently glinted with her own special brand of wise observation, which she seldom kept to herself. But there wasn't much evidence of brightness in her expression now. Her sorrow about Joseph and her tender compassion for Bertie shadowed her face.

Lilly Meyer was a strong woman who Bertie had always admired. After her husband's death, in the middle of the Great Depression, she'd refused to ask for help. Though neighbors had tried to do as much as they could, Lilly stood firm in her self-sufficiency.

She cared for her children the best way she knew how, with her garden and guesthouse, her innate business savvy and other talents.

Lilly could cook like a dream, and she kept her house spotless. Her guests ate like kings and queens, and the many entertaining activities she offered in her establishment brought the same folks back year after year from all over the country. That was how she'd supported her kids.

Though Red had seemed content to remain at home and help Lilly after his brother and sister flew the coop, Bertie guessed he simply could not bring himself to leave his mother without good help at the house.

"I've got a room ready for you at my place," Lilly said. "Had a traveling couple move on this morning, and—"

"That's very kind of you," Bertie said, "but I need to get home and settle in. I'm sure there's work that needs doin' around the place, what with—" To her embarrassment, her voice cracked.

"No problem there," Lilly said, gesturing toward Ivan, whom Bertie had caught watching Edith in his rearview mirror. "Ivan and Red plan to do those chores themselves. They're no strangers to hard work, and after what they've been through in the war, a little farming won't tire them out."

"But I know how to farm," Bertie said. "I've not forgotten how to work."

Ivan and Lilly exchanged a glance in the front seat. Bertie narrowed her eyes.

"Bertie, I sure could use your help at the guesthouse for a few days," Lilly said. "The men know all about farm chores, but they don't know how to bake. That's what I need help with right now."

Bertie gave her a suspicious glance.

"Those black walnut cakes of yours've won plenty of blue ribbons at the fair," Lilly said. "And we have guests right now who are a might too demanding for me." She slung her heavy arm over the seat and turned to pin Bertie with a long look. "Think you could do that for me, just this once?"

Bertie knew she was being had, but she couldn't argue with Lilly. She didn't have the strength. "Not sure what I could bake that you couldn't do better."

"I've got me some black walnuts I held over from last year. We've got honey and molasses aplenty, though there ain't much sugar. Don't guess you'd have much trouble baking without sugar, knowing what a good cook your mother was."

"I have a recipe for molasses oatmeal cookies with black walnuts."

Lilly nodded. "Sounds like it'll work."

"It's at the farmhouse, so I'll have to go get it."

"What say we stop in there on our way to town?" Lilly suggested. "I know you want to make sure everything's being cared for, anyway. 'Sides, Red's out there, doin' him some huntin', and we could give him a lift back to town."

Bertie stiffened. "Hunting?" He'd rather go hunting than greet her at the railway station? "What's in season this time of year?" Didn't he care any more than that?

She felt Edith touch her arm, and she pressed her lips together. She couldn't let on how much it hurt that Red didn't seem to want to see her.

Again, Ivan and Lilly looked at each other across the front seat—a serious look of shared understanding.

Bertie leaned forward. "Is there something going on you two oughta be telling me about?"

Ivan sighed. "Well, I guess you could say some of us are taking the law into our own hands."

"What?"

"Red's huntin' tracks," Lilly explained. "Around your farm. Just seeing what he can come up with."

"What kind of tracks?"

"Human ones, Bertie," Ivan said, giving her a troubled look over his shoulder. "He's not let up since he got home and found your father on Monday."

She sat back in her seat, lips parting. "Oh." Some of her bitter disappointment eased, to be replaced by that tightening in her stomach that she'd felt so many times in the past two days. "He still thinks somebody killed Dad."

"He's not ready to agree with the sheriff that Joseph's death was some clumsy accident," Ivan said, then nodded toward Lilly. "Neither are we."

Edith placed an arm around Bertie's shoulder, protective and comforting.

"I called the sheriff yesterday from the train station in Albuquerque," Bertie said. "He told me he didn't find any evidence that would make him think there was foul play."

"I know what Sheriff Butch Coggins said." Lilly's tone told everyone in the car what she thought of the man. "Some folks in Hideaway have got other opinions, and I happen to be one of them."

"That's right," Ivan said, glancing over his shoulder at Bertie and winking at her. "You let us take care of things, buddy. You've gone through enough for a while. You've got friends here who are going to help you."

Bertie bit her tongue, touched, but at the same time frustrated by Ivan's attitude. Did he think she was so delicate she couldn't take the truth? Why couldn't they tell her plainly what they'd found?

But she let it go. There'd be time to get to the bottom of things after she got settled in. And she had to admit that she didn't feel quite up to facing much more today, though she wouldn't let on about that to anyone, not even Edith.

She would corner Red soon enough, and he would tell her what she needed to know, or she'd know the reason why.

Chapter Fourteen

Red frowned at a small mess of limbs scattered at the edge of the Moennig's wooden front porch. Joseph never placed his firewood next to any buildings, and he especially would not allow a stack beside his home. He'd taught Red that termites got into houses that way.

Besides, when Joseph stacked wood, whether it be kindling or chopped logs, he did it with the kind of precision Red had only ever seen before in the military. These limbs looked a mess, sticking out every which way, slender hickory switches too green to use for kindling.

He kicked one of the branches with the toe of his shoe, and then frowned. Hickory switches. Something about those little limbs…

He remembered feeling the sting of a hickory switch on his backside a few times when he was a kid. There was never any damage done, but it sure hurt.

There was something else hovering in his mind that he thought he should be gettin'. Some sign…some message… but for the life of him, he couldn't pin down what that could be.

He searched through the house for any clue about what might've happened, then walked around the yard again, in case he'd missed something.

Though Joseph Moennig took good care of his fields, his garden, his livestock, Red didn't figure Bertie's father had given up a lot of time to cultivate a green lawn—and there was not a lot of space left for a lawn after the heap of gardening Mrs. Moennig had always done. With the mature shade trees surrounding the house, the grass grew awfully sparse in some patches.

The Moennigs were practical. They'd used their cattle and mules to mow the lawn when the grass grew too tall. That made for some good fertilizer, too, and recent rains had caused what grass there was to shoot up in lush clumps.

In one patch of dirt a couple of feet from Joseph's bedroom window, Red discovered part of a heel print. Someone had been standing out here, watching Joseph.

If Red wasn't mistaken, the print matched one he'd found at the edge of the barnyard and in the backyard at home.

He didn't bother to collect this one. He had enough to convince himself that Joseph's death was not an accident.

Red stepped around the rear north corner of the house and stopped. Something pop-pop-popped through the trees, softly at first, like the wings of a moth flitting against the window on a summer night. Then it grew louder, more insistent.

Red's breath caught. He froze, clutched by fear as surely as a rat in a trap. He knew that sound. It was familiar, close and threatening. Snap-pop, snap-pop…the sound of distant artillery fire… It was drawing closer….

His hand lost its grip on the cane. He hit the ground quick as a burned cat, and tasted the grit of dust between his teeth, felt the pain in his leg as he rammed it into the ground, preparing to fight, even though he had no weapon.

The Germans couldn't have found him here, not in the middle of America. They'd surrendered. This didn't make sense.

He closed his eyes, waiting for the thud-crack of incoming enemy fire, waiting for the agony of metal slicing through him.

But as he lay paralyzed, his mind swarming over all sorts of things a soldier should do at a time like this, the sound began to change. Now it wasn't quite right.

He lay with his cheek pressed against the earth, unable to stop shaking, as he listened to that sound, which grew stranger as it grew louder.

It was still familiar, but not artillery fire at all. No, not at all.

It was the sound of rubber tires rolling slowly along the rocky road, a sound as recognizable to him from the war as it was here at home. The roads in Italy were dirt and rock—barely roads at all until they'd been worn down by the hundreds of tires of advancing troops.

He looked up and saw the black hood of Ivan Potts' Chevrolet skimming above the hedge of sumac growing along the roadside.

Before the car could reach the clearing and all the passengers could see him lying in the dirt like a whimpering cur, he scrambled to his feet. Shaken by his reaction, he brushed as much of the dust as he could from his clothes, then limped quickly toward the front porch.

How could he have lost his senses so totally? He'd heard stories of shell-shocked men coming home from the war, but he'd never realized how completely convinced he could be that he was back in Italy, like that bad nightmare coming back to tap him on the shoulder in spite of the sunlight streaming from the sky.

He was standing on the steps, watching the road, when the car came into view. His gaze shot to the shining blond hair of the woman in the backseat.

Bertie. His beautiful Bertie. He couldn't look away.

Even when she stepped out of the car, he couldn't do anything but stand there staring. She wasn't a figment of his imagination this time—not wishful thinking. Bertie was here. He'd thought about this moment, longed for it, ever since he'd seen her last, crying at the train station.

He wanted to run to her and touch her face, catch her in a hug, tell her she was even more beautiful than he'd told the guys. He wanted to tell her that she'd saved his life. She was the reason he'd fought so hard to stay alive. She was what kept him going. Her faithfulness. Her sweet letters. Just knowin' she was there…he wanted to tell her all that, but he just kept staring.

She looked up at him, her face filled with all the spirit she'd written into her letters to him, and her hand raised in a wave. She took a couple of quick steps to circle the car, her eyes filled with sudden, wild joy.

Then her gaze dropped to the cane in his left hand. She gasped, and looked back up into his eyes, her own eyes widening. The joy vanished, and the expression that replaced it stabbed at him. The disappointment was obvious. The hurt. Her lips parted, and he heard a soft cry.

Bertie grabbed the car fender and held on to keep herself from falling over. That cane! Red wasn't just holding it, he was leaning on it. Heavily.

Dozens of thoughts leapt through her mind, and to her

shame, some of them were not sympathetic. She realized those thoughts were plain on her face, because she saw Red wince.

Fancy that. A man who had experienced the horrors of war for three years made anxious by one small woman with hurt and anger in her eyes.

This was why he hadn't written? Would he have ever contacted her again if not for her father's death? No one had even told her he was coming home.

Was she nothing more than a goodtime girl to him? The fears she had confessed to Dr. Cox, had they come true? Maybe Red didn't want her hanging around now that things had gotten tough. Maybe he didn't think she was woman enough to handle it.

All this time, she'd thought she meant more to him than that.

Stop it, Roberta Moennig. He's been wounded. Think about someone besides yourself.

And yet…when had he been wounded? Why had no one told her about it?

She shot a look over her shoulder at Lilly and Ivan through the windshield of the car. Neither could hold her gaze. She looked at Edith, and found strength in her calm dark eyes, encouragement in her gentle nod.

Bertie nodded back at her friend, who was silently communicating with her eyes: *You can do this. This is why I came with you.*

Bertie had never known a dearer, more stalwart friend than Edith Frost. As the world seemed to shift and crash, Edith understood because her own world had crashed three and a half years ago.

Odd how those folks Bertie had known and trusted the longest had let her down, while someone she'd known for only eight months could be so solid for her now.

But that wasn't the whole story. It couldn't be. Bertie knew she was overreacting.

Just yesterday, as they sat watching the countryside go past them on the train, Edith had said, "Grief's a strange beast, Bertie. Sometimes you'll think you're through with it, that all is well and you've dealt with your loss sufficiently, and then it will come back, stronger than ever."

"Well, we won't have to worry about that yet," Bertie'd said. "I don't feel recovered in the least. Fact is, I feel smothered with sorrow, wonderin' if it'll ever end."

Problem now was that the sorrow just seemed to expand to include everyone in her life.

Gripping his cane, Red stepped down from the porch and came toward her, limping, leaning hard on that metal support. She could see the pain in his expression, but she didn't know if it was physical, or emotional, because he felt exposed, walking in front of her like this—she, from whom he'd tried so hard to keep this secret. But why?

Except for the cane, he almost looked like the old Red, in his worn blue-denim overalls and red-and-gray plaid shirt. Work clothes, covered in dust. No sign of the Army uniform.

She ached to run to him, to put her arms around him, to ask what had happened—but since he hadn't told her about it, he obviously didn't want to talk to her about it.

Even after all their years of friendship, she wasn't an important enough part of his life to be told about an injury. He could tell her how much he missed her, and talk about home all the time, but he couldn't share this.

He drew closer, his steps awkward. The lines of fatigue in his face, the circles under his eyes, became more evident.

She swallowed hard when he reached her. She hadn't seen him in a year, and even at that time they'd had only short stolen moments together each evening, busy as he'd been helping his mother around the guesthouse, busy as Bertie'd been helping her dad with haying and tending the cattle, garden and house after her regular job at the Farmer's Exchange.

As she studied Red closer, he seemed…hardened somehow, his physique more corded with tight muscles. There was a new darkness in those blue eyes she'd caught only glimpses of last year. Here was no farm boy. There was no boyishness left in this man.

She searched his eyes for the twinkle she'd always known. It was gone, as if it had never been.

"Hi, Bert," he said.

She swallowed again, nodded, suddenly unable to find any words, unwilling to look at the cane.

"Hi, Red." Her voice betrayed her, quivery and hoarse. She knew anything she said would make it sound as if she pitied him. He'd hate that.

"Done with your hunting, Charles Frederick?" Lilly called through the window, her voice a little high-pitched, revealing tension.

Bertie glanced over her shoulder at the woman, and saw the concern in her eyes. Of course, Lilly had read Bertie's reaction. Who could miss it? What must Red be thinking?

But what was he thinking when he decided not to tell her? She didn't believe she'd've been more stunned if he'd backhanded her across the face.

Overreacting. I'm overreacting. This is the shock over Dad's death that's influencing my emotions. I've got to get over it.

"Got all I need for now," Red told his mother.

"Well, then, why don't you sit in the back with the ladies and ride to town with us?" Lilly said.

"Wait," Bertie said. "I have to get the recipe I promised you." She swung around Red like she was changing partners in a square dance and rushed toward the front porch.

Though she heard Red's uneven steps behind her, she didn't slow down, but barreled ahead and pushed through the front door into the living room, where her footsteps echoed through the house. Strange to be pushing through an unlocked door. Usually, she and Edith kept the doors to their apartment locked at all times. In Hideaway, though, few doors even had locks.

In the middle of the room she stopped and caught her breath, overwhelmed by the scents that sharply recalled her father's presence: his pipe tobacco, the lingering aroma of onions, potatoes and ham, which was what he cooked most often when he was by himself.

Her father should come walking into the living room from the kitchen any moment.

The room smelled dusty, too. Dad never dusted, so it would have built up for the past eight months, mingling with the smoke and ash from the woodstove.

She sniffed the scent of old wood smoke as she closed her eyes. *Oh, Dad. How could someone take you away from me like this?*

Chapter Fifteen

Red tried not to make noise as he entered the front door of the Moennig home behind Bertie. How many times had he done this over the years when he and Bertie were growing up? Of course, most times he and Ivan and John had come through the back door with Bertie, like family.

Cecil and Dixie Martin, John's brother and sister, were usually with Bertie's brother, Lloyd, and all together they formed a rowdy gang of kids who loved to play in the Moennig barn because it was bigger than the others and far enough from town so their yells and screams didn't bring out a posse of parents. The hay was always deep in the Moennig barn, perfect for kids swinging from rafter to floor on the rope that Joseph had hung for them.

Bertie's mother, Marty, always had enough cookies and candy to feed the army of youngsters who flocked to their farm.

Red closed his eyes, choking up at the memories. Sometimes this place had seemed more like home than his own, where he had to keep his things picked up and his manners polite because of the lodgers. There were times a fella just needed to be himself, without all the strangers to consider.

He glanced at Bertie, who stood in the middle of the room, her shoulders slumped—Bertie's back was usually ramrod straight. Her hands covered her face.

The front door, its wood swollen from recent rains, thumped against the frame as it attempted to close behind him. Bertie stiffened, half-turning, her face pale.

Red cleared his throat. "I shouldn't've yelled at you over the telephone."

"No, you shouldn't have." Her voice was still quivery, hoarse.

"I could've kicked myself ten ways to Christmas for doin' that," he told her.

She straightened her shoulders.

"But you shouldn't've hung up on me without giving me a chance to explain," he said.

Her lips pressed together in a firm line. She turned to face him as she caught and held his gaze, her eyes narrowing.

He stared back.

She spread her hands out to her sides. "Well?"

He blinked at her. "Well what?"

"There's still time to explain, if that's what you've a mind to do. What's going on around here? Nobody wants to tell me anything, like I'm some weak sister who doesn't have a brain in her head and will fall apart with one wrong look or word."

He sighed. "Nobody's sayin' you're weak, Bertie. You're one of the strongest people I know."

"Then treat me like it."

"But I had good reason to want you to stay away for a while." If only she knew how badly he wanted to protect her, how it tore at him to see her hurtin' like this.

"Because you didn't want me to get in your way while you were investigating *my father's* death?"

The woman sure knew how to rile him. "You think you can do it all yourself?"

"Did I say that?" Fire shot from her eyes. "Stop putting words in my mouth. I think I can help."

"The sheriff isn't even letting me help. I'm doin' this on my own. I don't even know what I'm gonna do next, much less how you can help."

Her gaze burned into his, but the annoyance gradually faded from her expression. For the first time he noticed the darkness beneath her eyes, which was more noticeable because of the paleness of her face. Sorrow replaced her irritation.

"And you might not think it's important," she said, "but I had to be here to say my final goodbye."

Red swallowed hard. Why couldn't she understand that it might not be safe for her here? "Funeral's tomorrow at noon, so you'll be able to say it then. Farm's being taken care of, and the sheriff won't be helpin' anybody investigate Joseph's death, since he don't think there was anything suspicious about it."

"I know that much." She glanced quickly at his leg, then away, as if looking at his injury was painful to her. Havin' her see it was sure painful to him. Was she seein' him as a cripple?

"Then I don't know what it is you think you can do about it," he said. "Bertie, you need to catch the train out of here as soon as you can and go on back to California. It's the best place for you right now." It was the safest place, too. For both of them.

Red could stick to his resolve more easily without her nearby, muddying up the waters, making him wish for something he shouldn't have.

She set her hands on her hips, and he could tell what she

thought about his advice. "What would you say if I told you I didn't want to go back to California?"

What would he say? He wanted to tell her to stay, to never leave again. But he couldn't do that. She had too much power over him.

He scowled at her. "My mother said something to me the other day that stung, but she was right, and you could use a good dose of her wisdom."

Bertie matched his scowl with one of her own. "What did she say?"

"Something about how stubborn pride ain't a pretty sight. She oughta know, because she knows me. But it isn't any prettier on a pretty woman than it is on a stubborn, ugly ol' red-headed soldier."

She blinked at him, and her eyes suddenly glimmered with moisture. With another quick glance at his cane, she turned and walked toward the kitchen.

Red wished then that he could've kept his mouth shut.

She would not cry. She *must* not cry. She pulled the recipe drawer out and fumbled through the messy stack of handwritten notes until she found the black-walnut recipes. Several of them. If Lilly wanted black-walnut desserts, she'd get enough to feed the whole town. While Bertie was working on the desserts, she'd copy each recipe down for Lilly so she'd have her own set.

The front door opened and closed in the other room. Red had obviously left the house. After telling her again to leave, then insulting her, he'd left the house without another word.

She shoved the drawer shut, hugging the recipes to her, staring around the large kitchen. The long oak table had seen so much laughter and happiness in the past. Bertie and Red and their friends had spent so many hours at this table, eating Mom's cookies, laughing, playing games and teasing each other.

She had thought, when they were growing up, that she'd known Red so well. How could she suddenly feel as if she didn't really know him?

All this time—three years—she'd thought she was falling in love with one of the sweetest, kindest, funniest men in the state.

She'd shared her heart with this man. She had thought she would be willing to share the whole rest of her life with him, and now it had come to this.

"Oh, Red," she whispered into the empty kitchen—to that long ago memory of his smiling face at the dinner table, "What's happened to us? Didn't we promise each other we'd never let anything break up our friendship?"

For one moment she considered stepping to the front porch and waving for Ivan to drive on to town without her. She had a perfectly good bicycle in the barn, and it would take only a few minutes to ride it to Lilly's guesthouse. It would mean she'd have her own transportation. She wouldn't be dependent on anyone.

Then she looked down at her skirt, and shook her head. Of course, that would be unthinkable. Down deep, she knew the real reason she didn't want to ride in Ivan's car was because she would be sitting beside Red. She'd wanted so badly to throw herself into his arms and kiss him and tell him she loved him.

How far different her dreams were from reality.

She walked back through the house, her footsteps echoing on the hardwood floors, through the only home she had ever known—the home no one wanted her to return to.

By the time she reached the car with recipes in hand, Red was sitting in the middle of the backseat. She slid in beside him, noticing that his overalls and shirt had a thin layer of dust over them, as if he'd been rolling in the dirt. She wondered why.

She swallowed hard and forced her voice past the growing lump in her throat. "Been gardening?"

"Not today." His deep voice held a new quality that she'd never heard in it before. There was a sharp edge, almost of anger, or some other deep emotion.

She glanced at his shoes. "Herding cattle?"

"Nope."

She looked up into his tight face. He wouldn't meet her gaze. She studied the curve of the cane at his side, resenting his attitude.

Not everything about him had changed. He was still the same Missouri mule when he wanted to dig his heels in about something, and he obviously wanted her gone.

She could be just as stubborn.

Red sat staring straight ahead, miserable and not knowing how to fix things. Maybe he shouldn't try. She was mad at him now, and maybe she needed to stay that way. Thing was, he'd never figured on losing a friend when he decided against the romance. This wasn't what he'd had in mind.

Ordinarily, Bertie would be nagging him about getting his wound seen to by a doctor or demanding he take one of her treatments with crushed onions or tree leaves or some other such concoction that she believed would help him heal.

Not this time. She hadn't even mentioned the cane, just looked at it—and at him—with pity. So on top of her anger, there was also pity. What could be worse?

An ugly voice told him she was avoiding the obvious subject of his injury because the Red Meyer who wasn't whole and healthy wasn't the Red Meyer she wanted.

But why should that bother him, since he'd been thinking the same thing himself?

"Your mother has talked Edith and me into staying at the guesthouse a couple of days," Bertie said.

He looked at her, nodded, looked away. At least she was being sensible about that, not staying at the farm.

"I'll walk out to the farm later," she said. "After Edith and I get settled in and I change my clothes. I need to get my bicycle out of the barn so I won't have to depend on anyone else to get where I want to go."

Ivan glanced over his shoulder at her. "I'd be glad to drive you wherever you want to go."

Red scowled. Good ol' Ivan, always helpful to a lady in distress.

"Thanks," Bertie said, "but I've got two strong legs, and I need to—" Her voice broke off. As if against her will, she glanced at Red's leg, and color crept up her neck and into her face.

If it hadn't been so awkward, he'd have laughed. If it hadn't been so painful, he'd have at least smiled. He could almost see the pity forming in her eyes.

"I'll be fine," she said quietly. She looked so sad all of a sudden. She leaned forward and touched Lilly's shoulder in the front seat. "So, Lilly, you said you wanted to do some baking. Would this afternoon be good for you?"

His mother paused. "There'll probably be a lot of visitors over to see you soon as they find out you're home. I'll spread the word you're stayin' with me. With that much company, doubt you'll have time for much baking."

"I'll get to work on some cookies when I can today," Bertie said. "That way there'll be something to feed the visitors."

"Let's see how much time we have," Lilly advised.

"I'll deal with everything a whole lot better if I can keep my hands busy," Bertie said. "Farming or baking, I might as well keep on the move, so if you don't need me to help with the bakin', I'll hop on out to the farm and get to work in the garden."

"Ought to stick to baking for the time being, then," Red said, unable to keep his mouth shut about it, though he knew Bertie wouldn't like what he had to say. "Leave the farm to the men."

He wasn't surprised when Bertie's small, strong hands clenched together until her fingertips showed white around the nails. Good. The anger looked better to him right now than her pity.

"I've not been gone from the farm that long," she said. "I still know how to take care of the stock."

"Stock's not what I'm worried about—though I can't see you handling the hay fields all by yourself." He wanted to put his hand over her bunched fists, remind her that this was him she was talkin' to, not some stranger. But he didn't want to push himself on her.

"I can hire help if I need it," she said. "Lots of men coming back home to the area from the war."

He winced at her words. "What do you think *I* am—" he snapped before he could think "—a goat?"

He heard her small gasp, saw his mother's quick, warning look over her shoulder, and cringed when Ivan laughed. He'd as much as told Ma on Monday that he wouldn't be much help on a farm, though he'd discovered since then that there were lots of chores he could still do, they just took him a little longer than they used to.

He realized Bertie was still looking up at him, gaze steady, as if she was searching into his very soul to see what was really going on with him. "I'd say that was a pretty fair description right now," she said quietly.

Ivan laughed again, this time so hard he nearly ran the car off the road.

Chapter Sixteen

Bertie sat beside Red on the very short drive into town and listened to Lilly, Ivan and Edith chatter about Ivan's funny experiences in the Pacific—only the funny ones. Edith asked question after question, drawing Ivan out, complimenting him on his poetry, and wanting to know what had inspired each poem she'd read.

Bertie was glad no one talked about the bad experiences.

Was she a horrible person for wanting to avoid the depressing stories right now? These men had risked their very lives for their country. Didn't she owe them a listening ear if they felt a need to talk about the horrors they'd endured for her safety, her way of life?

Sitting so close to Red, forcing herself not to look at his leg, trying hard not to think about it, she didn't feel she'd be able to bear to hear about what he had suffered. She would want to know later. Right now, with Dad not buried yet, she couldn't face more.

Laughter once again bounced through the car. Was it as obvious to Ivan and Lilly as it was to Bertie that Edith was keeping Ivan talking to cover the silence between Bertie and Red?

Bless Edith's kind soul.

And bless Ivan, too. He'd never liked dwelling on depressing things. Like Red, he'd always glossed over hardships or conflict with a distracting joke.

Bertie wanted to share in the laughter, but it caught in her throat.

She stole a glance at Red from the corner of her eye, and saw him staring out the windshield, his eyebrows drawn together in a grimace. Was he as painfully aware of her beside him as she was of him? Or was he off in another world entirely, remembering the experiences that had wounded him in the war?

From time to time, her insides seemed to spin like the belt on a lathe, and she couldn't tell if it was her stomach or her racing heart. It wasn't supposed to be like this. She should be sitting here with Red's arm around her, planning what kinds of treatments would best work to heal him. She felt as muzzled as a mad dog.

Oh, the countless hours she had daydreamed as she worked at the plant. She'd imagined her father's smiling face when he welcomed her home, the feel of the humid Missouri air on her skin, the smell of the wildflowers that grew along the wooded section of the farm and the tart taste of one of Lilly's gooseberry pies.

She'd also dreamed about the first time she and Red would see each other again, how handsome he would look, and how eager to catch her in his arms and promise never to leave again.

Not only hadn't he caught her in his arms, he'd shoved her away from him, even before she'd come home.

She closed her eyes. Reality was nothing like those silly

dreams. Yes, Red was alive. But this man sitting beside her wasn't the same man who'd written to her, with whom she'd grown up, and teased, and dated.

That man held gentle laughter inside that came out with the slightest encouragement. This man was prickly and bossy.

She grieved the loss just as she grieved her father's death.

From the corner of her eye, she studied Red's grim expression, the firm tilt of his jaw, and she figured he was worrying this situation as she was, like a dog gnawing on a hard bone.

"Well, here it is," Ivan said, glancing at Edith in the rearview mirror as the road curved around the side of a cliff and the sleepy village of Hideaway came into view.

The lush growth of trees, flowers and healthy victory gardens encircling each house reminded Bertie of an easier time, when she, Red, Ivan, John and John's sister, Dixie, would ride their bikes through town.

"You remember when we'd snatch flowers?" Ivan asked, looking in the rearview mirror at Bertie. "You were the worst of the bunch, Bert, making the prettiest bouquets from flowers you snitched from different gardens."

"Nobody missed 'em," she said.

"She didn't keep 'em for herself," Red protested. "She left 'em for the elderly folk to find on their front porches." He looked at her then, almost reluctantly, before quickly dropping his gaze. "Then she'd knock on the doors and ride away before she could get caught."

Bertie felt surprise, then a flush of pleasure at Red's defense of her actions.

"I heard about that," Lilly said, chuckling. "But their worst bit of troublemaking came when Bertie and Red went fishing one Friday afternoon and caught 'em a mess of fish, but did they bring that catch to me for a fish fry? Nosiree."

"I remember that," Ivan said. "I was with them. We left the fish on Mrs. Murphy's front porch, because Mrs. Murphy loved a good mess of fried striper."

Lilly clucked her tongue. "Well, when Bertie rode her bicycle past Mrs. Murphy's house on Monday, the fish were still out there, stinking to high heaven. Mrs. Murphy had been out of town with her daughter that weekend."

Edith's delighted laughter lifted Bertie's mood only slightly. "Bertie's always bragging about how pretty her town is, and I've always wanted to see it. She never told me the half of it."

Ivan drove his Chevrolet around the square, showing off their tiny town to Edith. Bertie suspected he also wanted to show off the car his parents had given to him as a reward for returning home in one piece.

Gerald and Arielle Potts would do about anything for their only child. If there'd been a new car manufactured this year, they would have bought it for him.

Everyone had known for many years that Arielle's plans for her son included an internship in Baltimore, Maryland, at her brother's bank. What most folks didn't know—what only a few of Ivan's closest friends had known for years— was that he had no intention of going to Maryland.

He had worried about the problem since high school, but he had been granted a reprieve by earning a scholarship to the state university in Columbia, Missouri. The war had claimed him immediately after college graduation, but Bertie knew he would soon be expected to take that long-awaited journey to Maryland. If he didn't, it would break his mother's heart.

Ivan loved his mother dearly, but as he'd told Bertie once, he "was a homegrown man," with no interest in venturing into his mother's native world. He identified far more with his father, who liked a good hunting trip, loved to fish, and whose highest ambition was to be mayor of Hideaway as he earned a living with the MFA Exchange feed and farm supply store—a lucrative living by local standards, though not quite what Arielle had in mind when she'd married Gerald.

Three old friends from church waved at them from the sidewalk, and twice Ivan had to stop the car when someone gestured him over to the edge of the red-brick street.

Everyone wanted to talk to the soldiers who'd come home from the war…and everyone wanted to hug Bertie and sympathize with her about her father's death. They also wanted to meet her friend from California. Mrs. Jarvis eyed Edith with suspicion, as if she was some foreigner, but then she warmed to Edith's southern charm in no time.

As Edith explained, no one was actually a native of California. She, herself, had been born and raised in Mobile, Alabama.

The sudden homecoming crowd on the town square was startlingly different from the anonymity Bertie had experienced in California, where everyone she passed on the street was a stranger. She glanced at Edith, and smiled at her friend's expression of growing disbelief.

"You're right, Bertie," Edith said quietly, under cover of another conversation between Lilly and Mrs. Thomas, the owner of Mode O' Day ladies' wear shop. "People are wonderfully friendly here."

Bertie shrugged. "As you've pointed out to me often enough, when folks are isolated from the rest of the world by a long drive and hard times, they learn to depend on one another. They have to socialize."

Bertie risked a look at Red, and for once, he returned that

look. Still no twinkle, no light of welcome in those blue eyes, only a brooding watchfulness that tore at her. But there was something else…some barely detectable look of…what? Tenderness?

Her imagination was running rampant.

She wanted to tell Edith that sometimes, no matter how well you knew someone, there was still a stranger inside. No one was ever completely knowable.

They drove past the Methodist church, and Lilly turned to look over her shoulder at Bertie. "We'll have the funeral at noon tomorrow." She pointed toward the cemetery, where the grave had already been dug.

"The Methodist church?" Edith asked, leaning forward to glance at Bertie. "But you attend the Lutheran church in California. I thought you were Lutheran."

"Dad was Lutheran when he came to this country with his family as a teenager," Bertie said. "But there was no Lutheran place of worship in Hideaway when they got here. Dad's parents would never adapt, but my parents started attending the Methodist church after they were married."

"How did that go over?" Edith asked.

"There was a culture clash," Bertie said. "The Germans liked to drink their beer at town gatherings, so there were a lot of eyebrows raised at my parents. But my parents never got used to women not properly covering their arms and legs, even at church."

Bertie remembered some of those conflicts from her childhood. People laughed about it years later, of course, but at the time those differences in customs and attitudes had fueled the German Americans' sense of exclusion in their new country.

At the Meyer Guesthouse, neighbors and friends started

bringing food and lingering to talk, reminiscing about old times with Dad. The house gradually filled, and Bertie realized there would be little time to bake anything this afternoon.

That was okay. She had other things she wanted to do, as soon as she could slip out of the house.

Chapter Seventeen

Red wasn't surprised that the first visitors through the front door were Gerald and Arielle Potts, followed by Ivan, who carried a large covered plate. Red knew that the plate would be filled with tiny sandwiches and quiches, bite-sized cakes and meringues, Arielle Potts's specialties.

Red always wondered how the Potts men could be so hale and hearty. Those dainties Arielle made usually wore off in about an hour, and a fella was starving again.

Gerald had met Arielle at college in Baltimore, where she had been born and raised. Both had been smitten at once, and they married as soon as they both graduated. According to Ivan, it'd been quite a shock for his mother when Gerald brought her back to his hometown of Hideaway to settle and have a family.

It had been an even deeper shock, and a huge disappointment to her, when she'd been able to produce only one child.

In spite of these initial disappointments, however, Arielle Potts had been quick to set about maintaining her pride of heritage, and even in Hideaway, she'd tried to instill a sense of community spirit for the past. She'd attempted to convince Ivan to attend the same college in Baltimore she and Gerald had attended, but she'd been thwarted and disappointed when Ivan didn't abide by her wishes.

Her next great plan for her son was to see him taken under the wing of her brother, a banker, as soon as this war was over, to be established in business.

Ivan was smart, he'd done well in school, in spite of a bit of rebelliousness, and she wanted to see him in politics, maybe even the governorship someday.

She'd always encouraged the friendship between Ivan and Red—she was partial to Red, which baffled him, being a homegrown boy in every way. But Red knew that even after all these years of being a citizen of Hideaway, the wife of the mayor, and running the library, Arielle Potts still didn't have any really close friends. Leastways, not according to Ivan. For the most part, the townsfolk still treated her like an outsider.

Once, when she didn't realize Red and Ivan had come into the house after school, they had overheard her complaining to her husband about the town's "hillbilly mentality." That had been after Gerald had run for mayor and was being criticized for some of his new policies.

Red felt a little sorry for Ivan's mother. She was like a princess who had come to a town of commoners and could never become one of them, hard as she tried. Red suspected a bit of jealousy might be part of the reason she wasn't fully accepted—because of her looks. Arielle Potts was a pretty woman, still slender, with blond hair and dark brown eyes.

Some folks said Gerald had been elected mayor in spite of his uppity wife. Some folks were plain ornery and envious.

"Arielle!" Bertie called to Mrs. Potts, stepping from the kitchen with a platter of corn muffins to set on the table.

The two women hugged each other, and Red thought he saw tears in Arielle's eyes. She murmured something into Bertie's ear.

It seemed, ever since Bertie's mother died in '42, that both Red's and Ivan's mothers competed over who would take Marty Moennig's place in Bertie's affections.

"So," came Ivan's voice from behind Red at the fireplace, "first of all, are you going to tell me why you're covered in dirt? Second, when are you going to change clothes? And third, when are you going to start showing Bertie how much you missed her?"

With a grimace, Red looked down at his dirty old clothes. "Guess I oughta get out of these things."

Ivan put a hand on his arm. "Not until you answer my questions. What are you up to, Charles Frederick?"

Red scowled over his shoulder at his fair-haired friend. "Still checking things out."

"Did you fall out there at the house?"

"Not exactly."

"So what happened? Don't tell me somebody jumped you."

Red gave a long-suffering sigh. "If you must know, Mr. Noseypants, I thought I heard artillery fire, and I did what any good soldier would've done."

"Hit the ground." Ivan's puzzlement turned to obvious concern. "Somebody shot at you?"

"Nope." Red felt a flush creep up his neck. "Let it drop, okay?"

Ivan seemed about to press.

"And I'll deal with Bertie my own way, if you don't mind." Red crossed the room to Ivan's mother. "Mrs. Potts," he said softly in her ear, "mind if I ask you a couple of questions?"

She smiled up at him. "You're calling me *Mrs. Potts* now?

This sounds serious." She gestured toward the sofa in the parlor where Red had sat plotting an investigation with Ivan and John on Monday. "We can close the French doors and talk about anything you like," she said. "Will a little privacy meet your requirements?"

He nodded and led her there, gesturing for her to be seated, then closed the French doors and sat across from her on a straight-backed chair. "I was wondering, since you know so much about history, if you could tell me anything about the Bald Knobbers."

Her perfectly arched eyebrows raised a fraction of an inch. "You want to talk about local history at a time like this?" She turned and peered through the windows into the other room, where Bertie seemed to be in deep conversation with Mr. Potts near the fireplace. "And here I thought you were coming to me for a little advice about romance."

Red said nothing, but glancing toward Bertie, he felt a tug of frustration. "I think the most important part of romance is keeping that loved one safe."

Arielle returned her attention to him. "Well, of course, but safe from what, Red? Do you perceive Bertie to be in some kind of danger?"

"Haven't decided yet, but I aim to do my best to find out." He forced himself to stop casting quick glances toward Bertie like a love-struck schoolboy and focused on Arielle. "I know the Bald Knobbers hung out around Hideaway sometimes. I thought, you knowing so much about local history and such, you'd have a little information about them."

She nodded at Red, her eyes bright with curiosity and concern. "Don't tell me you're thinking of resurrecting that vile group of fiends."

"No, but maybe somebody already did."

She leaned forward and placed a hand on Red's arm. "I remember how much you and Ivan and your friends loved to play Bald Knobbers down in the caves below the Moennig farm. You children found trouble more times than I care to remember for playing where it wasn't safe."

He knew what she was talking about. Those caves had been flooded half the time, and Cecil Martin had almost drowned there ten years ago.

"It was always John Martin's idea to play there," Red said. "He was always hung up on the Bald Knobbers for some reason."

"He might not have been so eager to idolize that gang if he'd known how roughly *they* played."

"Maybe not, but his grandpa told us the caves were an outlaw hangout at one time, so we couldn't resist goin' down there. We'd heard the story about the Bald Knobbers raiding the place sometime back in the early nineteen hundreds."

"Those wouldn't have been the original Bald Knobbers," Mrs. Potts said.

"Tell me what you know about them."

"The stories are quite embellished, and I think they might be much more legend and myth than fact now."

"So you're saying you think the tall tales about those vigilantes is a load of hooey?"

An affectionate smile lit her face. "Trust you to put it that way, Red Meyer. What kinds of things do you wish to know?"

He shrugged. "Mr. Cooper told me the Bald Knobbers was the meanest, cruelest bunch of men in Taney County."

Mrs. Potts leaned back, resting her elbow on the armrest while managing to keep her posture straight. "Actually," she said, her voice taking on a lecturing tone, as it often did with him, "the Bald Knobbers were a bit of a mixed baggage, or at least the original ones were."

"They sure made a name for themselves," Red said. "Folks still talk about them in these parts, even this far from their hangouts around Forsyth."

She nodded. "They made a lot of people anxious."

"I think I learned in school that one of their methods of warning a victim that they were out to get him was to place a bundle of hickory switches at their door."

She nodded. "If that didn't straighten the poor victim out, then they'd sometimes use those switches on him." She stopped and cleared her throat, obviously uncomfortable with the subject. "These weren't gentle little taps, either. They drew blood. They intended to injure with those switches."

"What would you say if I told you I saw those very same kinds of switches on Joseph's front porch?"

This definitely caught her attention. She leaned forward. "Red, are you certain? Couldn't you have just seen some branches the wind whipped up? Because I have to admit this theory about a resurrection of the Bald Knobbers seems a stretch for me."

"I know, but just listen," Red said. "I heard that sometimes the farmers would have their livestock run off their land when the Bald Knobbers wanted them to leave their property. Joseph was missing livestock, and someone even let Ma's horse out of the stable the day I arrived. There have been several incidents like that, which is why I keep wondering if someone's trying to hide behind a Bald Knobber hood. They was thieves."

"They *were* thieves."

"That's right. And murderers. Masquerading as men providing justice, when they really hurt a lot of innocent people."

She nodded, her dark eyes narrowing at him. "Red, are you trying to compare Joseph Moennig with Bald Knobber victims sixty years ago?"

"I think I remember hearing about copycat groups that sprung up after the first one was disbanded. These folks was more vicious than the originals."

"Were, Red. They *were* more vicious."

"Yup."

She looked pained for a moment, then shook her head. "What we're thinking here is pure conjecture, unsubstantiated by dependable sources."

"I know, but there's still enough old folks around these parts who remember what went on back then."

"Memories can become faulty with the passage of time," she warned him.

"Did you hear about that brick someone put through Ma's window last week? And Earl and Elizabeth Krueger and their five kids seem to have took off. I just heard today that nobody's seen aught of them since. They disappeared in the middle of the night, the same day Joseph died."

She looked down for a moment, then slowly shook her head. "That still doesn't convince me that there has been a revival of the Bald Knobbers. Have you spoken with the sheriff about any of this?"

"The sheriff don't seem interested in my ideas, or anybody else's. So Ivan, John and I plan to check it out for ourselves."

"Well," she said, leaning forward, the affectionate smile back in place, "you're always welcome to visit me at the library. We have some books there you're welcome to check out. I plan to go straight there as soon as we leave here."

He nodded. "I just might do that."

Her expression betrayed her doubt. Red had never stepped

foot inside the library except when he helped Ivan and Gerald build the shelves for her.

"I need to change clothes and get a haircut first, then I might check that out." He stood up. "Thanks for answering my questions."

She offered him her hand, and when he took it, she let him help her up. She was always doing little things like that, teaching him how to behave like a gentleman without making a big deal out of it. She'd been the one he'd gone to for advice before his first date.

As if reading his mind, she asked, "I suppose you're thrilled to see Bertie again. It must have been lonely without her." There was no missing the friendly curiosity in her eyes.

He glanced into the living room, where Bertie sat on the sofa, talking to Gerald, who sat across from her in an over-stuffed chair. "It was more than lonely."

Arielle patted his arm. "Don't expect to pick up where you left off the day you went away. Bertie's as true as the flow of the James River, but give her time to adjust."

She didn't look at his leg, but he knew what she meant. He decided not to tell Arielle, yet, that he wasn't going to even try to pick up the romance where it had left off. Bertie loved somebody who didn't exist anymore.

Arielle gave his hand a final pat, then stepped out to speak to some neighbors who had just arrived with more food. To avoid the growing crowd, Red slipped out to the back hallway. He would change his clothes so nobody else would ask him if he'd been rolling in the dirt, then he'd hightail it to the barbershop, before surprising Arielle by actually stopping in at the library for those books. He nearly smiled when he imagined her reaction.

Chapter Eighteen

Bertie's arms became tired after hugging so many folks who'd decided to "just drop by" to say hello, welcome her home and offer condolences on her loss. She was grateful for Lilly's warm hospitality, and for Gerald Potts, who stayed nearby, such a comforting presence, strong and supportive as the crowd grew.

"Lilly told me you and your friend are staying here instead of at the farm," Gerald said.

"I don't think the choice was ours. Lilly pretty much insisted."

"Good," he said. "I don't feel comfortable about this whole situation yet."

"You, too?" She sat down on the sofa, and Gerald sat beside her. "Are you saying you don't think Dad's death was an accident?" she asked softly.

He glanced around the room. "I'm not convinced about anything yet."

"Then, as mayor of the town, can't you ask Sheriff Coggins to check further into the case?"

He grimaced and reached down to pat her hand. "Let me tell you a little about being mayor of Hideaway. If you ever tried to herd a flock of chickens, then you know it can't be done. The position of mayor in our town doesn't pay, and it doesn't earn a person any respect. If anything, it makes a man the object of jokes and a dartboard for any complaints."

"So the sheriff won't listen?"

"He doesn't think there's a case."

"But Red does."

Gerald nodded. "That's right."

"He doesn't even want me to go out to the farm to do the chores, but Red Meyer is discovering he doesn't get everything he wants."

"I'd be honored to take care of the animals for you, but I think Ivan and Red have already taken that task on themselves."

"I would like to go out and get my bicycle, but Red doesn't even seem to want me to do that."

"He's worried about your safety, and I don't blame him. If I'd had a pretty young lady like you waiting for me for three years, you can bet I'd do everything in my power to keep her safe."

Bertie allowed herself to smile at the compliment.

"I know you've had very little time to make plans for the future," Gerald said gently. "But if there's any way I can help, you'll let me know, won't you? After all, you were my best worker at the Exchange before you left, and there'll always be a job for you if you want it."

"Thank you, Gerald. I appreciate that."

"Have you considered further schooling?"

"I'm a certified machinist."

"I'm talking college, Bertie. You're young. You have a

whole future ahead of you, and there's plenty of equity in your farm to help you with that."

She nodded. "I'll be thinking about it in the next few days."

What she intended to do as soon as possible was collect a batch of comfrey leaves from the lower forty acres, which overlooked the James River. She just wouldn't say anything to anyone when she went. If she did, she believed she'd be hogtied and dragged back to town.

Gerald gestured toward the front porch, where Ivan and Edith were holding a lively conversation.

"My son doesn't seem to be able to drag his attention from your friend. She was all he talked about on our way here."

"You noticed that, did you?" Bertie said dryly. "She's been my roommate in California for eight months, and she insisted on coming with me when Red called with the news about Dad."

The screen door opened, and two familiar figures stepped into the entryway of the guesthouse. Bertie suppressed a scowl. Gramercy and Drusilla Short.

"Here comes trouble," Gerald muttered.

Drusilla waddled beside her husband across the living room toward Bertie. There was no smile of greeting on their faces, and no expression of grief over Bertie's loss. Dru was broad at the hips, with heavy legs, which made her waist seem smaller than it actually was. With her gray-blond hair and muddy yellow eyes, her unfortunate coloring made her look as if she was always scowling.

That wasn't the reason Bertie had never found her to be a pleasant person.

Gerald stood. "I think it's time for some crowd control," he said. Then he walked toward the Shorts and greeted them, his voice clear and firm.

From the edge of her vision, Bertie could see Red slip from the sitting room into the back hallway. Escaping the crowd, no doubt. She wondered how many times he'd been forced to explain his leg injury since he'd arrived home Monday. Hideaway folks were a curious bunch.

She figured if she listened for a few moments to any nearby conversation, she was likely to learn more about his injury than she'd heard from him.

Arielle Potts walked across the living room to join Bertie in the sitting area in front of the fireplace. She gave Bertie another warm embrace and sat down beside her on the sofa, offering no explanation about her private discussion with Red.

"Bertie, you can't know how happy I am to see you home again." Her voice, as always, was musical and throaty. She glanced around the large, crowded living room. "Lilly is a gracious hostess, and I know you'll want to be near Red, but you must remember that you'll always be welcome in our home, as well. You may want some peace and quiet after all this."

Gerald reappeared from his welcoming duty and sank down in the chair across from his wife. "That was one of the most pleasant visits I've had with the Shorts."

"Why?" Arielle asked. "Because it was so brief?"

He clucked his tongue and pointed at her. "You've hit the nail on the head. I've been asking Bertie about her plans for the future."

"And what was her answer?" Arielle looked at Bertie.

"So far she's giving me the runaround."

"Now, Gerald," Bertie teased, "you know that isn't true. I'm not sure what I'm going to do yet."

"I think she should stay in Hideaway," Gerald said to his wife. "If she and Lloyd can sell the farm, Bertie would be able to attend college with her portion of the proceeds, and have a nice nest egg to tide her over until she decides what she wants to do with her life."

"But what if she decides she wants to keep the farm going?" Arielle asked, giving her husband an enigmatic look. "What she needs right now is time to recover."

"It never hurts to plan ahead," he said.

"Her father's funeral is tomorrow, and she shouldn't have to make any big decisions right now. She has a good head on her shoulders, and she'll know when the time is right to make any kinds of changes."

Bertie silently blessed Arielle for her support. Gerald, with his thick, broad shoulders, firm jawline and piercing blue eyes, was the kind of man who made solid, quick decisions, who got things done and did his best for the town, whether or not his efforts were appreciated. His wife provided the tender heart and wisdom, and she wasn't afraid to voice her opinions to her husband. Sometimes firmly.

They were a good balance, even if they did strike sparks off one another from time to time.

"There you are, Bertie Moennig." Louise Morrow, one of her closest—and nosiest—neighbors, rushed to the sofa with a plateful of food. She nodded to Gerald and Arielle, sat beside Bertie, giving her a one-armed hug, and then handing her the plate. "This is for you. Thought you'd be famished. Lilly mentioned you hadn't eaten yet."

Bertie accepted the plate with sincere gratitude.

"How are you holding up, honey?" Louise's graying brown hair was tied back neatly in a bun, her gray-green eyes soft and slightly out of focus—she'd always hated wearing her glasses.

"I'm fine, Louise, thank you." Bertie picked up the fork and cut into the thick slice of meatloaf. With a silent prayer of thanks, she savored the food. Fried potatoes and gravy, cornbread and green beans fresh from the garden, cooked with bacon. The neighbors had gone all out.

She ate without talking for a few minutes while Louise, Gerald and Arielle talked around her, and she caught a few snatches of conversation here and there from others in the room who had already greeted her and offered their condolences.

Bertie had lost friends and loved ones before. She had experience with grief. But missing someone she knew she would see again someday was a far cry from that cold fear that she might be saying goodbye forever. Thankfully, she knew she would see Dad again. He'd had a strong, enduring love for his Lord, as had Mom.

But even though Bertie knew they'd be together again, it wouldn't be here on earth. She already missed him with a deep sense of loss.

She picked up on the conversations around her.

"…was a good man, dependable and honest…"

"…can't understand why Butch isn't checking this out better…"

"…never seen the like…don't know what this world's coming to…"

"…best food in the four-state area!"

"…oughta try the mountain oysters…"

"…what's the filling in the fried pies? Tastes like some kind of berry…"

After only a few bites, Bertie realized her appetite wasn't as keen as she'd first thought.

Arielle gave Bertie another hug, and rose to her feet. "Everyone is going to want to talk to you now that you're home. We'll give you some time to get your bearings, but you must remember that our home is always open to you, Bertie."

Gerald held up his hand. "One more thing, Bertie. I really could use some help down at the MFA Exchange this summer. We're busier than we've ever been, and I need someone in the office with knowledge about farming."

Arielle gave her husband a look of exasperation.

Bertie hesitated. "If I decide to run the farm myself, I won't have time for any outside work, Gerald."

He grimaced. "A young woman like you shouldn't have that kind of burden." His wife tugged on his arm, and he shrugged good-naturedly at Bertie. "We'll see you tomorrow at the funeral."

As Gerald and Arielle walked into the crowd, Louise leaned close to Bertie. "I wouldn't let anybody talk me into selling yet, honey. Wait a while. Talk to your neighbors."

"Don't worry, I won't make any decisions without talking to my brother first."

"That's good. And if you do sell, be sure to come to us first. Honey, I don't know what to say about your father. I feel so awful, after talking your ear off Sunday night when your dad didn't answer your call. I should've known something was wrong, but he's always been such a strong man, so sure of himself, a body doesn't expect something to happen to him." Louise paused for a breath.

"I don't blame you, Louise," Bertie said quickly. "You and Herbert have always been good neighbors." She hesitated. Well, that wasn't exactly true. Dad and Herbert Morrow had argued often about the fence that connected their properties at the back forty.

Dad had never been one to mince words, and he'd thought Herbert was just plain lazy about upkeep. Few people, however, were as diligent about keeping their fences, barns, cattle and homes in as good a condition as Joseph Moennig.

The other farmers who lived and worked on the five-hundred acre section of land closest to Hideaway—the Jarvises, Morrows, Kruegers and Fishers—were hard workers. But they never quite matched Dad's meticulousness when it came to caring for the land. He'd always seen his work as a calling from God—the real oldest profession and the most blessed. He took that calling seriously, which was one reason Bertie had so much trouble accepting his death as a careless accident.

But it was even harder to hold any of their neighbors in suspicion. Sure there had been times in the past when her father's gung ho attitude had rubbed some folks the wrong way, but no one she knew would have resorted to attacking him.

"Louise," she said softly, "did Dad ever mention any problems he might have been having with someone? Another neighbor, maybe? Or someone from town? Have there been any newcomers in Hideaway recently besides tourists?" No one Bertie knew would have paid as much attention to the comings and goings of strangers as Louise Morrow.

Louise leaned back on the sofa, looking as if she intended to settle in for a nice, long conversation. "He hadn't said much recently. You know how he kept so busy. There wasn't always time to sit and chat, besides which, Joseph was never much of one to visit of an evening. I'd heard about the cattle that went missing from his place. He'd asked Herbert about those cows." She paused, leaned closer to Bertie, lowered her voice. "You know I don't mean any disrespect, but I had the feeling Joseph might've thought my own Herbert took the cattle, which of course is ridiculous."

"He never said anything to me about that," Bertie assured her.

"I know the Kruegers *said* they lost some cattle, as well."

Bertie frowned at her. "You didn't believe them?"

Louise spread her hands to her sides. "It isn't for me to say. Herbert went out and checked on our stock when he learned there might be cattle thieves in the area, but we didn't lose any." She leaned close again. "Herbert did tell me about something he overheard at the Exchange the other day. Somebody thought the Kruegers might've—"

She stopped suddenly, as if realizing who she was talking to. "Oh, Bertie, listen to me jabber on. You don't need to be burdened with all this, what with your father's funeral—"

"Louise, what did Herbert hear about the Kruegers?"

"Oh, you know how those men down at the Exchange like to tell their tales."

Bertie nodded, waiting.

"Well, okay, but you need to take this with a grain of salt, and it's probably not even worth that much." Louise glanced around them hesitantly, then scooted closer to Bertie. "I'm not going to mention names, mind you, but some folks have actually come right out and suggested maybe Krueger was the one who took those cattle in the first place. Half the town knew he was struggling to make his farm payments, what with all the money he had to send back home to his parents in Germany."

"What else did they say?" Bertie asked, hearing the quaver in her voice.

Louise patted Bertie's hand. "Now, honey, don't you worry yourself about such gossip. Like I said—"

"They're saying Krueger was the one who killed Dad?"

Louise blanched, eyes startled. "All guesswork. Nobody knows for sure."

"But it would be an easy conclusion to draw," Bertie said, though she couldn't bring herself to believe it. "People are probably wondering why else Krueger would take his family and disappear in the middle of the night."

Louise hesitated, then nodded.

"Can anyone remember seeing any of the Kruegers after Dad was found Monday?" Bertie asked.

"Well, you know, I thought I saw somebody out in their garden that morning, but with that eighty acres between our house and theirs, it's kind of hard to know for sure."

Bertie nodded. She would have felt badly for pressing Louise, but she had the distinct impression that Louise didn't mind at all. In fact, she seemed to want to be pressed for more details.

Bertie got up, taking her plate with her. "Thanks for telling me this, Louise. I know it's just hearsay, but at least I'll know what people might be thinking when they talk to me, and what they're saying when I'm not around."

Louise patted her arm. "You let me know if you ever need to talk about anything. You know where I am."

Bertie carried the half-empty plate into the kitchen, which was unoccupied for the moment.

Louise was a kindhearted soul, but Bertie couldn't see herself confiding in her...unless, of course, she wanted to spread news to everyone in Hideaway and half the folks in Hollister.

At one time, Arielle Potts had decided to start a Hideaway newspaper. With Gerald's help, she'd compiled six pages of up-to-date news and information, using the efforts of several high-school students. She'd used a printing company in Hollister, and had, of course, included some of her own son's poetry, which had embarrassed Ivan half to death.

Most townsfolk bought the first couple of weekly editions for the novelty of it. But it soon became apparent that they couldn't find much in the paper that they didn't already know by word-of-mouth. They did, after all, have radio now, and relatives who kept them informed with phone calls and letters.

Bertie had been sorry to see Arielle's efforts get off to a rough beginning. That paper had been skillfully edited by Arielle, herself, and every word could be trusted as truth.

On the other hand, Louise Morrow never bothered to edit the words that came out of her mouth, and she didn't always bother to check her facts with people who might actually know the truth.

Bertie placed her plate in the sink, ran some warm water and washed the dishes that had already been brought in from the other room. She had managed to speak with everyone who had come to see her. Soon, she would put on sturdier shoes and take a walk.

Chapter Nineteen

Red stepped out of the barbershop, reeking of aftershave and itching around the collar of his shirt. He'd never liked going to the barber, so he always let his hair grow a little too long before getting it cut. In the Army, that hadn't been much of a problem.

As he walked from the barbershop to the MFA Exchange for some grain for Seymour, short hairs continued to poke at his neck. Time to take a bath as soon as he got home—if he could get past all the visitors without being drawn into some conversation or other.

As usual, when he reached the MFA Exchange, he saw a handful of farmers loafing around the large dock where the farmers unloaded their excess crops and loaded up with things they didn't have. Some would've brought grain in to sell, others, like Red, were there to buy it.

The MFA Exchange, the barbershop and the diner down the street were the three favorite places for the men to catch up on local news, find out the going price for grain and let off some steam every once in a while.

A telltale haze of pipe smoke greeted Red before he caught sight of Gramercy Short sitting on a hay bale, jawing at anybody who'd listen.

Not many ever did. Gramercy's word was about as dependable as a cow pie in a hailstorm. But Red did eavesdrop on several conversations as he limped along the aisles of farm supplies, sniffing the sweet grain laced with molasses, the sunbaked hay, the smoke from various cigarettes and pipe tobacco.

"...sure keepin' to himself since he got back..."

"...thought they were sweet on each other before he left. Think they'll get married now that he's home for good?"

"...going to try to run that farm all by herself?"

"...oughtn't to be buryin' a Nazi in a Christian graveyard..."

He stopped and looked sharply toward the sorry soul who'd made that last remark. Of course. Gramercy Short was still hunched down low on the hay bale, muttering to his wife, Drusilla, who stood beside him. Far be it from ol' man Short to let his wife have the only available seat.

True to form, Dru didn't seem to be listening to a word her husband said, but stood thumbing through last year's copy of the *Farmer's Almanac*.

Red's hands clenched at his sides. Gramercy Short, that old hog-nosed bully, had always been a few rows short of a plowed field. What right did he have to call anybody a Nazi? Or complain about who was buried in the church cemetery? He never went to church, or even funerals, unless the dead person was close family, and no Shorts had died around here in a coon's age.

Not that Red wanted harm to come to any of them, but they sure did cause a heap of trouble for the rest of the town with their constant bickering and their troublemaking ways. Dru was the one that had upset Ma so badly, accusing Red of being AWOL on his last leave from the war.

Red caught Gramercy's eye and held a staring contest with him until the scoundrel looked away. As he walked past the man, he checked Gramercy's shoes. Old work boots, about the right size, cracked at the edges. The shoes looked almost as old as Moses, and probably didn't give much protection to the scoundrel's feet.

Resisting the urge to ask Gramercy to pick up his foot, Red passed by him with a nod.

After buying the grain—Seymour was going to be a happy horse, because Red was the only one who knew what kind he liked—Red greeted most of the other farmers by name, and stood and jawed awhile. Homer Jarvis, another of the Moennigs' neighbors, wasn't as talkative as he used to be. Red having been gone to war for the past three years, could be he'd missed a gradual change in the man. But Jarvis had never been an overly friendly sort.

It was well-known in town that the Jarvises needed more land to grow what they needed to raise their flock of kids. Homer had approached the subject with Joseph a few times, hinting that Joseph might consider selling his land to a neighbor he could trust.

Red couldn't see anyone killing off a trusted and respected farmer for a few measly acres of farmland.

He left the way he came in.

He happened to walk past Gramercy's old Model T Ford, parked across the street from the Exchange. No telltale shoe prints around the driver's side, but he did see one print near the passenger side. A large print, like that of a work boot. There was a ridge on the dirt that could've been made from a cracked sole, but it didn't tell him much.

Red glanced toward the sheriff's car, parked now in front of the barbershop, and strolled back in that direction. He studied the damp earth around the parking area across the street from the shop. Right there in mud he saw another footprint with that telltale crack in the heel, like the one outside the guesthouse, and the one outside Joseph's house. But footprints in the dirt wouldn't be enough to convince the sheriff to open this case again.

Red would have to do more than that. But what?

He limped back to his horse, tied the feed bag on the back of the saddle, fighting off Seymour's curious, snuffling nose and thick, seeking lips.

Red wasn't finished yet.

Bertie wanted to check the farm for herself. Sure, she trusted Red to go over it with a fine-tooth comb and scare up any evidence of foul play that might be there. But she would know if something was wrong, perhaps, simply by walking through the house on her own, seeing if something was out of place, or if Dad might've been worried about something he hadn't mentioned to anyone. She'd been in too big a rush to check any of the rooms while everyone waited for her in the car earlier.

She also wanted to check and make sure the hunting rifle was still in the place where Dad had always kept it, or if, for some reason, he might've moved it from the pump house and taken it into the house with him for protection.

Another thing she wanted to do was hike to the spring above the cliffs over the James River and see if the comfrey still grew there as thickly as it once did. Even if Red resisted her attempts to treat him, she wanted to be prepared.

Right now, Red was making her feel useless, treating her

like a brainless little woman who didn't know how to think for herself. She didn't need rescuing. She did need to be kept in the loop about what Red might've found out about Dad's death. Was it simply a tragic accident? Or had someone actually attacked him out of vengeance, or had they made an error of some kind? Did someone really think Dad was aligned with the enemies in Germany?

Ordinarily, Louise's inquisitive nature repelled Bertie, but this time she wondered if it wouldn't be a good idea to learn a little more about the goings-on in the neighborhood recently.

But first, it was time to do some investigating for herself—if only she could manage to slip away for a little while.

The coast was clear. The kitchen was empty for the time being. Bertie had slid on her best walking shoes and come back downstairs, and had actually made it to the back of the house without being stopped by any of the guests, who continued to chat in the living room.

She had stepped out the back door and turned to pull it shut when she heard a loud male voice behind her on the porch. "There you are! Bertie Moennig, it's hard to catch you without a whole roomful of people surrounding you." It was John Martin. She recognized the deep sound of his voice before she even turned around and saw him, dark brown hair combed back and held into place with enough VO5 hairdressing to pave the road in front of this house.

"Why, John, I wondered where you'd gotten off to." She hugged him with a little more enthusiasm than she ordinarily would. "I figured you'd be working on the farm, with school being out."

She couldn't tell if his flush was from her exuberant greeting, or from a little too much sun recently.

"I've been working some extra in town when they can spare me from the farm. The school's growing with the rest of the town, and we're building some new classrooms during summer break." He raised his hands. "When I'm not kept busy picking blackberries and gooseberries for my mother."

She saw his hands were scratched, the left sleeve of his denim work shirt ripped and stained black. "Those vines can be hard on skin and clothes." He glanced down at her walking shoes. "Headed out somewhere?"

"Just needed to get some fresh air. If you're hungry, there's plenty of food inside."

He nodded. "Knew everybody'd come to see you." He hung his head. "Bertie, I sure am sorry about your dad. He was always so good to us kids. We'll all miss him."

"Thank you, John. That's a comfort to hear." She gestured toward the back door. "Why don't you go on in and get some of Lilly's German chocolate cake before it's all gone." Her own mother had made that cake for years, using black walnuts in the filling.

John grinned. "No kidding? I guess I'll have to go have a taste before Ivan eats it all. Bertie, you be careful out here." He glanced around the backyard, nodding toward the back fence. "Someone nearly brained me last week with a brick through the back window." He pointed to the largest window at the back of the house, where there was a small sitting room for those who preferred privacy from the rest of the guests.

Bertie gasped. What *else* had they all decided not to tell her about? "Did it hurt you?"

He pointed to a partially healed wound on his forehead. "Got some glass, but at least the brick missed me. We swept on that floor for what seemed like hours to get all the glass up."

"It didn't hurt anyone else?"

He shook his head. "I was up late, and everyone else was in bed. Your father came over the next morning and helped us patch up the window until Lilly could get a new pane. That came in on Wednesday."

"It looks as good as new. Did Red repair it?"

John nodded. "I helped."

Bertie nodded toward the house. "You'd better go ahead and get some of that cake. I'll talk to you a little later."

He nodded to her and walked through the kitchen door.

With relief, Bertie turned away, wondering again how many other things had happened in this town that Red and others were "protecting" her from.

The guesthouse was nearly twice the size it had been before Lilly had started taking in boarders. It had been an ongoing project for the family to build on an extra room any time they could afford the material. The sitting room at the back of the house had been Red's sister's bedroom until she went off to college.

Bertie walked over to examine the large picture window that John told her had been broken. He and Red had done a good installation job.

She walked through the garden and inspected the back fence, which was made of hog wire to keep stray dogs out of the yard. Anyone could have gotten into the backyard either through the horse stable, or by climbing the apple tree, the trunk of which was being used as a fence post.

Bertie had climbed this tree many a time. She'd also helped mend the fence when she or Red or one of their friends had come down on the wire and torn it loose from its moorings.

For old times' sake, she grabbed a low branch and swung herself up and over, then slid easily to the other side. With a quick glance toward the house, she started to turn away when a voice arrested her from inside the horse stable.

"Where are you off to, young lady?"

For an instant, Bertie froze. Then recognizing her roommate's voice, she relaxed. "Spying on me?"

Edith stepped out of the stable. She, too, had changed into her jeans. "That's what I'm here for." She turned and looked again at the building. "How I miss my own horse back in Mobile."

"I thought you grew up in the city."

"I did, but we always kept horses at a stable in the country. I dreamed of living in a place where I could get up in the morning and go for a ride before school." She climbed over the fence and landed beside Bertie. "You haven't told me where you're going."

"For a stroll."

"Crowd getting to you?"

Bertie cast a wistful glance toward the road. "It's good to see everyone, it really is."

"But sometimes it can be too much." Edith nodded. "I know."

Bertie hesitated.

"Don't let me stop you," Edith said. "I'm well aware that you want to be alone right now, but this is as alone as you'll get today." She looped her arm around Bertie's. "Where to?"

Bertie suppressed a sigh of frustration. She knew better than to argue, because with Edith, she usually lost. "I want to go home."

Edith's arm tightened around hers, and the humor died in her eyes.

"Just for a few minutes. Please."

Edith raised an eyebrow, her eyes narrowing as she held Bertie's gaze. "We should call Red or Ivan to come with—"

"No. Not this time. I don't need either of them breathing down my neck right now. They hover too much, and I can't focus when Red's around. Besides," she said, gesturing toward the stable, "He's obviously gone somewhere on the horse."

"So it seems."

Bertie glanced toward the house again. "I want to do my own investigating, and I want to find my father's hunting rifle, and even gather some comfrey if I can find it. Red's leg obviously needs some help healing."

"Then let's get there and back before the posse can catch us," Edith said gently.

Bertie wanted to hug her. Instead, she led the way around the house to the road.

Chapter Twenty

The birds serenaded Red as he urged Seymour toward the library. Some loud whippoorwill sat in the top of a gnarled old oak tree halfway up the side of the hill Hideaway was built on, not wanting to shut up—probably the same one that had kept him awake half the night. A mourning dove joined in the song, followed by a mockingbird.

What Red wouldn't have given to hear this chorus when he was skulking through a deserted Italian town, expecting any minute to hear the whiz of bullets or feel the burn of metal in his flesh.

And when he finally did get hit, the physical pain had been nothing compared to the damage down deep inside.

The morning he was shelled, he'd closed his eyes and thought of home…of the sounds of the birds in the trees, the smell of the lilac bushes in full bloom, Bertie's smiling face. All he'd had to get him through that day, when the Germans were watching too closely for the medics to get through to him and pull him to medical care, was the bundle of Bertie's letters, which he'd carried right here in his front right pocket.

Could be she'd saved his life that day.

A small voice deep inside asked him why, now that he was out of danger and back home, he couldn't tell Bertie how much those letters had meant to him. How much *she'd* meant to him.

As he rode beneath a tunnel of trees that overhung the road—sycamores and oaks, maples and willows—dappled sun warmed his face and neck, creating gold patches of light against the gray shadows beneath the trees. He allowed Seymour his head once again. The horse knew this road as well as anyone, and Red had more important things to do than tug on the reins.

He pulled a letter from his pocket—the one letter he would never forget, and which had caused him more joy than he'd ever felt in his life. In the past weeks, it had also been the one letter that caused him the most pain.

Sunlight shot through the trees and reflected from the top page with such brightness for a moment that it nearly blinded him.

Dear Red,

I can't believe I've already been in California for over six months! Every day when I go to work, or look at a calendar, I remember how long we've been apart. I know it must seem silly to you, reading about the things that are happening in my life right now, when you're in Italy's trenches, fighting with your life for your country's safety and freedom.

He didn't know how many times he'd read this part, and it always made him feel good. She'd been thinking of him, about how much time they'd been apart. A woman as special as Bertie could've had any number of men callin' on her, but she'd waited on him.

He fingered the sheet and continued reading.

To keep hope alive, I can only think of the future, how good

*it'll be once we're both back home. Knowing of your sacri-
fice urges me to keep giving blood, even when I'm still feeling
weak from the last time I gave. The hope keeps me knocking
on doors, urging folks to buy war bonds. Doing without sugar
and meat and nylons is such a small sacrifice, when I think
about what we could be doing without... our very lives.
You're a hero, Red Meyer, and I've never been prouder to be
able to tell people I know you.*

He looked up as Seymour reached the town square.
Hideaway had a different city plan than any other town Red
had ever seen. It was built with the storefronts and offices all
facing outward onto a bricked street that surrounded it on all
four sides. The town itself was built into the hillside, and
overlooked the James River below, which wrapped itself
around the hill on three sides in its lazy route to the White
River.

He steered the big bay gelding to the right, then relaxed
the reins again and continued reading.

He'd discovered a few months ago that Bertie was not only
writing to him, but to a few of his buddies. She'd also convinced several of her girlfriends to write, as well. She was
like a one-woman campaign to keep the soldiers supplied
with letters from home.

At first, he'd been jealous, and had let her know about it.
Then he'd been ashamed.

He especially liked the ending to this letter.

*Red, you know I miss you something awful, and the months
that go by make it harder and harder. Writing to other men
fighting for our freedom makes me feel I'm that much closer
to you, but don't you worry. You get the most letters, and
you're the one I think about so often every day. You're the one
in my prayers and in my heart. Always and forever in my*

*heart. You hang in there and come back home to us. The one
thing I want more than anything else in the world right now
is to see you again, healthy and whole.*

He winced at that, then refolded the pages and slipped
them back into his pocket. She always signed her letters
Yours with love. He knew it'd been wrong to ask her about
the other guys she was writing to, but he couldn't help
himself. He'd never been jealous before.

He reached the library and slid from Seymour's back.
Time for some more research.

"I don't know where Lilly's going to put all the food people are bringing," Edith told Bertie as they strolled along the
deserted road toward the farm.

"Don't worry, it'll be eaten soon enough." Bertie stepped to
the edge of the road, where, if she looked just right, she could
see the curve of the river below. "Though none of my relatives
are coming in for the funeral, we won't lack for people. They
almost always have a dinner on the church grounds."

"Good, because I'm eager to taste a botten cake."

Bertie cast her a curious glance. "I'm sure you've had
those before."

Edith looked at her blankly. "Not that I can remember. I'm
hoping to taste gooseberry pie, and fried mayapples and
mountain oysters, as well—whatever those are. I thought I'd
tasted everything the world had to offer, but the Ozarks offer
foods I'd never even heard of in Hawaii or California."

Bertie grinned to herself.

"So, what is a botten cake?" Edith asked. "Mrs. Jarvis
brought one. I've heard of chocolate cake, pound cake, fruit
cake and wedding cake, but—"

"You're going to be disappointed." Bertie chuckled, pitying

her poor, proper-English friend. "Edith, you have too much school teacher in you. Have you met Arielle Potts, Ivan's mother?"

"Not yet. I helped Lilly in the kitchen for as long as I was needed this afternoon."

Bertie chuckled. "Mrs. Jarvis simply bought her cake at the store instead of baking it at home."

Edith blinked, her dark brown eyes mirroring confusion. "Boughten."

Edith frowned.

"Store bought."

"You realize, of course, there's no such word as boughten."

Bertie smiled. "You realize, of course, that we're hillbillies who sometimes make up our own language," she said, mimicking Edith's southern accent. "Don't worry, though, you'll still have plenty of new things to taste. I daresay you haven't had black-walnut cake."

"I've had plenty of black walnuts. I'm from Alabama, you know. Have you ever eaten boiled peanuts?"

Bertie made a face. "No, and I don't intend to. As I said, I really think you should meet Arielle Potts. She was a school teacher, she has a college education, she's the town's only librarian, and the two of you speak the same language."

"Well, by all means, I hope to meet this delightful lady. Ivan's mother, you say?"

"That's right," Bertie said. "She's quite a lady. She's also busy, and the library is one of her top priorities. You might stop by there sometime soon."

Edith nodded. "I may do that."

When they reached the farmhouse, Bertie paused for a moment inside the front gate. This had been the only home she'd ever known. Mature elm, maple, broadleaf pine and dogwood trees shaded the house, keeping it cool in the summertime. Or at least as cool as it could get in the humid Ozark climate.

Edith touched her shoulder. "Are you okay, honey?"

Bertie nodded and led the way up the porch steps, frowning at the limbs scattered along the far end, which she hadn't noticed earlier in the day. She didn't know where those had come from. She'd have to ask Red.

She opened the front door and went in, once again accosted by the poignantly familiar smells that threatened to bring tears.

Edith followed more slowly. "You people don't believe in locks, do you?"

"No reason to use them. We've never had a break-in here." Bertie stopped in the middle of the living room, frowning at the closed door in front of her.

"What's wrong?"

"That's odd. I know I left the door open between the kitchen and the living room when I left here this morning. And Red went out before I did."

"Maybe Red came back after he left the guesthouse." Edith stepped up behind her, sniffing. "Did something die in here?"

Bertie sniffed, grimacing. "That doesn't smell like a dead animal." She pushed open the kitchen door, and the smell attacked her.

She stepped backward. "That's propane gas."

Edith caught her arm. "Must be a leak. We should get out of the house."

"No, wait." Bertie pulled away and went to the stove. She was shocked to find the burner knobs all opened to the widest setting. She turned them off and reached for the back door to air out the room.

Before she could get the door open, however, from the corner of her eye she caught sight of a thick thatch of golden fur wedged between the stove and the back wall.

"Herman!" she dropped to her knees, gagging at the stench of the gas as she reached for her father's barn cat.

"Bertie, what is it?" Edith asked. "We have to get out of—"

"Get the back door open, quickly!" Bertie lifted the cat into her arms. "He's still warm."

She felt the animal's body arch, and then sharp claws buried themselves in her arm as he yowled.

"Ouch!"

"Here, bring him out." Edith shoved the door wide and braced it as Bertie fought the suddenly struggling animal.

She couldn't hold him. When she dropped him into the grass, he scrambled away from her, footsteps as unsteady as a drunk's.

"What was he doing in there?" Edith asked.

Bertie reached for an old washtub at the corner of the house to brace the door open. "I have no idea. He sure wasn't there earlier today, and Red wouldn't've let him in."

"He also didn't open the gas valves on that stove," Edith said, "And he didn't blow out the pilot light."

Bertie turned to her friend as the implications sank in. "Someone's been here."

Eyes wide with alarm, Edith glanced around the yard, looked toward the barn, and looked back at Bertie. "And someone might still be here."

Bertie started back into the house. "We need to call for help."

"Not here." Edith grabbed her by the arm. "What if whoever did this is still in the house? Or what if the gas has spread enough to ignite? Isn't there a water heater in the house, with a pilot light?"

Bertie closed her eyes, focused on her breathing. "I can't believe this is happening."

Edith looked down at Bertie's arm, then released her. "You're bleeding."

"Cat scratched me." Bertie's heart thrummed in her chest. The cat had also ripped the dressing from her sutured finger.

"We'll get you taken care of as soon as we get back to Lilly's," Edith said. "But we need to get there as quickly as possible." She cast another glance around the yard, and then she looked at the kitchen window. Her eyes widened, and much of the natural color drained from her cheeks. "Oh, Bertie," she whispered.

Bertie looked up at the window. Scrawled in thick red lines were the words *Nazi gas chamber.*

Edith grabbed her again. "Let's go. Now! Let's get back to town!"

Chapter Twenty-One

Red opened the library door and stepped inside. The Hideaway library was little more than a large room out back of City Hall. There'd never been a library at all before Arielle married Gerald Potts and came to town.

She had a lot of pet projects—special classes on charm for the young ladies, establishing a town newspaper, hosting a weekly ladies tea, but the library seemed to be her biggest source of joy, other than her son, Ivan.

Here at the library, she prided herself in keeping a wide variety of reading material, with the latest novels and periodicals. The magazine rack was especially well stocked with news about the war, and she always had more than one copy of *Stars and Stripes*, because it was so popular.

She was carrying a stack of books in her right arm and pushing one book into place on a shelf with her left when Red walked in, and he got a lot of satisfaction from the look of surprise on her face when she saw him.

"Fooled you, didn't I?" he said.

The surprise turned to welcome as she smiled at him and

set down the books she'd been shelving. "And here I'd done all my research on the Bald Knobbers because I was sure I'd never see you in here doing it for yourself."

He hid his relief. He didn't have time to go searching through all the books for something that might not even be here. "Are there many books on the subject?"

She pointed to her desk, just inside the entrance. "A total of two. The original vigilante group of men who called themselves the Bald Knobbers formed in the mid-eighties, many years after the end of the Civil War in '65." She picked a book up from the desk and held it out to Red. "What began as a good thing, to enforce law and order, soon turned evil when men allowed their greed for land and power to control their actions. It's much the same today, of course."

Arielle Potts had been a teacher of high-school history for a brief time before Ivan was born—and before she discovered she didn't possess the brute strength it took to corral a schoolhouse full of wild "hillbilly" kids. She'd always taken an interest in history, especially in this area—probably from a need to understand why the Ozarkians were so different from Easterners.

"Just in case you didn't have time to read these books, I've written some notes for you." She opened the cover of the top book and slid out two folded sheets.

Red recognized her neat, very precise handwriting. "Thank you, Mrs. Potts. Do you think my hunch might be right?"

"About a revival of the gang?" She frowned. "There are some similarities, of course. The Bald Knobbers formed after the Civil War because so many men had been killed there weren't enough to contain law breakers. Our war with Germany recently ended, which is a similarity, but we have law and order here. Times aren't the same."

"But we don't even have a police force here in town. We have to rely on the sheriff, and if you don't mind my saying, he ain't the best."

She gave an elegant grimace. "Why don't you let me talk to Gerald about this? He would be the best person to speak with Sheriff Coggins."

"That'd be fine." Red didn't tell her he planned to keep searching for Joseph's killer, no matter what the sheriff decided to do.

Bertie and Edith reached Lilly's guesthouse, winded and perspiring, but safe.

"We can't go inside with this," Bertie said, holding up the rifle she had insisted on grabbing from the pump house.

"I can't believe I let you waste time getting that thing!" Edith said. "What would we have done if we'd been shot?"

"Well, we weren't." Bertie skirted around the outside of the fence toward the corral and stable.

"We've got to tell the police about this."

"Not yet. I've done some thinking about it, and I don't think that's a good idea right now."

"The sooner someone gets out there, the less likely it will be for the intruder to escape," Edith said.

"That intruder's long gone, Edith, you know that. It would've taken some time for the cat to be affected by the gas, and no one's stupid enough to hang around that long. Nobody knew we were going out there."

"Someone at least needs to go inside and check to make sure the whole house doesn't explode with all that gas," Edith said.

"The doors are open."

"You should at least tell Red."

"Not yet." Bertie reached the corral fence and handed Edith the rifle, then climbed into the corral. The stable was still empty, which meant Red wasn't back yet. "First of all, I don't know who's doing this, and so we really don't know who we can trust."

"You can trust Red. You know that."

"And what's he going to do? Ride out to the house just to find that no one's out there? After the funeral tomorrow, I'll tell Red all about it, but I can't risk having him hear about it, and deciding to drag me right back to the train station at Hollister."

"You don't have to let him do it."

"I don't want a big brawl the day before Dad's funeral." Bertie glanced around the stable.

"What are you looking for?" Edith asked.

"Someplace to hide this rifle."

Edith glanced toward the house. "Someone might have already seen us with it."

"I've been trying to keep it out of sight." She reached for it, and Edith handed it to her then climbed the fence after her. "Edith, I didn't want to drag you here in the first place. It's proving to be too dangerous."

"You didn't drag me, I came of my own free will, and I'm not going back without you. My main focus is my best friend, who needs me right now."

"Well, then," Bertie said, carrying the weapon into the shadows of the stable, "your best friend wants to know if you're any good with a hunting rifle."

"I sure am."

"You are? I thought you were a city girl."

"My husband wasn't. Harper grew up in rural Alabama, and he knew how to shoot practically before he could tie his shoes. He taught me how to handle a rifle before we got married, and I was good." She frowned at Bertie, the strong lines of high cheekbones and firm jaw tense with seriousness. "Whom do you want me to shoot?"

"I told you, I don't know yet. I hope nobody, but if we have to shoot to protect ourselves, can you do it?"

"I guess we'll see, won't we?"

Arielle raised a slender finger and pointed it toward the cane Red had leaned against the table. "Now, suppose you tell me about this injury of yours. I have a cousin in Baltimore who is one of the finest surgeons in Maryland. What can we do to get you healed?"

He shook his head. "Already seen too many docs. The Army surgeon says I should be fine."

"But you obviously are not fine."

"One doc tried to tell me it was all in my head."

"Psychosomatic?"

"He didn't say I was psycho, he said I was imagining pain that wasn't there."

Her lips pressed together with disapproval. "I don't agree. I think the Army may need some new surgeons who can do their jobs correctly without blaming it on your mental acuity."

He nodded. "I appreciate that, Mrs. Potts, but I don't think there's gonna be any more healing."

"I've noticed you and Bertie seem to be avoiding each other this afternoon."

Red tried not to scowl. "Lots of folks want to see her, and I've got things to do."

Arielle shook her head at him. "Don't forget whom you're talking to, Mr. Meyer. I've known you since you were a baby, and there's something wrong. I know the war has changed you, but you haven't been yourself at all today."

"She just got here today, and we haven't seen each other in a year. Give it time."

Arielle leaned forward and rested a soft hand on Red's arm. "Young man, you've fought in the war for three years, with very little leave. If I had been separated from Gerald for three years when we were courting, no one would have been able to keep me away from him—or him from me. Don't tell me there's nothing wrong."

Red shrugged. "War changes things, Mrs. Potts."

"It certainly does. You seem to have forgotten that I prefer to be called by my first name by those whom I perceive to be my friends. Do you suddenly have a problem with that?"

"No, Arielle." How could he have forgotten her habit of opening his life up like a book, reading and discussing whatever page she chose to light on?

She smiled at him. The smile was warm and kind, and he decided he really didn't mind having this lady with a good heart turning a few pages in his life's book.

Chapter Twenty-Two

Streaks of red, blue and white lights raced across the night sky and a deafening firestorm exploded in the blackness in front of Red. He dove for cover, smelling the stink of the explosive, tasting the grit of wet earth as he landed face-first in the bottom of the foxhole. Mud filled his nose and ears, blinding and choking him.

He reached out to feel for the side of the foxhole, and he felt something else. Something soft and cold.

It was human flesh, stiff with death.

He jerked away, dashing the mud from his eyes. Another streak of light flashed past him. He looked down at the body and saw Joseph Moennig imprisoned in the thick, black mud.

Red cried out and scrambled backward, only to fall against another body. Bertie's lifeless eyes stared past him.

Screaming, Red lost his footing and fell…and kept falling.

The mud wasn't soft and deep this time, but hard, flat, painful. He opened his eyes to darkness, and he froze, his breath loud in his ears, sweat dripping down his face. He waited until the square of his bedroom window took shape in the blackness of the wall. His leg hurt, and so did his shoulder and hip where he'd hit the floor. He'd fallen out of bed.

He swallowed to keep from throwing up, and stared out the window at the fading stars in the early morning sky. Why couldn't the dream disappear, like the mist that rose from the river?

The dreams were getting worse instead of better. How much longer would they haunt him like this?

He hoped he hadn't disturbed any guests. If he kept having these nightmares, he'd end up sleeping with the horse in the stable.

In fact, that might not be such a bad idea. At least if he was watching Seymour, no one could turn the horse out of the corral again without getting caught.

Someone knocked at his door, and he groaned. He'd been heard. His mother had moved his bedroom to the first floor of the house, in spite of his protests that he and his cane would be fine upstairs. She'd insisted that she wasn't worried about him and his cane, what she was worried about had something to do with a handsome, single man sleeping too close to his future bride. Folks would talk.

Red had warned his mother time and time again not to get her hopes up about a wedding, but would she listen to him? Nope. She still treated him like he was her rambunctious little boy. Not only did he want to protect her from disappointment, but he wanted to protect himself, as well.

Everything had changed. She'd have to get that through her skull.

The knock came again, and his door handle jiggled. "Red, you okay in there?"

He squeezed his eyes shut. It wasn't Ma outside that door, it was Bertie, and though relief washed through him afresh—

proof stood right outside the door that his dream was nothing more than that—he knew he had to keep his defenses up.

"I'm fine," he said. "Just a dream." One of the worst nightmares yet. He needed time to get over it. What he didn't need was Bertie asking questions he didn't know how to answer, when he wasn't thinkin' straight.

"You fall or something in that dream?"

He grunted. A fella couldn't even make a little noise without somebody running to check on him. A person would think he was a cripple or something.

He scrambled to his feet, reached for his robe, then his cane, and was halfway to the door when the handle jiggled again.

"Red?"

He couldn't tie the belt of his robe while handling the cane, so he didn't tie it. His pajamas were decent. Yanking the door open with his free hand, he braced himself for the sight of her. She held a lit candle in her right hand. She held more than that, though. She held the power to convince him to do things he knew he shouldn't.

"Woman, you're not my nurse. Do you think I'm an invalid?"

She caught her breath and took a step backward, the candle fluttering, and he felt all kinds of a heel.

She recovered quickly enough. Her eyes flashed. "Not physically," she snapped. "You might be a little soft in the *brain* sometimes. I heard a thump, and it scared me. For all I knew, somebody'd hurled another brick at the house."

Red grimaced, partly from a sudden pain in his bad leg, partly because Bertie knew about the brick. Too much stuff happening these days. If she'd stayed in California, she wouldn't have all this extra worry heaped on those shoulders.

"You shouldn't have been told about the brick," he said, hearing the instinctive gentleness in his own voice. "You've got enough on your mind. I'm okay."

"No you're not. You're hurtin', I can tell."

He looked away, suddenly thinking his breath must be rank enough to water her eyes, and then wondering where that thought came from.

Still, it was one thing to wake up in the morning with a bunch of battered soldiers who hadn't washed in maybe two months. It was another thing to face Bertie in the bare morning light before he even had a chance to brush his teeth.

He couldn't help noticing she didn't have any trouble with bad breath or an untied sash. In fact, she looked wide awake with her hair all in place, as well as he could tell in the candlelight.

"You already up for the day?" he asked.

She glanced down the hallway, toward the front window that overlooked the road, where the night still held sway, then she shook her head.

He took a step closer, and thought he saw dark circles under her eyes, the skin of her face pale—too pale. "Mercy, girl, you look like something the cat dragged in." She needed some sleep. She looked like she hadn't had any. Was he the reason for that?

She turned her scowl back on him. This was the old Bertie. The one he'd grown up with, who could fight like a boy when she needed to, and hadn't been afraid to punch him in the jaw once when he was eight and she was six and he locked her in the outhouse at school.

"I'm going to gather some comfrey out on the farm today," she said. "I tried to do it yesterday, but…I got sidetracked."

"You went out to the farm yesterday?"

She hesitated, looking away. "Sure did."

"What for?"

"I wanted to see the house without you breathing over my shoulder and everybody waiting for me in the car."

"I thought I made it clear it wasn't safe—"

"Yes, you made that crystal clear, Red."

He blinked at the sharpness in her voice.

"What you didn't make clear was *why* you didn't think it was safe," she said. "You didn't tell me about the brick, you didn't explain what all those limbs were doing on the front porch, and you never gave me any reason for why you think Dad was killed. What else didn't you tell me?"

He couldn't hold her gaze.

"That's what I thought," she said, voice softening. "Anyway, comfrey'll be the best thing for that leg."

Something inside him relaxed, some burning pain eased that he hadn't even realized was there. She'd been thrown for a loop, seein' him like this yesterday without any warning, but now her nursing instincts were kicking in. She did still care about him.

As soon as the thought came to his mind, he dashed it away. He had no right to her healing touch. He had no rights at all.

"No need to do that," he said.

"I'll boil some of it into a tea, and the rest I'll—"

"I don't like comfrey tea." He hated the stuff. "Your mother made me drink that nasty brew when I broke my arm. I hated it then, too."

"It's not for your enjoyment," Bertie said. "It's for you to start feeling better. I'll sweeten it with honey, and then I'll make a comfrey-leaf poultice for that leg, and—"

"No, you won't." He wanted to grin, but he kept his face

straight with effort. She didn't need to go gallivanting over the countryside, what with her father's funeral today. She especially didn't need to go alone.

"Sure I will," she said. "We'll see if we can't pick up where the doctors left off."

He placed a hand on her shoulder, and then realized this was the first time he'd actually touched her in a year. Her shoulder was so slight…so delicate. She didn't need to be takin' care of him, she needed takin' care of.

Now that he'd crossed that great, cold gap between them, he didn't want to let go. He wanted her so much closer.

And yet, he didn't have a right to touch her. He didn't have a right to be giving her hopes about a future together, even if she still wanted that future.

"Don't take to meddlin'," he said, releasing her reluctantly. "And you need to get some sleep." He wanted to take her in his arms and kiss her hard and long and wipe that look of hurt from her face.

He wanted so much more. He wanted things to be different, but they weren't. They were what they were.

Ma was right to move his room.

"I think Ma's gonna need help with the guests this morning," he said. "She's cooking a batch of beans for the funeral dinner, but she wants to bake some cracklin' cornbread and a heap more things. You know what our funeral dinners are usually like."

"I asked her last night if she'd need help, and she said—"

"You know Ma, never one to ask."

Bertie's eyes narrowed. "You're trying to distract me, Red Meyer." But she didn't sound angry. He could hear the slight lilt in her voice.

He suppressed another grin. "Why don't you see about

helping her? We'll talk about comfrey and tea and stuff like that later, after this whole thing is over today."

She stood watching him. "You promise?"

"I said we'll talk about it."

"You will let me try to help you?"

"Now, Bertie, you know I don't make promises I might not be able to keep, and I hate comf—"

She pressed her fingers to his lips, and that soft touch sent a warning shock through him. He jerked away.

"Don't press me, woman." He couldn't believe the sharpness of his own voice, but he also couldn't believe how tempted he was, how weak he felt. "Do you know how many doctors told me my leg would be as good as new? I got my hopes up every time, and it never happened." He slapped his leg. "It's not fixed, and a few leaves and a swig or two of nasty-tasting tea won't do any more for me than the doctor's best penicillin, so don't start on me."

"Red, you've seen it work before."

"We'll talk later," he said, then closed the door and leaned hard on his cane, listening for sounds that would tell him she was leaving.

For a few seconds there was no movement, and then she walked slowly back to the staircase and up the stairs—the boards creaking with every step.

He'd have to get the floors fixed around here. Right now, though, he had other things to see about.

Soon as he could get his heartbeat back under control.

Chapter Twenty-Three

Bertie stepped silently through the bedroom she shared with Edith. She couldn't even cry, for fear of waking her friend.

How had it all come to this? Not only didn't Red want her here, he didn't want her to be close to him, to try to help him heal.

He knew she was knowledgeable about the herbs in these parts. Her mother had taught her everything she knew. But he didn't want to try. Not even for her.

She felt the sting of that through and through.

She stepped to the window overlooking the river and stared into the dim gray of the coming dawn. Time to get control of her thoughts. She was tired and overwrought. Edith was a silent sleeper, but the bedroom had only one double bed, and each was accustomed to her own bed.

Bertie had expected to sleep heavily last night because of her sleeplessness on the train, but her mind had flown from worry to worry, and she'd tried hard not to toss and turn for fear of waking Edith, which had made her more uncomfortable.

Every time she'd begun to drift off, a new problem would occur to her—how was she going to run the farm all by herself? How could she stand on her own two feet and run anything, if she wasn't even allowed to go to the farm alone?

And how could she expect Edith to go with her? Edith didn't know how to cope with cantankerous bulls, or cows with an overly developed protective streak for their calves.

Things would look better once she'd had some rest, surely.

With a quiet sigh, Bertie realized Red was probably more right than she wanted to admit. She *wasn't* ready to make any major decisions right now. The shock of Dad's death was too fresh. She didn't want to make a move that would turn out to be the wrong one.

She leaned against the window sill and gazed into the hollow as it grew dove-gray with morning light. Red had let her know how little he wanted her in his life right now. She'd seen the irritation in his eyes when he opened his door to her, and nobody could've missed the way he'd reacted to her touch. Like she was poison.

Why had she even gone to his room? If anyone else found out, she'd be mortified. A young lady did not go to a man's bedroom. Period.

But this wasn't any man, it was Red, and she'd heard him cry out. She'd do it again in a heartbeat.

"You've been standing there half the night," came Edith's groggy voice from the bed. "Don't you think you should try to get some sleep?"

"I can't."

There was a rustle of covers as Edith pushed back the blankets and stepped into her bedroom slippers. She padded across the floor to Bertie and placed an arm across her shoulders.

"How about some nice, warm milk with honey? That works for me when I can't sleep. Of course, it takes more than milk and honey to get a woman over a man."

Bertie grimaced. "Meaning?"

"Red isn't exactly welcoming to you right now, is he?"

"He's grumpy as a bear in the springtime, if that's what you're gettin' at."

Edith squeezed Bertie's shoulders, chuckling. "When Harper and I were dating, we had an argument about college. I wanted to go, and he didn't want me to. He thought a woman's place was in the home."

Bertie rolled her eyes. "How'd you two ever end up married, then?"

"It took a while. I told him a woman's place was anywhere she wanted to be, and if he didn't like it, he'd better tell me before we got more serious, because I wasn't about to play second fiddle to anyone, much less a man who didn't value me as a human being."

"What happened?"

"We stopped dating for about six months."

Bertie caught her breath. She'd been alone for nearly three years already. If she and Red had that kind of fallin' out now, would they ever get back together again?

Of course, it couldn't get much worse than it was right now.

"Then what happened?" she asked.

"I started dating someone else," Edith said. "Don't get me wrong, I loved Harper, but I knew that if he didn't respect my wishes before we were married, he sure wouldn't respect them afterward. I knew the kind of life I wanted, and it included a college education."

Bertie leaned her head against the window sill. "I don't know if I could date someone else. Red's the only one I've thought about for three years." She hesitated. "In fact, Red's the only man I've ever wanted in my life."

Edith gave Bertie's shoulders another squeeze, then released her and stepped to the window. "Harper was the only man I ever wanted, too. I still dated other men. And I started college."

Bertie knew this. Edith had been in her third year when Harper Frost was killed. Then she'd quit. She'd never returned.

"You must really miss him still," Bertie said softly.

"I do, but I'd go through all of it again, even knowing he would be killed. What we had was worth the heartache."

Bertie looked up at her friend, whose strong-yet-beautiful features were outlined by the bare dawn light that stretched across the eastern horizon, turning the river below the house to a silver stream of mist.

Edith had dark brown hair, dark eyebrows and eyes that sometimes seemed to reflect the night sky.

That pretty face turned to Bertie. "We both have our whole lives ahead of us, Roberta Moennig. If you want to be a wife and mother, then you need to decide now that you will be the best wife and mother you can be. If you want to be a business woman, like Lilly, then you learn all about the business, and don't let anyone tell you what you can and can't do. Not even Red Meyer."

"That'll be kind of hard. What I want to do is find out what happened to my father, and Red's being awfully bossy about it right now. Thinks he's protectin' me."

"Red strikes me as the kind of man who can get the job done if anyone can, and he seems determined to take care of that job, himself. I still think we should tell him about what we found at the farm yesterday."

"I'll tell him later today. There's nothing he can do about it now, anyway."

Edith gave an impatient sigh. "I don't know why I let you talk me into this secrecy. So what else do you want in life?"

"To get Red well, back to his normal self," Bertie said, frowning down at her hands. "Not so broken. That's what'll be hard."

"But that's exactly what you need to do," Edith said. "No matter what it takes."

With a nod, Bertie turned from the window. She threw her arms around Edith and hugged her. "I don't know why God blessed me with such a good friend, but I hope this friendship lasts for a lot of years."

Edith chuckled and patted her back. "I do, too. Now, you need to get to bed for a few hours. Can't go without sleep forever."

Bertie did as she was told, snuggling beneath the covers, feeling calmer than she had in days. It would work out. God had brought her this far, and He would see her through everything.

But as she drifted off to sleep, she once again saw those words scrawled across the kitchen window. *Nazi gas chamber.*

Who in the world would ever believe the Moennigs were Nazi sympathizers?

Chapter Twenty-Four

The Friday morning sun had barely begun to peer through the trees along the hillside above Hideaway when Red saddled Seymour and headed into the valley. He used to ride the horse bareback, but he couldn't jump nearly so high with this blasted gimp leg, and so he had to use a saddle now to get on the horse. Besides, he needed someplace to tie his cane.

Aside from the cane and the saddle, Red could close his eyes and just about feel like a man again. He could almost pretend he wasn't lame.

The fresh June morning air cooled his skin as mist drifted above the James River, swirling around the trees and hiding the water. The scent of lilacs drifted around him like the finest perfume. The sun crept higher, making a red background against the black-lace pattern of the treetops. Seymour's hoofbeats echoed against the cliffs.

If he could forget everything but this moment, he could convince himself the world was right again.

But the memory of Bertie's touch on his lips kept intruding—and the look of hurt in her eyes that came and went, as if her very heartbeat depended on him. He felt squeezed in a vise, and the nasty situation with Joseph's death turned the crank. He'd done the right thing with Bertie, and yet it had hurt her bad—the very thing he didn't want to do.

Why's it got to be so hard, God?

The prayer of complaint slipped from his mind before he could catch it. What was the use? God sure wasn't listening to him.

He let Seymour have the lead, sighed and sat back, willing the early morning beauty of his hometown—the home he'd longed to return to for so many months—to soothe the ache inside him.

Though Hideaway was a tiny town, far off the beaten path and on a gravel road except for the bricked street that surrounded the town square, it had a goodly share of visitors. The James River was great for fishing and floating, and Hideaway was built high enough above it that even the worst of flooding could never reach the town. There had been some lollapaloozas in past years.

Besides the fishing and floating, there was a lot of good huntin' in the woods around here, and Red knew the best places to find everything from coon to deer to wild turkey. He even knew where to find wild honey, and had supplied his mother with plenty of the sweet stuff over the years.

Before the war, the grocery and dry goods store had been well-stocked for such a small, out-of-the-way place, and the weather was so good the merchants catered to tourists three seasons of the year. Red knew these things well, since his livelihood for so much of his life had depended on those tourists.

He passed the Jarvis home and heard Mrs. Jarvis calling the chickens out back. Her husband, Homer, stepped out on the front stoop, letting the screen door slap shut behind him at the same time Red reached the gate.

Red gave him a polite nod. The Jarvises had never gotten on well with Dad when he was alive, but after he died they'd helped Ma out as much as they could, like the rest of the town.

"What you doin' out so early this morning, young soldier?" Homer asked, settling onto the porch steps with his spittoon can and a plug of tobacco.

Red didn't stop the horse. "Just checkin' a few things out."

"You heard any more talk about that dam the U.S. Army Corps of Engineers is planning for Branson?" Homer asked.

That made Red pull back on Seymour's reins. He stopped in the middle of the road. "I thought they scrapped that idea."

"Only 'cause of the war. Now that it's almost over, I hear they're getting interested in it again. There's talk, anyhow."

"War's not over yet."

"I said *almost*. My sister and her family live down along the White River. A dam like that upriver from them would sure change things. It'd stop all the floodin'. Can't beat that."

Seymour jerked on the reins, eager for a good morning walk. Red pulled back. "You hoping to live on a lake?" he asked Homer.

"Cain't say that I am."

"If they build that dam, the whole holler below us'll be flooded." All that hunting, and the good fishing would be wiped away. There'd be different fish altogether in a lake, with the warmer, sun heated waters.

"Don't see how you figure that." Homer ripped off a little plug of tobacco and slid it between his lip and bottom teeth. "They're damming White, not James." He'd become so good at talking with his mouth full of tobacco, he didn't even slur his words.

"James runs into White, and that dam's gonna be bigger than you and I ever dreamed," Red told him. "It'll reach this far, easy."

Homer shook his head. "You know how many miles we are from Branson?"

"Not far enough to avoid the lake," Red said. "It'll cut us off from Hollister. In fact, it'll cover the whole road. We'll have to drive twice as far to get anywhere."

"Who told you that?"

"I know how to read maps." Red shook his head. "Guess it's okay for some, but it'll sure change things for us around here."

Homer spit into his can. "I can tell Joseph's been talkin' to you. He and Earl Krueger thought the water would flood their fields."

"Joseph was right," Red said. "Can't blame a fella for wantin' to protect his livelihood."

"Well, if they was to have lakefront property, it'd probably be worth a pretty penny."

Red knew Joseph hadn't been interested in having lakefront property. All he'd ever wanted was his farm. Red had been relieved when the plans for the dam were scrapped. He wasn't one to take to change. Seemed like the whole world had changed too much in the past few years, and he couldn't help wonderin' if it'd be destroyed completely before the war ended. Folks who hadn't been in the front lines of the war—who hadn't seen Italy or Germany or the rest of Europe—didn't know what destruction was.

He waved to Homer and nudged Seymour on, passing by the Moennig farm this time. He'd investigated all he could there. He'd stop and count the livestock on his way back home, but first he wanted to do a little more investigating. He had a hunch that kept sinkin' its teeth into him, and he couldn't shake it.

The Krueger family had lived downhill and across the road from the Moennig place. By the time Red reached their farm—a flat plot of land with good dirt for crops—the sun had begun to warm the air.

This was the farm where Earl and Elizabeth and their five kids had a victory garden so big they'd supplied enough vegetables to keep Hideaway in produce all summer long. Before the war, when the depression was weighing down the rest of the country, the Kruegers had followed Joseph Moennig's example and grown fields of tomatoes for the local canneries.

Red had heard later, though, that they'd still come close to losing their farm a time or two in the past years.

Using his cane so he wouldn't have to climb down from the horse, Red unlatched the front gate to the Krueger place and rode on into the yard. The family had apparently taken their two yappy little dogs with them. Their cattle and chickens, interesting enough, had ended up in the farms of their closest neighbors. If Red hadn't started seein' to Joseph's livestock, he had no doubt they'd've ended up with the neighbors, as well.

Finally, Red reached the porch and slid from Seymour's back. He tied the horse to the front post and limped around the side of the house. Straightaway, he saw something that stopped him.

Someone had scattered limbs at the far end of the enclosed porch. They were small, more switches than thick limbs.

He noted the color, the texture of the wood. Hickory switches. Like the ones Red had seen on the Moennig porch.

He shook his head and glanced around the yard, as if somebody might still be lingering this long after the Kruegers left.

With the aid of the growing sunlight, Red found something else he was looking for—familiar footprints, etched in the thick, congealing mud alongside the house. It had rained last night enough to moisten the earth, but not enough to erase these prints. They were probably made with the style of heavy work boots a farmer might wear, and they were like the ones he'd found in Ma's backyard, and at Joseph's house, and across the street from the barbershop.

The more he thought about it, the surer he was the crack across the left heel had come from an ax head. Someone who chopped wood might've stepped on one. That didn't tell him anything, though. Everybody in the country had an ax.

He shook his head and gazed around the place. This made three homes of German immigrants that had been attacked in a week. Ma had suspected the Kruegers might've been threatened by someone, but Earl Krueger had always been a close-mouthed guy, a little too proud to let anyone know if he was having trouble. If he hadn't been forced to visit the neighbors asking about his lost livestock, nobody'd have known about it.

Earl and Elizabeth hadn't come to this country until a few years ago, when they could no longer ignore the Nazi threat to their peaceful little rural town in Southern Germany. They spoke with a heavy accent, but until the war began, they'd been treated with as much kindness and dignity as anyone else in town. Lots of folks had accents around these parts.

Other German families who'd recently come from the old country to America had been sent to detention camps. Could that be what had happened to the Kruegers?

But then, why wouldn't anyone know about it? Whole families didn't disappear in the middle of the night for no reason. And there were other German immigrant families in town. He'd not heard they were having any problems.

The switches bothered Red a lot.

Those nasty rascals, the Bald Knobbers used to bully men and teenaged boys into joining their vigilante gang by leaving switches on their front porches to warn them what would happen to them if they refused to join.

It was obvious why the Bald Knobbers did that. The more men who were involved in their terrorizing of the countryside, the fewer there would be to oppose them.

But how would anybody expect Joseph Moennig or Earl Krueger to even know about something like that? Joseph might have heard about it from elderly neighbors, but Earl wouldn't have any way of knowing about it. Not unless somebody'd told him a little about this area's history.

Red walked back around the house to the front porch. Unlike Joseph's porch, this one wasn't open to the wind, but had a rock wall enclosing it from the elements. Those limbs…

As he studied them again, a shape took form that froze his blood—something he should've seen sooner. Leaning heavily on the cane, he went up the steps and walked across the porch to stand over the switches.

There were eight of them placed together. At first glance, he'd thought they were scattered haphazardly, but these were not. He had a feeling Joseph's hadn't been, either, but the wind would've had more chance to scatter them out of order.

Someone had made a rough Nazi swastika with those switches. It surprised him that he hadn't recognized the shape as soon as he saw it, even though some of the limbs were askew.

The symbol that had stamped his nightmares for three years had been used in an act of terror against these German Americans. He gripped the curve of his cane in anger. He wanted to stomp these switches, to break them into tiny pieces and burn them. He raised his foot…and then he put it back down.

Never destroy evidence.

With shaking hands, he tested the front door of the house, found it unlocked, and went inside. In the kitchen, he found a couple of small, cracked saucers Mrs. Krueger had left behind, and he carried them outside.

Carefully, he scooped the familiar section of footprint into the saucer, and studied it. He figured it to be about a size ten, heavily worn on the outside, but the most helpful mark was that cut in the heel.

No telling how many men had been to the barbershop the past few days. The prints there might not tell him anything, and just because those prints were there didn't mean the man had even gone inside the shop. Red had noticed Ivan had gotten a good haircut in the past couple of days, but then so had his dad, and John Martin, and likely half the town, freshening up out of respect for the dead at the funeral today.

Even tobacco-spittin' Homer Jarvis looked as if he'd had his ears lowered recently.

The one person Red wanted to suspect, Gramercy Short, didn't even go to Bernie's barbershop. Those two'd had a falling out years ago over a fence between their properties, and Gramercy hadn't forgiven Bernie yet. His wife Dru cut his hair, and it showed. On the few times a year he got a shearing, he looked like a shaved billy goat.

Red would have to start paying more attention to shoes for the next few days. One way or another, he was going to find Joseph Moennig's killer and bring him to justice.

Chapter Twenty-Five

Bertie awakened several hours after dawn on Friday morning to the sound of a loud thump that jerked her up from her pillow. Morning sunlight streamed through both bedroom windows, the lace curtains throwing delicate shadows over the polished wooden floor.

The bedroom she shared with Edith was in the second story, front corner of the large guesthouse. It overlooked the road that skirted the front of the property at the edge of the bluff, and Bertie could see the James River from the front window.

She realized the thump had apparently been the slam of a car door. Noticing that Edith had already risen for the day—probably already working in the garden, an activity she loved—Bertie turned over and covered her ears with the pillow. Just a few more minutes of slumber…

But she still heard the footsteps of someone climbing the concrete steps to the wooden front porch below the window. It was too hot in this upstairs room to leave the windows closed at night, and so they opened both to create a cross-

breeze. The James River Valley caught that breeze and seemed
to direct it upward and into the open windows in the evenings.

Yesterday evening that breeze had been most welcome,
because, when not entertaining company, Bertie had spent her
time helping Lilly in the kitchen, sorting dried beans for overnight soaking, helping with mincemeat pies and baking black-
walnut cookies. And worrying, worrying, worrying about the
gas in the farmhouse and the message on the kitchen window.

But she couldn't let herself think about that right now. In
a few hours would be Dad's funeral.

Dad used to love Mom's dishpan cookies, made with
oatmeal, molasses, chocolate chips and black walnuts. In
fact, there wasn't much Dad hadn't loved about Mom, which
was why Mom had gone out of her way to please her
husband. The love they'd shared had always been an inspi-
ration to Bertie when she was growing up, and it was why
she'd been so surprised to discover that other marriages
weren't always as happy as Mom and Dad's.

Last night Bertie, Edith and Lilly had baked a huge batch
of the dishpan cookies, and Lilly had crowed with delight
when she'd taken her first bite. They'd be serving the cookies
at the funeral dinner today.

Lilly had fretted about the grieving daughter being forced
to cook for her own father's funeral, but Bertie had reassured
her she needed the activity to keep from thinking about many
things.

The spring on the screen door downstairs groaned as it
opened. Someone stepped inside—a man, by the heavy sound
of footsteps. A moment later, Lilly called out a welcome from
the dining room, her footsteps making the floor creak downstairs.

"Help you, sir?" her generous voice boomed.

In a very short time, Bertie had gotten used to hearing every conversation that took place in the living room, as the staircase directed sound up to this bedroom like a megaphone. It was why she'd heard Red holler and fall out of bed early this morning.

She frowned again at the memory—at the rejection. It was the only thing she could call it. Why should she even bother with Red? He didn't want her. He'd made that clear enough yesterday, when he'd left the house and not made an effort to talk to her the rest of the evening.

The man downstairs asked for a room for himself and his wife.

"Sorry, sir," Lilly said, "but we've got guests filling the house all weekend."

He offered to pay double.

Lilly didn't hesitate. "I'd do it if I could, sir, but we can't turn out our other guests."

Bertie was out of her bed and throwing on her clothes by the time the screen door slapped shut, and the footsteps echoed the visitor's return to his car. She daren't run out into the road half-dressed, though it frustrated her to let him get away. It was because of her that he hadn't been given a room.

She caught Lilly in the kitchen, heaving her bulk from stove to kitchen table with surprising agility as she started preparations for the large country breakfast she always advertised in the Hideaway weekly newspaper. While cooking breakfast, she was also working on the huge pot of beans, and had a cake pan of cracklin' cornbread ready to go into the oven.

Lilly was famous for her breakfasts on Friday and Saturday mornings, which were open to the public. She'd told Bertie last night that she'd begun to make almost as much income from her breakfasts as she did for her rented rooms.

"You can't keep doing that, Lilly." Bertie finished buckling the belt around the waist of her dark blue denim pants as she joined Lilly at the kitchen table. "You can't turn down paying customers like that. It's your livelihood."

Lilly handed Bertie a bowl of flour, a wooden spoon, buttermilk and a crock of freshly churned butter. "Think you can bake me up a batch of biscuits that'll keep our customers comin' back for more?"

Bertie took the items and laid them out on the table. "'Course I can, but you don't need me livin' here with you to do that."

She paused. If they'd had this conversation yesterday morning, she'd have insisted on staying out at the farm and riding her bike in every morning to help with the household chores. But she knew that would be out of the question. At least for today, until after the funeral, she needed to keep her mouth shut about what she and Edith had found.

"Arielle Potts invited Edith and me to stay with them while we're here," she told Lilly. "I hate to see you give up good income for a room."

"I want you here," Lilly told her. "With no college tuition to pay anymore, and no kids to take care of except Red—who's more help to me than anyone could be—I can afford to do what I want with some of my rooms, and I want to let my special guests stay here. That's final." Lilly nodded firmly.

"Then at least let me—"

"And don't even start on me about paying."

Bertie pressed her lips together. "Thank you." She sifted the flour and baking powder, mixed them and added the buttermilk. "Somehow, during any free time I can find today, I need to search through the woods and fields for some comfrey leaves to treat Red's leg."

Lilly gave her a pointed look. "You think that'll help him?"

"Sure it will. Mom used comfrey a lot. It can't hurt anything."

"I heard that it could. Wrap his leg with those leaves and it'll heal the outside fine, but the infection inside the leg would then be trapped, and he could lose his leg."

"Not if we give him comfrey tea along with it. That'll heal him from the inside out, while the leaves work on his wounds from the outside in. Besides, the infection should be gone." Bertie focused on the task Lilly had set before her, taking comfort in the familiar recipe for biscuits. In her mind's eye she followed a trail through the woods back of the farmhouse, where her mother used to gather plants for treatment.

It had been well over a year since she'd been there, but Bertie knew what she'd need. She and Edith both agreed that whoever had been at the house yesterday wasn't likely to linger there. She would probably be safe.

She hoped.

Leastways, she couldn't let a little fear stop her from making sure Red got the treatment he needed to heal.

"Lilly, do you have any idea why Red would refuse to have his leg treated?"

Lilly looked up from her frying. "You talk to him about the comfrey yesterday?"

"Early this morning, actually, after I heard him fall out of bed."

"He fell?"

"Nightmare."

Lilly fixed her with a stern look. "Young ladies don't go to the bedrooms of young men."

"I thought he might be hurt, and I couldn't let him lay

there. Anyway, Red's behaving strangely about his leg. Don't you remember that time he broke his arm?"

Lilly continued to level a stern look at Bertie for a few more seconds, to let her know how serious her transgression was. Then she nodded, relenting. "I sure do. Why, he loved all the attention that got him from friends. He made a big joke out of it."

"Of course, he complained about having to drink that comfrey tea Mom gave him," Bertie said, "but he did it, and he knew it helped him heal. Now it almost seems as if he's ashamed of his war wound, which is crazy, and he doesn't seem to even care if it heals."

A war wound like that was something a man would be proud of, wouldn't it? But Red had not mentioned much about the war, had stayed quiet yesterday when Ivan was entertaining the ladies with stories. Where Ivan was proud of his uniform and his medals, and wore them yesterday, Red wore his old work clothes.

Something was eating at Red, and Bertie aimed to find out what it was.

Red couldn't put his finger on what bothered him as he mounted Seymour again and rode back to the Moennig place. The beef cattle were out in the pasture, with plenty of grass to graze on and a pond full of water to drink. He counted them from the road. All were there.

The milk cows, of course, were already together in Ma's small pasture between the house and the river. Red and his mother had moved them on Monday afternoon so they could be milked more easily and watched more closely.

He guided Seymour across the front yard and up to the porch. Sure enough, the hickory switches looked like they'd been blown around by the wind. There were seven switches on the porch itself, and when he checked, he saw another one on the ground.

Somebody wanted to play Bald Knobbers, and they were smart enough to make sure their victims got the message.

He started to turn back to the road, but then he noticed the front door wasn't completely closed. When Bertie came out yesterday with her recipes, he'd watched her pull the door firmly shut.

Had someone been out here since then?

He nudged Seymour around the side of the house to the back door. It stood wide open. Something red caught his eye from the kitchen window. He froze when he read the words.

Chapter Twenty-Six

Bertie slid a large batch of freshly cut biscuits into the oven and closed the door before the heat could escape. Most folks around Hideaway cooked with a woodstove, but Lilly had the wisdom to know she needed the most modern kitchen setup she could buy, with all the people coming in and out, needing to be fed. She had a gas stove and a nice, large icebox.

There was a smokehouse out back of the house, where Lilly kept hams and bacon and sometimes smoked pork chops and sausage. She rendered her own lard in a huge kettle whenever she butchered a hog. She kept frozen meat at the meat locker on the town square; potatoes and apples, carrots and turnips in the root cellar; and jars of food she canned in the pump house. Lilly was a busy lady.

Bertie knew her way around this kitchen, too. She should. She'd been here enough times over the years.

She washed her hands at the sink and turned to Lilly, who stood carving thick slices of bacon from a slab she had brought out of the smokehouse yesterday.

"I've made my decision, Lilly," Bertie said. "You know

Edith and I are beholden to you for letting us stay here, but I'm not planning to leave Hideaway after the funeral. Maybe never. You can't keep giving us free hospitality while you turn away paying customers."

Lilly pulled a cast-iron skillet onto the front burner and turned the switch. Blue flames licked up around the metal. "I think you oughta let me decide how I'm gonna use my own house."

"I've got a perfectly good home, with three bedrooms and indoor plumbing."

"Your pa told me that sometimes the electricity shuts off on him."

"I can work with that. We still have a backup hand pump behind the house, and our old outhouse is still upright."

Lilly paused in her work and placed her hands on her wide hips. "Roberta Moennig, I'm not discussing this with you anymore. Red doesn't want you staying alone out there until he's cleared up this mystery, and that's the way it's going to be. Now, I know you're a modern, independent woman, but you've got to understand that a man's gotta be made to feel like a man, especially when he…when he might have reasons to doubt his abilities."

"But he's a war hero, Lilly," Bertie said softly. "How could he doubt that?"

Lilly turned back to her work, draping strips of bacon into the skillet. They spattered, sending a rich, smoky aroma into the kitchen. It would bring the guests in to breakfast, for sure. Until last year, folks in America had done without a lot of meat so it could be sent to the boys overseas—as it should have. But Lilly had always taken good care of her own right here at home.

Lilly suddenly turned again and looked at Bertie, wiping

her hands on the towel. "That shell hit more than Red's leg, Bertie. It seems to've ripped into his heart."

Bertie nodded. "I think more happened than that injury."

"Sure it did. He's decided he's not the man you need, now. He doesn't think he's gonna heal any further, and he doesn't want to burden you with a cripple."

Bertie wouldn't've been more shocked if the stove had suddenly turned purple. "He told you that?"

Lilly gave her a grimace of a smile. "Didn't have to. Don't forget, I'm his ma."

Bertie closed her eyes. *Oh, Red, no.* "He must know me better than that. Does he think I waited for him all this time to walk away when the goin' gets tough?"

"It ain't you that's makin' the decision, Bertie."

"He's not getting away from me that easy."

"Then you oughta have a little talk with him."

"He'll hardly talk to me."

"Keep tryin'. He needs to be showed you're made of sturdy stock, and you can handle anything he was to throw at you."

"I haven't changed."

"Red has. And besides, a feller doesn't want to be a sympathy case."

"I've never seen him as that!"

Lilly put the towel down. "I know you ain't, but he's not thinking straight right now. He's got a lot on his mind, especially while he's tryin' to figure out what happened to your pa. Red'll get to the bottom of things, you know."

"I know," Bertie said.

"Ivan Potts and John Martin think they're helping, but they don't know tracking like Red does," Lilly said.

Bertie felt suddenly chilled in spite of the heat in the kitchen. "Red knows how to take care of himself, but if the wrong person knows what he's doing, he could be putting himself in danger."

"He's still a soldier. He's doing what he has to."

"Lilly," Bertie said, "how long should I let someone frighten me out of living in my own home? I thought that was one reason we went to war in the first place."

She was talking more to herself than to Lilly now. Yes, she was afraid. Terrified. She didn't know if she would be brave enough to go back into that house after what she and Edith had found there yesterday, and yet it made her mad. She didn't want to let anyone do that to her.

"I didn't think I had any enemies in this town," she murmured.

"Your pa didn't have no enemies," Lilly said. "He might've been cantankerous sometimes, but he for sure didn't have no enemies in this town. None we knew of, anyways. That's what makes it dangerous. We don't know who to trust."

"How can it be any more dangerous out on the farm than it is right here?" Bertie asked. "You had that brick thrown through your window."

Lilly's lips parted in surprise, and her blue eyes widened. "Who told you about that? After all you've gone through, you don't need to be worryin' about—"

"John Martin told me yesterday afternoon, and I'm glad he did. I'm not a child, Lilly."

Lilly dabbed at her perspiring forehead with the back of her hand. Her plump cheeks were rosy with the heat. "Never said you was, darlin'. You don't need to get all worked up about other things right now. What you need is time to recover." Lilly gave a firm nod. "I can't stop you from movin' out, but I can sure refuse to rent a room in my own house.

It's your room, and it will be 'til I say different. No one else will be stayin' there, whether you and Edith stay or not. I take care of my own."

Bertie raised an eyebrow. "Your own?"

Lilly rested her hands on the table and fixed Bertie with a level look. "The way I see it, one way or another, you're gonna be my daughter."

Bertie sighed, shaking her head. Oh, the stubbornness of mothers. And yet, she hadn't felt this loved and protected in a long time.

Sudden laughter reached them from the garden, and they both glanced out the back window to see Edith and Ivan gathering vegetables.

"You noticed those two together?" Lilly asked.

"How could I not?"

"Ivan is a true gentleman from a good family. Edith's an educated lady. They could do lots worse. Don't hurt to do a little matchmaking, does it?" Lilly asked.

Bertie shook her head. "Not at all." She watched Lilly working, and marveled at the fact that she felt closer to her father right now than she had in a long time.

Lilly had such faith in God's provision. Sure, she'd gotten a brick through the window, had lived without a husband for twelve years, and had a son wounded in the war, but she'd had a thriving business all these years, and she knew how to smile, how to have fun, how to treat her guests with kind hospitality.

The lady also had a bent toward romance. In fact, Bertie had discovered about a year ago that Lilly might even have been interested in Dad. They'd spent a lot of time together, laughing and talking. Lilly had taken several dishes of food up to the house when Dad was alone. Bertie knew this, because Dad had told her about it, and he wasn't unhappy about it, either.

Bertie remembered teasing him about Lilly a couple of times over the telephone, and he hadn't protested. In fact, he seemed to enjoy it.

She glanced up to find Lilly pulling a chair out and sitting down at the table. The smile, so characteristic of her all the time Bertie was growing up, was gone, and lines of sadness creased her face.

Now that she thought about it, Bertie realized Lilly's laughter, though still there, had been forced, her smiles lacking the usual happiness that radiated from her. She had always been such a powerful force in her family's life— because she had to be, and because she was naturally gifted with a joyful spirit. Seeing Lilly so tired and sad jolted Bertie.

"It must've been awful for you and Red to find Dad like that on Monday," Bertie said.

Lilly bowed her head with a somber nod. "He was a fine man."

"I'm so sorry, Lilly. Here I've been grieving my own loss and not given much thought to how Dad's death is hurtin' others. I know Dad thought a lot of you and Red." She hesitated. Should she even mention it? "I even got the feelin' you and he might've gotten to be pretty close…if you—"

Lilly took a breath and straightened her shoulders. "Now, don't you start that. Joseph was a good friend. He helped me here at the house any time I needed it. With Red gone, I couldn't do everything myself, and Joseph knew that. He was always checkin' up on me because he was such a good man, and that's all."

Bertie couldn't suppress a smile. "I heard tell you fed him a few times for his trouble."

Lilly nodded.

"Well, I know…knew Dad pretty well. With Mom gone

and Lloyd living far away, Dad and I did a lot of talking. He admired you, spoke of you quite a few times, when he could be sure the neighbors weren't listening to our calls."

Pink crept up Lilly's neck, and she fanned herself with the dish towel. "Roberta Moennig, don't you go teasing me like that. Your pa could've landed himself pert near any woman he'd want in this town. No reason he'd be lookin' at a fat woman like me for a wife. We was good friends, and that's all we was."

Bertie shook her head. Lilly sure didn't see herself the way most other folks in town saw her. Anyone who knew her saw a charming woman with a strong and loving spirit.

Lilly got up and reached to turn the bacon, then sliced more from the slab. "Roberta Moennig, I know you and your tomboy ways, and you'd fight a wild boar if you had a mind to, but there ain't a lot of women around like you."

Bertie watched her, waiting.

"I don't want you to up and decide you're gonna move into the farmhouse in spite of what Red thinks, or what I think."

"Okay. I won't."

Lilly gave her a suspicious look. "You promise?"

Bertie nodded. "Promise."

Lilly nodded. "Folks'll start coming in soon. I've got to finish laying out breakfast on the sideboard. How about whipping me up some of that delicious cream gravy like your ma always used to make?"

Bertie got up, glad for the work to keep her occupied.

Chapter Twenty-Seven

Edith came through the back door carrying a burlap bag of garden produce. She had dirt under her fingernails, mud on the shoes she kicked off outside the door, and a thoughtful smile on her face, the likes of which Bertie had never seen before.

Lilly was in the dining room setting the long table, and Ivan had gone in to help her with the other two tables she used for the breakfast crowd. Their voices could be heard from the dining room, Lilly teasing Ivan about something, and Ivan's laughter filling the house.

Edith glanced over her shoulder at Bertie. "That Ivan Potts is one of the nicest young men I've met in a long while."

"You don't say," Bertie said dryly as she spooned all but a few tablespoons of hot bacon grease from the huge cast iron skillet. "With the heart of a poet, no doubt. Was he quoting his poetry to you out there in the garden a few minutes ago, when you picked green tomatoes instead of ripe ones?"

"Oh, you wipe that smirk off your face," Edith warned with a chuckle. "All I said was he's nice. He has a good head on his shoulders, he's funny and he's literate. And yes, the man can quote a poem off the top of his head about something as mundane as a carrot."

"I don't know many men who'd care enough to try."

"I don't know many men who could do it even if they wanted to."

"That's our Ivan, all right," Bertie said.

"I told him his talent would be wasted in a stuffy old bank, and that he should be a school teacher."

"Well, maybe he should marry one," Bertie said. "He's going to be a banker. His mother already has the plans made."

Laughter and additional voices reached them through the swinging door between the kitchen and dining room.

"Speaking of Ivan's mother," Edith said, "he told me that Red had been by to see her at the library yesterday afternoon."

"The library? You don't say. I wonder what's up there. Red's hardly ever stepped foot in the library."

"Maybe she's doling out advice for the lovelorn," Edith suggested.

"Then she might oughta think about giving her own son some advice before long, you think?" Bertie sprinkled flour over the grease and stirred until it thickened, then started adding fresh milk to the mixture. She realized, after several seconds, that Edith still hadn't responded.

She glanced around to find Edith staring down at the vegetables she'd picked. Just staring.

"It's not a sin to find a fella attractive, you know," Bertie told her.

Edith picked up a bunch of dirt-covered carrots and set them in the sink to run water over them. "I don't suppose you've given any thought about what you're going to do in the next few days."

"I sure have. Lilly talked me into staying on here for a spell. Changing the subject? You must really be taken with Ivan."

Edith looked up from her work. "You're staying for good, aren't you?"

"I'm leaning in that that direction more all the time." In fact, down deep in her heart, Bertie wasn't sure she'd even considered going back to California. Not seriously. How could she leave again, with Red here in Hideaway?

"That doesn't surprise me," Edith said.

Bertie stirred the gravy, adding salt and pepper. "I'm needed here, and I'm not about to let somebody run me off the land our family worked so hard to cultivate. The question is, what will *you* do now?"

"I told you I wasn't leaving you until I knew you were settled. Nothing's changed since Monday, and I sure don't see you settled yet."

Bertie grinned at her. "I don't suppose Ivan could be giving you a little more reason to stay."

Edith turned to look at the garden. "How far does Lilly's land go?"

"It goes back about an eighth of a mile. The road in front of the house divides her acreage. The rest of her land stretches downhill between the road and the river. She had a lot more before she sold off acreage to the town for the city's expansion. Folks say this town's gonna double in size in the next few decades." Bertie rubbed some dried sage between her fingers over the gravy as she stirred. "Edith, I'm serious, it's not wrong to be attracted to another man."

"It's more complicated than that."

"How?"

"I promised myself at Harper's funeral that I'd never marry another man in the armed forces, or a policeman or anyone who might die on me. I don't ever want to go through that again."

"And Ivan's headed back to the war next week," Bertie said softly.

"That's right."

"So what's the problem? There won't be enough time for you two to fall in love, but you could sure enjoy his company while you're both in town."

Edith placed the carrots carefully on the dish drainer and reached for some snap beans. "You've lost loved ones, Bertie. You know how it rips something apart inside you."

"Yes, and it hurts somethin' awful. And I know I haven't lost a husband like you have, so I've no room to be telling you what to do or who to date."

"Well, I can tell you that losing the person you love most in all the world is like being ripped apart, then being left on your own to grow back."

Bertie knew that. Losing both her parents in the space of three years had been like that.

"And then people think you should be fine in just a few months," Edith said.

"I never thought that," Bertie said.

"For me, it's been three and a half years, and sometimes I think I haven't even begun to heal." Edith picked up a scrub brush and worked at the carrots until part of their skin was worn off, exposing the brighter orange beneath. "Ivan told me Lilly makes the best fried green tomatoes in the state."

"That's right. She has several recipes for green tomatoes. I know folks here in Hideaway who are addicted to Lilly's green-tomato preserves." Bertie looked out the window and saw Red riding Seymour into the corral.

He wore his work boots and jeans with an old plaid shirt

that Bertie remembered was his favorite before he joined the Army. It stretched too tightly across his shoulders now.

He stumbled when he got off the horse, but caught himself quickly, reaching for the cane tied to the saddle.

He glanced over his shoulder toward the house, as if ashamed of his weakness and hoping no one had seen.

For some reason, she stepped away from the window. If he hadn't wanted her to know about his injury in the first place, he for sure wouldn't want her to see the weakness. She watched him lean the cane against the stable door and uncinch the saddle, a little unsteady on his feet. At that moment, she felt such a rush of love for him, and pride in him, because she understood. Charles Frederick Meyer was an honorable man. That part of him had never changed. The war had injured him, but it had also taken the good man he'd been before the war and fired him into an even better version of himself. That was what testing did to good men.

Red was doing all he could, with only one good leg, to find her father's killer. Most men who were whole and healthy couldn't do what he was doing. And he was trying to protect her through it all.

Why hadn't she seen?

"Oh, Edith, I've been such a fool."

Her friend joined her at the sink. "How is that?"

"I was angry with him for not telling me about his leg. I did everything wrong yesterday when I saw him, but I was so hurt that no one had told me."

"I heard from Ivan that no one knew. In fact, Ivan didn't even realize it when he first saw Red on the train."

"That's because he didn't want me to know," Bertie said. "If anyone in town had known about it, I'd have heard, and he wanted to wait and tell me himself. And I was so angry with him. It was a horrible way for me to treat a war hero. Especially the man I love."

Bertie slid the skillet from the burner and glanced at Edith. "Do you think you could—"

"I'll find a gravy boat. You go on out and talk to Red. Better hurry, though. I hear people coming in the front door."

Bertie didn't hesitate.

Chapter Twenty-Eight

R ed ran a currycomb down Seymour's withers, feeling the tremor of flesh beneath the metal. The horse loved to be groomed.

"What do you think we oughta do now, boy?" He smoothed the glossy hair with his hand. Seymour hadn't even worked up a good sweat this morning, but combing him gave Red a sense of peace that he couldn't seem to find anywhere else right now. "I can't just go around town asking people to show me the soles of their shoes."

He thought about the tracks he'd seen at the back of the house, leading from the kitchen door, and the words scrawled on the window, and he gripped the comb so hard he thought he might hear it crack.

A soft sound of a footfall came from behind him, and he jerked around to see Bertie as she reached the whitewashed corral fence. Her hair was tied back with a blue bandana, and she wore a blue plaid shirt and blue jeans.

She climbed the fence instead of walking around to the gate, and he had a good view of her shoes. Sturdy walking shoes.

He ran the comb down Seymour's back. "Sure some good smells comin' from the kitchen," he said. "Guess you helped Ma with breakfast this morning."

"Guess I did. Have you been out looking for more evidence?"

He nodded. "May've found some, too."

"Where?" She reached for the currycomb.

He held it out of her reach. "You don't need to take my work away from me. I can still groom a horse."

"Sorry."

"Why don't you let me do a little more investigating before you start asking questions?" He kept his voice gentle. Her father's funeral was today, and she didn't need to be yelled at.

"I'm not trying to check up on you, I just want to know about my father."

He gave the horse a final swipe with the comb, patted him on the haunch, and hung the comb on a nail in the wall. "I'm checkin' a few things out." He pointed down at her shoes. "For instance, I was out at your house a while ago. Seems you were there before me."

Her eyes widened, and her lips parted in dismay.

"I thought we'd decided you wouldn't go out there by yourself." Still, he kept his voice gentle.

"I didn't."

"Who went with you?"

"Edith."

He took a deep, slow breath. "What happened?"

"I guess you saw the words on the window."

"Yes. Were you the one who left the back door wide open?"

Seymour chose that time to nuzzle Bertie's hair, and she reached up to rub his nose. "Yes. We wanted to air the house out."

"Air it out?"

She crossed her arms in front of her. "I'm sorry I didn't tell you about it, but I was so sure you'd try to pack me up and haul me back to the train station before I could even attend Dad's funeral, that I decided to wait until after the funeral to tell you about it."

He gritted his teeth. She must think he was some kind of bully. He didn't mean for her to feel that way, but how else could he keep her safe without watching her every minute?

"I wouldn't have hauled you to the train station," he said.

"Good, because I wouldn't have gone, anyway. I just didn't want to fight with you." She took a step toward him, her gaze gentle and…what was the word? Vulnerable? "That's the last thing I want to do, Red."

"Why did you want to air out the house?"

She bit her lower lip and jammed her hands into the back pockets of her jeans. "Someone had turned all the gas jets wide open on the stove, and the pilots were out. All the kitchen doors were closed, and I found Herman lying between the stove and the wall."

He closed his eyes as horror washed through him. She could've been killed! "That's what the words on the window meant. *Nazi gas chamber.*"

She nodded.

"The cat okay?"

"He came to pretty quickly." She held her arms out, and he saw the scratches on them.

He reached for her hands. "The cat did *this?* Are you okay? Did you doctor these—"

"I'm fine, Red." She looked up at him, a tiny smile touching her lips. "Edith and I ran all the way back here."

"Looks like whoever wrote that message used an old tube of lipstick from the house. I found it on the ground."

"But no idea who put it there?"

"I know who I suspect. Good ol' Gramercy. But it can't be that easy."

"Why not?"

"Nothing's ever that easy. Bertie, you've got to promise me one thing." He resisted the powerful urge to take her by the shoulders and shake her. He would shake her gently, of course. But he needed her to see reason.

"I know," she said. "I can't go back out to the house alone."

"Or drag poor Edith out there and risk both your lives."

"Before we ran back here yesterday, I made a side trip to the pump house and got Dad's old hunting rifle and a box of bullets. Edith and I both know how to shoot."

Red grimaced. That didn't make him breathe any easier. Sometimes this woman made his head want to explode. "Did you call the sheriff?"

"I didn't call anybody. Edith wanted me to tell you."

Sure she did. She at least has the sense God gave a goose. He glanced toward the house. "No use in arguing. What's done is done."

"I turned off the gas."

He nodded. "Like I said, no use arguing. And like I also said, breakfast sure smells good. Guess I'd better get washed up and get some of this horse hair off me before I try to sit at the table."

He turned to walk toward the house. Bertie followed him. "Red, you've got to stop telling me to go back to California."

His steps slowed, but he didn't turn around. *Now what?* He saw his reflection in the window he'd installed Wednesday. He looked grim, jaw jutting out, red brows drawn into a heavy frown. He tried to relax his expression a little, but it didn't do much good.

"I've decided I'm not going back," she said.

He stopped. In the window reflection, his frown deepened. He saw her standing behind him, and knew she could see how her words were affecting him, same as he could.

"If you'd been here the past year," she said, "I'd've never left in the first place. With you back home, I'm stayin' right here where I've always belonged. And don't go trying to change my mind." She paused, swallowed. "I don't know about you, but nothing's changed for me in three years."

He wanted to groan out loud with frustration, and at the same time he had a hard time keeping a sudden grin from popping out on his face. What *was* it about this woman that could make him act like a five-year-old kid?

He bowed his head, kicking at a stone on the ground with his bad leg. "It won't work, Bertie." It amazed him that he was able to keep his voice quiet, gentle, sane.

He turned around, leaning hard on the cane as he looked at her. "Please don't even try it."

He saw the sudden hurt in her eyes, but she shook her head. "I'm not trying anything, I'm telling you my plans. I'm staying. I know you've got to have time to recover some from the war, but I'm going to be here waiting when you do."

"You didn't ask for a cripple," Red said.

Her eyes flashed with a brief show of her typical spirit. "And *you* didn't ask to *be* crippled."

"You deserve more."

"I deserve better than the treatment I'm getting from you right now. I deserve the man I waited for and wrote to all this time. I deserve a hero."

"That's not me."

"It sure is."

"Not now."

"Lilly told me you've got a whole drawer full of medals you earned over the last three years. You have a Purple Heart. You risked everything for your country, and if your letters were telling the truth, you risked all that for me. I'd like to know who in that army is a hero if you're not."

"Bertie," he said quietly, trying to derail the freight train before she could work up any more steam, "you don't know what all went on over there."

"What makes you think you're the only one who ever went to war?" She glared up at him. Plenty of the ol' fire left in her. "My heart traveled right along with you, into those foxholes and on every dangerous mission. My prayers followed you every step of the way. My body might've been safe here in America, but the rest of me was right there with you."

"You didn't do the things I did. You didn't kill—"

"I devoted myself to you before you ever left for the war, and—"

"Bertie, this kind of thing's exactly why I never made any promises or asked any from—"

"You can't tell my heart what to do, Red!" She stood with hands on hips, face flushed. "And you can't toss it away like so much garbage because you don't know how to deal with it anymore. You're going to have to learn again."

"I can't—"

"Don't try to tell me you can't do something." Bertie bit her lip and looked away. Her chin wobbled very briefly, but she met his gaze again. "You've always been able to do anything you set your mind to, and you can do this. I know your injuries aren't just physical. A fella can't go through a war and come back unchanged. But I'm here to tell you, even if the old Red doesn't ever come back, this Red right here," she said as she reached out and smacked him none-too-gently on the shoulder, "this is the one I want. I'm taking you as you are right now."

She continued to stand there glaring at him for another second or two—or it could've been an hour. Right now, he wouldn't've known the difference. Then she shoved her hands into the pockets of her jeans and turned and stalked into the house.

He felt as if he'd just had another kind of war declared on him. This was one war he suddenly wasn't sure he could win. And he wasn't sure he wanted to.

Chapter Twenty-Nine

Bertie still burned with shame as she sat in Ivan's car once again, this time in the front seat at his insistence, in honor of her loss. Lilly weighted down the back on the passenger side, Red was once more in the middle of the backseat, and Edith sat behind Ivan.

What must Red be thinking now? Of all the cockeyed things to do. A man was supposed to pursue the woman, not the other way around.

And this wasn't the time to be thinking about such things. *Bertie Moennig, you have the worst timing!*

Edith's dark hair was in perfect order, her dress the latest fashion, formfitting and attractive, military style with broad shoulders and slim waistline. It was one Bertie had helped her make from pieces of an old dress with a McCall's pattern.

Bertie's dark gray dress had been made from the same pattern, with some adjustments by Edith, an expert seamstress, who had sized down the pattern for Bertie's smaller, shorter frame.

Both men wore their military dress uniforms—Red with

great reluctance, and only because Lilly and Edith had both begged him to show some pride in his country and his own service to them. He still didn't wear any medals. It was as if he was ashamed of them.

The drive took barely a couple of minutes. Lilly had protested that they could walk to the church faster than they could all get situated into the car, but Ivan wouldn't hear of it. Any other time, Bertie would've teased him about inventing a reason to see Edith again.

Though the funeral wasn't scheduled until noon, a crowd had already begun to gather at the church by eleven-thirty, with folk huddling in small groups on the grass outside the building. Some strolled around in the church cemetery, visiting at the gravesides of departed loved ones.

"Is there something else happening at the church today?" Edith asked when Ivan pulled in front of the church.

Bertie looked back at her blankly. "No, just the funeral."

"You have this kind of turnout for a funeral?" Edith asked, glancing around at the crowd with interest. "We don't even do this in Mobile. It looks like a party setting up."

"I told you," Bertie said. "Things are a little different here." She didn't know about Mobile, but in California, where everybody was from somewhere else, very little family was present to honor their dead.

Ivan parked at the edge of the church cemetery, where Bertie glanced toward three graves decorated with military headstones. Fresh flowers covered the gravesites, blooming in multiple colors. The families of James Eckrow, Larry Peterson and William Lewis were keeping the memories of their boys alive, though the bodies were destroyed in the

Pacific Theater two years ago. The town still mourned the three young men whom Bertie had known in school.

Joseph Moennig was to be buried beside his wife, Martha, near the edge of a bluff that overlooked the James River at the far corner of the cemetery.

Bertie noticed that her mother's grave had been well-tended, with flowers growing around the headstone. Ever the practical man, Dad hadn't been much interested in growing flowers around the house, but when it came to his wife, his practicality had often flown out the window in favor of their strong bond.

Mom had been the one to convince him that they needed electricity and indoor plumbing long before most of the rural residents had anything but outhouses and oil lanterns. Even during the Depression, Dad had worked extra hours to make sure his wife had a few extra things—material for a new dress, even lace handkerchiefs from time to time.

"We've brought in a load of chairs from City Hall," Ivan said, drawing Bertie from her memories. "Dad had them hauled over earlier this morning."

Bertie nodded. It would be a packed church.

Ivan got out, opened the back door for Edith, then rushed around to the other side to help Lilly and Bertie. Lilly, of course, had already helped herself from the car and was halfway to the front door of the church.

"You doing okay?" Ivan asked Bertie softly, under cover of Lilly's greeting to some friends congregating near the door.

"I will be."

"Your father was a fine man," Ivan said. "None better."

"Thank you." Bertie felt the heaviness of grief settle over her again. She'd done very well yesterday, with so many friends around to comfort her and so many things to distract her. But today was different. In spite of the presence of so many, she weakened under the impact of Dad's death. He wasn't coming back. She was on her own.

She glanced over her shoulder toward Red, who had climbed out of the car and limped to the cemetery fence, gazing toward the gravesites of his fellow soldiers. "I can't help thinking of simpler times, when there wasn't a war, when we were just wild kids with living parents and the only thing we had to worry about was whether we'd get into trouble for getting our clothes wet paddling the river."

"Or putting a daddy longlegs in the teacher's desk," Ivan said.

"Or carving initials in the outhouse wall," she said.

Ivan grinned. "You were the one who did that? I thought it was Red. You know he was sweet on you all through high school."

Again, she glanced toward Red, and found him watching her. He looked away quickly, but not before she saw, once again, a deep sadness in his eyes.

Her cheeks burned as she thought about her bold behavior this morning. Not just once, but twice. She'd never pushed herself on any man—never thought she ever would. Sometimes things changed that made a person change with them, and Lilly's words had kept running through her mind.

"He's crazy about you, kid." Ivan put an arm around Bertie's shoulders and hugged her.

She allowed herself to lean against him and accept the comfort of another one of her longtime friends. "He doesn't want me here."

"That's right, but you know why, and it isn't because he's suddenly stopped caring. He wants you safe, same as the rest of us do."

Bertie groaned. "And here I'd hoped I wouldn't hear that tired line for the rest of the—"

"You just listen to your ol' Uncle Ivan." He gave her shoulders another squeeze and released her. "The day we came home, I surprised Red on the train. He was reading a letter from you, concentrating so hard he didn't even see me coming. The thing was worn to a frazzle."

Bertie looked up into Ivan's dark brown eyes. "You sure it was one of my letters?"

He nodded. "You've written me enough, I should know your handwriting by now."

"This isn't a good time to tease me, now, Ivan Potts."

"I may tease about a lot of things, but not this, Bert. You know me better than that. For Red, the sun rises and sets in you. It's always been that way for him."

She sighed. "He's pushing me out of his life as sure as I'm standing here." She'd talked a brave talk to Red in the backyard this morning, but she wasn't nearly as sure of herself as she'd pretended to be.

Ivan glanced toward his friend, and Bertie followed his gaze, saddened once more by the loneliness she saw in the figure that stood apart from all the rest.

"We're talking about a man who's trying to come to terms with too many awful memories," Ivan said.

"I knew it was hard on him," she said. "He didn't write about it often, but when he did, I could tell it was tearing him up, but it tears everyone up."

"You can't know what it was like unless you've been there," Ivan said. "Red's doing what he can to see to it you don't have that same experience here. He's behaving the way a man would behave if he was in love with a woman and wanted her safe."

She glanced at Red again. "He's acting like a man who's only half alive."

"That's what war does to a man, especially someone like Red." Ivan pressed his hand against her back and urged her to walk toward the church, where Lilly stood chatting with Mrs. Cooper and Edith.

"But he's so different," Bertie said. "It's like he's another person completely."

"I think that's one of the things that's keeping him at arm's length from you," Ivan said. "He knows he's changed, and he doesn't want you to accept him back home as if it were your duty."

"I don't believe Red's changed for good," Bertie said, glancing in Red's direction. "It'll take a while, but the shock of things he's seen will fade over time. Someday he'll even find where he put his sense of humor."

Ivan followed her gaze. "Give him time."

Bertie nodded. Time was exactly what he deserved. Time and patience.

"Mom has the meal planned," Ivan said. "We heard the minister who's doing the service is long-winded."

"Folks'll get hungry, sure enough," Bertie said.

"And they'll want to stick around and visit afterwards, since you've been gone so long."

"And they'll want to visit with you and Red," Bertie said.

Lilly turned back to them, as if just now realizing they weren't right behind her. "Ivan, I've got a big batch of ham and beans cooking on the stove that we'll need to collect after the funeral."

Ivan looked disappointed. "No chicken and dumplings?"

"For the whole town?" Lilly laughed. "I may not be hurtin' too bad, but I can't afford that. Don't you worry, though, you'll get more before you have to leave again." She winked at him. "I did make some cornbread and some gooseberry cobbler."

Ivan grinned and kissed Red's mother on the cheek. "Lilly Meyer, will you marry me?"

As the two continued to tease in their old, familiar way, Bertie caught sight of Ivan's parents, Gerald and Arielle, directing the setup of tables in the shady yard at the side of the church.

Arielle, tall and slender with graceful movements, wore a stylish black suit. Her pale blond hair was drawn back in a chignon, with a black hat and black netting over her face.

In contrast, Lilly wore no hat, and though her navy dress was only a few years old, it stretched tightly across her ample hips and shoulders. Lilly typically dressed more comfortably in roomy house dresses and flats, cooking a feast for her guests. Edith had spent some time beautifying her this morning, and now her golden red hair was neatly gathered in a bun on the back of her head.

Arielle most likely had cooked something far different from Lilly's pot of beans and cornbread. In all these years living in Hideaway, Arielle hadn't grasped the mindset of the typical Hideaway farmer.

Bertie loved Arielle's tartlets and finger sandwiches, but most folks hadn't quite caught on. They wanted something that would fill their stomachs, even if it was ham and beans. Too many still struggled with the aftershock of the Depression.

There had always been a sharp contrast between Arielle Potts and Lilly Meyer, and there'd been times after Mom died that Bertie had felt a little like a rope in a tug-of-war between the two women. Both had been worried about their sons fighting overseas, and their need to mother someone was strong. Bertie had become the object of affection of both women.

Though Bertie had been a grown woman of twenty when Mom died, Lilly and Arielle had paid visits to her at home and at work ever since, until Bertie left for California. Arielle had shared her favorite books with Bertie, while Lilly always seemed to be cooking up a "little too much" for her guests, and needing someone to help her eat the generous leftovers.

Bertie felt more comfortable with Lilly's down-home ways and blunt honesty, but there were times when it was nice to have a little of Arielle's sophistication and social grace.

Edith stepped up beside Bertie and looped an arm through hers. "It looks as if the whole town's coming."

"You wait and see," Lilly said. "That church will be packed in a few minutes, and there'll be folks sitting out in the vestibule and out by the windows. Folks around these parts loved Bertie's pa, and they'll turn out for his farewell."

Bertie glanced at Red, who continued to stand at the edge of the cemetery, as if the rest of the world didn't exist—or maybe he only wished it didn't.

She stared down at his hands, clasped on the hook of the cane. Tightly. It was as if Red Meyer held everything inside as tightly as his hands gripped the wood.

She thought about the words he had written to her from Italy. He'd thought he might die before he saw her again.

How right those words had turned out to be.

Bertie believed in the resurrection of Jesus. What she had to ask herself was if she believed that very same Jesus was strong enough to resurrect Red Meyer, because he seemed so dead to her that she barely recognized him.

Chapter Thirty

Red studied the graves of the men who'd died in the Pacific—friends he'd hunted and fished with and shared farm chores with. He'd visited the parents of all three on Tuesday, not knowing what to say, though it didn't seem to matter. His presence seemed to bring them comfort.

He could've ended up in the cemetery with his friends. What would that've done to Ma? To Bertie? He thought about what Ivan had told him on the train Monday—about bein' better off dead. But what would that have done to Gerald and Arielle?

He heard his mother's strong voice carry across the yard, and glanced around to find her and Bertie looking toward him. He turned away quickly.

What were they talking about? Why had they suddenly gotten quiet? He'd not been able to stop thinking about Bertie, nor keep his gaze from straying her way ever since her declarations this morning.

All through breakfast, while Edith helped Ma serve folks, Bertie had sat at the far end of the table, as far from Red as she could get. Every time he'd looked at her, she'd been watching him, and once she'd nodded at him, as if to assure him she meant what she'd said about staying.

He knew his behavior was hurting her—had hurt her for weeks. She couldn't understand why he was drawing away. If he'd had any doubts about her feelings for him, he sure didn't now. She'd never been one to hide what was in her heart.

"Hello there, soldier," came the familiar voice of Gerald Potts, and Red turned to greet Ivan's father.

Gerald pounded him on the back and shook his hand until it nearly tore off at the wrist—even though they'd seen each other yesterday. Ivan took after his father; both men were built like draft horses and were as friendly as hound pups.

Gerald's thick, graying hair was slicked back, his gray suit jacket too tight across his shoulders.

"Will Bertie and her friend be at the guesthouse for the duration of their stay?"

Red wasn't sure what to say. He didn't feel like announcing to the world that Bertie wasn't going back to California. "I'm not sure."

"Well, I don't think it's safe for them at the farmhouse just now. They'd both be welcome with us for as long as they want to stay."

"They're welcome with us, they know that. But if Bertie takes a notion to move back into her own homeplace, there's not much I can do to stop her."

Gerald chuckled. "You know our Bertie. She can be strong-willed. I may have a talk with her, or have Arielle ask her and Miss Frost to lunch in a day or two."

"That's *Mrs.* Frost," Red said. "Her husband was killed at Pearl Harbor." He stepped in a hole, and grimaced when pain shot up his bad leg.

Gerald grabbed his arm. "Are you okay?"

"Fine. I'm fine."

"You're still tracking the mystery of Joseph's death?"

"That's right."

"Found anything yet?"

"Maybe a few things, footprints and such. You know about the swastika somebody left on our stable, but did you notice those switches on Joseph's front porch?"

"Yes, I saw them," Gerald said. "I didn't pay much attention. We'd had a decent storm the night before, and you know how things can blow up."

"There were also the same kind of switches on the Krueger porch. All hickory, all about the same length. They'd been placed there, Gerald. They were laid on the porch in the shape of a swastika."

Gerald regarded him with sudden gravity. "Well, that places a question on one theory."

"You thought it was Krueger?"

Gerald nodded. "Still could've been. He might have placed those switches on his own porch in order to misdirect."

"But what reason would he have for doing it? Krueger's whole family disappeared. And yet the threats are still being laid." Red told Gerald about what had happened to Bertie and Edith yesterday.

Gerald shook his head. "I've tried to talk Butch into re-opening the case."

"No luck?" Red asked.

"None. You know how stubborn he can be sometimes. I've overheard a few discussions down at the Exchange. Lots of crazy ideas, all the way from Joseph's neighbors doing the deed, to someone from out of town."

"I think Joseph Moennig and the Kruegers and my mother were all chosen because they're German," Red said.

Gerald's eyes narrowed in thought. "I wondered about that, too. Have you considered the possibility that the culprit is actually a Nazi?"

"You mean someone who's infiltrated the country? Gerald, that's the kind of thinking that's caused so much trouble with folks all around. It's why innocent families were forced into detention camps."

"How do we know all those people are innocent?"

Red didn't have an answer. He didn't agree with Gerald, but then Gerald wasn't German American.

"Red, I trust our government. If intelligence sources have concluded that there are infiltrators sent by that demon, Hitler, they could be anywhere. They could be in any town."

"But the Germans surrendered."

"Publicly, yes. But Hitler started making his evil plans to take over the world long before he started the war. His people and their families could have been indoctrinated for years. There could even be second-generation Nazis under cover, and if they haven't been caught, they might carry Hitler's standard as long as they can, even with Hitler dead."

Talk of such things gave Red a queasy feeling. "But why attack other Germans?" he asked. "And why here in Hideaway? We're so far removed from major defense plants and military headquarters."

"We have no idea how many spies Hitler could have sent to infiltrate," Gerald said. "Now that Germany's lost the war, they could be wanting to do as much damage as they can to their enemy out of revenge, and they see German Americans as turncoats. That's who they want to attack."

Red shook his head. "I don't agree."

"I don't want to think like this, Red. It's frightening to

consider that anyone in our neighborhood, any of our friends, could be the enemy, but we have to be realistic. We know what Hitler was capable of."

"But we know all our neighbors. Someone would've had to come here years ago, hide their accent, and have the downright meanness to hurt and kill their neighbors."

Gerald spread his hand, indicating the crowd around the church. "It takes all kinds to make a community, Red. Take your pick. Arielle's parents still have a Swedish accent, but you can tell she sounds purely American." He stood beside Red, studying the newcomers, most of whom walked to the church. "The infiltrators would be trained to blend in."

A large black hearse pulled to the front of the church, and Gerald nodded toward it. "I think we'll be getting started in a few moments. I'm a pallbearer, so I'd better be going." He patted Red on the shoulder once more. "Whatever you do, make sure Bertie doesn't get herself into trouble. I'd like to talk more about this later. Maybe tomorrow. I've already made plans for a fishing expedition later this afternoon down by the caves below the Moennig house. Fish are really biting there right now, and we have an empty drawer in the meat locker."

Red nodded and watched Gerald walk away, wondering at the things he'd said. Could there actually be someone among them who had been spying on their community for years?

He didn't even want to think about it. But he did.

Krueger hadn't been in town long. He'd left the day Joseph was found dead in his corral. Could he, as Gerald said, have placed those switches on his own porch to deflect suspicion from himself?

Though the sun shone brightly today, Red felt as if the whole town was covered by a thick cloud of gray.

* * *

Bertie watched from the front of the church as her father's casket was carried through the foyer by the pallbearers. She knew all these men. Ivan Potts and his father, Gerald, John Martin, Fred Cooper, Bernie Wilson and Leon Peterson.

She was grateful to them, and she knew Dad would be proud that such fine men would usher his body to its resting place.

During the funeral, Bertie sat at the front of the church and allowed the organ music to float over her, hearing the words of "How Great Thou Art" in her head.

She stared out the side window at the cemetery. Dad would be buried there in a little while…his body lowered into the earth, to be covered in darkness.

Lilly's arm came around her from the left, and Edith took her hand from her right. *Oh, God, how could You do this to us?* She thought of her brother. Medical science was coming a long way toward curing tuberculosis, but not everyone lived through it, even yet. The sanatorium, in Mt. Vernon, Missouri, was their only hope.

Dad had been the youngest in a family of four brothers. The others were dead, and Bertie's cousins, all boys, were in the Pacific Theater, risking their lives for their country, just as Red and Ivan had done. She had no family here.

She glanced past Lilly to the cane leaning against the pew in front of them.

The whole world was flying apart, and she couldn't keep from wondering if she was flying apart with it.

The service ended and people filed forward to view the body and greet her. She swallowed and forced a smile. So many friends loved her, were here for her. The church was full, and old classmates, former teachers, her church friends, all came by to tell her how sorry they were, and remind her about what a wonderful man her father had been.

As if she needed reminding.

The final person filed past. The funeral director—who had driven over from Hollister—bent toward her, gesturing for her to approach the casket.

But as she started to rise, she realized she couldn't do it.

Lilly gently urged her to stand.

Bertie wanted to shove her away, but she didn't. She just didn't stand. Edith, bless her, just sat holding her hand.

After a few moments, Edith said quietly, "You can't go with him, no matter how much you probably wish you could right now."

Bertie looked at her, saw tears in Edith's eyes, and realized she was reliving a loss of her own.

"Your time hasn't come yet. You have to keep going," Edith said.

Bertie nodded, then slowly stood. The people waited outside for the casket to be carried past and into the cemetery. She would go with it.

But the life she had known was over. What would happen next?

Chapter Thirty-One

Red stood apart from the crowd that circled Joseph Moennig's grave. He wished he could be strong for Bertie, holding her up and encouraging her the way Edith and his own Ma were doing, but try as he might, his mind was on the battle. He couldn't let it go, not even when he saw Bertie turn around and study the crowd, and her gaze lit on him.

She was probably seeing the old Red, with his threadbare suit and red hair slicked down for church. She was seeing the boy she'd grown up with, played baseball with, fished with, worked with.

She wasn't seeing what was inside him now. She used to be able to look at his face and know what he was thinking, long before they'd started seeing each other in a...romantic way.

Back when they were both in that ol' one-room schoolhouse out past this church, she only had to look at him to know if he was gonna go fishin' after school, or if he had to get home to the farm to help with chores.

But she didn't know him anymore. He was a soldier home from war, with one more battle to fight, and he didn't have the weapons he needed for this battle—wasn't even sure he could win this one.

It ate at him that he didn't have the strength to fight it alone, without this blasted cane.

A soldier had to be on guard all the time, and Red was.

John Martin stepped up beside him, looking even more awkward in his old suit than Red did. John had kept growing after high-school graduation, and the sleeves and legs of his jacket and slacks exposed a little too much of his long limbs. Fashions these days were skimpy on material, saving all the excess for the war effort. Even Gerald Potts, who could afford a new suit, wore one he'd had for at least ten years.

"I think you're hopeless, Charles Frederick," John said. "Bertie Moennig's a fine woman, and she needs you over there with her, helping her through her loss, not over here brooding by yourself."

"I'm not brooding, I'm thinking. Besides, Bertie needs something I can't give her."

"That's silly. It doesn't take much to stand beside her, let her know she's not alone."

"And how'm I gonna do that?" Red demanded, gesturing toward his ma, Edith, Ivan and Ivan's dad, who all seemed to be competing for Bertie's attention. "They've got her well in hand. I can't even get close to her right now. Besides, I've got other fish to fry."

"I don't see you frying any fish," John grumbled. "I see you avoiding Bertie because of that limp of yours. You're all hung up about—"

"You can't tell me how to behave with this leg if you ain't gone through it yourself," Red growled back.

John glared at him. "At least you got to come home as a wounded war hero, and you're still alive. Others came home in caskets. And still others are living in shame because they weren't counted worthy to fight for their country."

Red flinched. He knew John had tried to enlist more than once.

"I'm not a coward, Red Meyer," John said.

"I know that," Red said gently. John simply didn't know, and there was no way to explain it to him.

"I'd have done my part if they'd have let me. I'm doing my part here every time I can. I give blood so often I must—"

"Didn't say you was a coward," Red grumbled.

"Yeah, well, sounded different to my ears, but then maybe that's because of the chip on your shoulder. The words must bounce off that big old chip and sound like other words by the time they reach me."

Red sighed. He was tired of apologizing for being so tetchy, but he didn't know how he could manage to act differently. Right now, everything seemed to simmer below the surface, ready to boil over with one word, one wrong look. He knew it, he hated it. He wanted to do something about it, but what?

"You notice anybody who oughta be here but isn't?" he asked, shooting a look around at the crowd. Even the Shorts were here, unwelcome as they were with their foul thoughts and mouths.

"Kruegers aren't here," John said.

"Anyone else?"

"Other than that family, nobody's missing that I'd have expected to be here."

Red turned and studied the individual faces in the crowd. Could there be someone here who wasn't surprised by Joseph's death? Could someone here even have been the one who caused it?

* * *

Bertie stared at the casket as others wandered away, chatter growing louder as they prepared for the meal on the church grounds.

It was time to cry now. It was time to say goodbye. Even Lilly and Edith were sniffling beside her, and Arielle was holding a handkerchief to her eyes.

Somehow, though, Bertie's eyes remained dry. She felt as if the tears she had held inside since Monday had petrified in her heart like that forest had done in Arizona.

She stood over the place where her mother's body had been buried for more than three years.

Edith placed a hand lightly on Bertie's shoulder. "You never told me how your mother died. Do you realize she and my Harper died only a few months apart?"

Bertie nodded. She and Edith had never discussed death much. Thoughts of it were too close to both of them. "Mom died of polio. Hard as the doctors and nurses worked over her, nothing they did could save her. Dad and I had already tried every potion Mom ever used on the townsfolk and neighbors around Hideaway—hot onion poultices, hot mustard plaster, mullein, coneflower that grew along the roadsides. Nothing worked, even though these things had done the job many times before."

"You said your mother used to treat sick neighbors?"

"That's right. Mom was the closest we had to a doctor hereabouts, and folks came to her from all over. Hill folk, mostly, who didn't trust modern medicine."

Edith stood beside her in silence.

"In the end," Bertie said, "the doctor accused Dad and me of keeping Mom home too long. He said we were 'experimenting' on her with our 'crazy witchcraft.' I don't think that doctor could've done any more for her if she'd gone to him at the first sign of illness, because there'd been an epidemic in Hideaway, and three of the townsfolk died in spite of all the doctor tried to do."

"Your mother treated them?"

Bertie nodded. "That's the sad thing. Mom caught the polio from a neighbor who had it and refused to travel the long distance to see a doctor. Mom treated this neighbor with those same plants. The neighbor lived."

"Which neighbor was that?"

"Elizabeth Krueger."

After Mom's death, Bertie had cried for days, until she'd begun to wonder if she'd ever stop. Even last week she'd dreamed of Mom and had woken up teary-eyed.

Now she was afraid of those tears. She was going to have to be strong, stand alone.

"It sounds to me as if the herbs worked better than medical science," Edith said.

"But try to tell anybody that," Bertie said, glancing toward Red, who had wandered down toward the riverbank, leaning heavily on his cane.

Lilly placed her heavy arm around Bertie. "You said something to me this morning about treating Red with comfrey. It grows in the woods on your place, doesn't it?"

"Yes, above the cliffs over the James River, where the caves are."

The arm tightened. "Honey, it's about to break my heart, watchin' him brood the way he is. You really think it'll help that leg of his?"

Bertie nodded. "If he'd let me try it, I think it could help."

"I know most folks would scoff. They'd say no leaf could help where a doctor's best medicine won't bring healing, but

I'm desperate. It could be just your loving touch that'd help more than anything."

That was all Bertie needed. "I think I'll have another talk with Red."

"That's my girl." Lilly gave her shoulders a final squeeze, then looked down at Joseph's casket. "Your father was always so proud of you, Roberta Moennig. He had every right to be. You're the sweetest possible combination of your mother and your father, with a whole lot of just plain ol' Bertie thrown into the mix."

With those words, Bertie said her final goodbye to her father, then walked away from the burial site, past the church-yard, where most of the women, and at least half the men, were involved in setting up for the meal, while children played on the grass.

The ladies of the church knew how to set a table with all the best produce from their victory gardens. Lilly had already sent Ivan to the house to collect her beans, ham, cornbread and cobbler. John's mother, Cora Lee Martin, carried another cobbler, proud of the berries her son had picked.

You've got people who love you, Bertie. They'd told her that, and she believed it, but *someone* in this town didn't love her. It was hard to feel welcome with all that was going on.

She walked steadfastly toward Red's receding figure, not knowing what kind of reception she'd get from him. He was so moody lately, one minute making her think he still cared about her, and the next minute shoving her away from him, almost like she was poison.

No matter what happened between them, she'd do the best she could to help him heal—as much as he'd let her do—and she would stay in Hideaway. In spite of all the wondering about who might be behind Dad's death, in spite of the ugly messages someone had been leaving, this place was home. She loved California, sure enough. It was beautiful. The mountains and the ocean, which she'd never seen before this past year, made her think of God's majesty. His bigness. His power.

But these Ozark hills had been made by God, too. He had created the medicinal, nourishing plants that grew here. It was here, if anywhere, that Red would finally find healing.

The tears came then, as she realized how afraid she'd been this week. And she was still afraid of the future. Mom had always told her not to trust feelings, but to trust in the Word, because the Word would last through feelings. Mom had always quoted Job, "Though He slay me, yet will I trust Him."

But what was trust? Sure, Bertie knew she'd be in heaven when she died, but was that all there was to trusting Him? What about here and now, on earth, when loved ones died or went to war and came back changed?

Besides a happy afterlife, what did she have to look forward to?

As old, familiar voices of longtime friends drifted across the cemetery, Bertie fought the loneliness and fear with silent prayer.

Neighbors and friends had all spoken to her today, hugged her, told her, "If there's anything we can do, just holler."

She'd nodded and thanked them, knowing she probably would never holler. But also knowing that at least some of those friends would be there when she needed them.

Chapter Thirty-Two

Red was halfway down the bank to the river's edge when he heard soft footsteps behind him. He turned his head just enough to recognize Bertie's blond hair.

She didn't give up.

He turned around, leaning on his cane. "Been a bad week for you," he said.

She climbed down an incline and stopped in front of him, but didn't say anything. He knew that look in her eyes. She had something on her mind. Still, she needed to hear what he had to say.

"Awful bad week," he repeated. "I know you don't believe it now, but it doesn't always hurt this way."

She nodded and turned to step down closer to the water's edge. "I know you wouldn't say that if you didn't know it was true. But you still have your mother and brother and sister. Sometimes it seems I'm about to lose everything and everybody I've ever cared about."

He winced. "I know it does."

She kept walking.

"Bertie?"

She stopped and turned, looking up at him.

"I've done a lot of things wrong," he said at last, scrambling over some rocks to her side. "I shouldn't've been so hard on you this week. Seems like everything I say turns to—"

"You did fine," she said gently. "I know you've had a lot on your mind, too. I know you thought a lot of Dad. You're just trying to keep me safe and find out what happened at the same time. That's a hard job. I know all that."

He waited for a but. It didn't come, and he just stood there for several seconds looking down at her stupidly. "That's right. I'm glad you understand."

She held a hand up. "I understand that just fine."

Oh, no, here came the but.

"What I don't understand is why you didn't tell me about your leg."

He sighed. "What is it you want to know about it?"

She looked down at the cane, which he leaned on heavily. "Why didn't you tell me before I had to see it for myself?"

"I didn't want you to worry."

She frowned up at him, eyes narrowing. She could see through him better than anyone he'd ever known.

"I kept thinking it'd get better," he said, not able to meet her eyes. "Didn't want to worry anybody."

"You didn't want to *worry* anybody? Why did you stop answering my letters, then? You don't think I was plenty worried about that?"

He grimaced and looked out across the rippling water. "At first, I just thought I'd heal and it'd be fine, so I didn't say anything about it in my letters. Didn't want to sound like a whiner."

"And so when you didn't heal? Why didn't you tell me then?"

He still didn't look back at her. "You know me too well, Bertie. You'd've known something was wrong if I'd tried to write to you then. Besides, a lot of the time I was hurting too bad to do much but lay there and wish I was dead."

"You gonna tell me about it now?"

"Not much to tell."

"You got shot?"

"Got shelled."

"From what I hear, a shelling could blow a man's leg clear off. Or his head. Or make mincemeat of his whole body."

"It didn't. Just sliced through muscle and bone."

"When did it happen?"

He sighed. "Last of March. Medic couldn't get to me for a few hours, because of the battle, and it was daylight. Then they couldn't get me to a hospital because we were still under attack."

"It's a special blessing that your leg was saved."

He gritted his teeth. He didn't want to hear about blessings right now. "Guessed you'd say something like that."

"You're alive, Red. After everything I've read about the war, your very life's a special blessing. At least it is for me."

He looked at her then. When she was like this she could talk a stubborn mule into plowing the moon. "I don't see it that way," he said. "You don't have any idea where I've been or what I've done, so don't go talking to me like you know all about it."

She frowned at him. "Now you do sound like a whiner, and I know better. Red Meyer's never been one to complain about the hard things that had happened in his life, the things he'd had to do without after his father died."

"Red Meyer's always been healthy before."

"You're walking," she said. "Even if it is with a cane."

He shrugged. "They say penicillin's a miracle drug."

"I'm sure they're right, but just because they've treated you with their miracle doesn't mean God's other miracles are worthless now."

He nodded.

"So you'll let me use comfrey on that leg?" she asked. "I overheard Gerald say he's going fishing this afternoon. I know his favorite fishing hole is down on the river, just below the comfrey I need to collect."

"No."

"I'd be perfectly safe if he's there, too."

Red groaned and turned away. "Bertie, don't start this."

He heard her step up beside him, and he moved away. "I didn't come down here for company. I came down to do some thinking. Alone. You need to go back to the church." Without looking at her, he limped along the river's edge, leaving her behind.

Bertie watched Red's retreating back, feeling grief threaten to overwhelm her again. But she wasn't going in that direction this time. Instead, she allowed her loss to fuel a quick spurt of anger.

"Don't you dare treat me like this!" she called after him. When his steps slowed at the sound of her words, she caught up with him. "I'm only wanting to help you, and you're treating me like a pesky puppy."

"You don't know anything about this, Bertie, so just simmer down."

"Well, I *should* know about it." She risked his anger by stepping in front of him. "You don't think I've earned just a little more respect from you? I've been true to you for three years. With all those pages of letters I wrote to you, I could've written a dozen books."

He blinked at her, swallowed, nodded. "Maybe more." He didn't look mad.

"But I wanted to write to you. You're the one I've put all my hopes in, the one I've waited for."

"I didn't ask you to." It amazed her that such a harsh statement could be spoken with such gentleness.

"You said that to me this morning, too. I'm tired of hearing it." She heard a quiver in her voice, and that tiny sign of weakness made her mad all over again. "Something's bothering you that you haven't told anybody, because I know you better than this. You don't mope, and you're not the cranky type. Not the way you've been since I got back."

He grunted and closed his eyes. "You don't know me now."

"So you keep reminding me, and that's just ridiculous. A fella doesn't change the core of who he has been all his life. Maybe your outlook on life is changed, but who you are inside won't change. Not your character. Not the person God made you to be."

He shook his head. "You can't even guess, Bertie."

"Yes, I can. Up until a few weeks ago, I got letters from you all the time. You weren't afraid to tell me what was going through your mind. So something happened just before the end of things over in Italy." She gestured to his leg. "Something more than that. Don't shut me out like this, Red. It isn't fair to me."

He looked down at the cane in his hand, then turned and gazed toward the edge of the forest across the river.

For the longest moment, all was silent except for the birdsong echoing from the trees, and the sigh of the wind through the leaves.

"You're right," he said at last. "It isn't fair to you." He looked down at her and laid a hand on her shoulder, and all the love she'd ever seen in his eyes or read from his letters was suddenly, amazingly, plain on his face. "You need to understand why everything's changed, and then you need to let it go."

Chapter Thirty-Three

Before Bertie could respond to the touch of Red's hand, he pulled away, as if he'd done something wrong.

"A week before I got hit," he said, "our scouting team was captured by the German Army." The soft, matter-of-fact voice contradicted the shock of the message.

Bertie felt the jolt of his words all the way to her toes. She swallowed and didn't say anything, not wanting to break his momentum now that she had him talking.

He gave her a brief glance, then looked away again. "I haven't told anybody about this."

"You can tell me."

"I'd appreciate it if you…" he paused, then shook his head. "No, that ain't right. I can't dump bad news on you and then expect you to keep it bottled up. I did that to Ma."

"Red, I won't say anything to anyone unless you want me to." She reached out and touched his arm, and felt the hard muscles underneath the sleeve of his suit coat. Her Red. "Just tell me. I want so much to understand."

He hesitated. "I will, but you've gotta promise me one thing."

"You name it."

"Don't go giving me a sermon about how I should get over this and move on with my life. I don't want a pep talk."

"I promise."

"And don't go trying to remind me about the great blessing of life."

She flinched at that. "Okay. I guess it was pretty stupid of me to try to tell you about blessings when you're suffering so with your leg. I know how I felt yesterday when Mrs. Fisher sidled up to me and whispered about how happy I must be that Dad's now with the Lord."

His brows lowered. "She said that?"

"Yep, she did. I'm sorry, Red. I for sure won't do that to you again."

A bare nod as he looked toward the sky, jaw muscles working. She could see from the strain in his expression that he was suddenly reliving something awful.

She almost told him to forget it, that it wasn't any of her business, and it wasn't worth making him go through it all over again, but she needed to know. She felt, after everything, that it most certainly was her business. Maybe her very most important business right now.

"One of our captors was this young kid," he said at last, turning to stare back up the bank in the direction of the church, though the church wasn't visible from where they stood. "Looked to be fifteen, sixteen, mouthy and mean, always beating up on us, pulling ugly tricks on us, then laughing." Red took a deep breath. "Always stirring up trouble."

Bertie swallowed hard. She wanted to ask how long they'd been captured, just exactly how mean this soldier was, how they were rescued, she wanted all the details quickly. She pressed her lips together and squeezed his arm, wanting so badly to wrap her arms around him that it became a physical need.

But she knew he needed her not to. He was a grown man who didn't want mothering. He'd already made that clear enough this morning.

He looked down at her, as if memorizing the features of her face, then he looked away again. "Kid's name was Fritz. Blond hair, dark, snapping eyes, never took guff off anybody, even though he had to've been the youngest in his squad."

He closed his eyes. "He could've been a Moennig, Bertie. Could've been a bratty little brother of yours. He looked so much like you and Lloyd when we were growing up."

The thought stung her. She still had relatives in Germany, of course. But just because he'd looked like her didn't mean they had a blood bond.

"I decided to see if I could talk to him," Red said. "I know a little German I picked up from Pa's side of the family, and I tried a word or two on him."

"What did he do?"

"Laughed at me, mostly. Made fun of me to his buddies. I kept trying, anyway, for those few days they held us." Red looked down at his leg, then turned and walked along the rough track beside the river.

Bertie held on to his arm and walked beside him.

"He released us all one night."

She stumbled on a rock, and felt Red's arm tense beneath her hand, steadying her. "The bully released you?"

Red nodded, not breaking his stride. "Came to us while we were sleeping, untied our bonds, and kicked us awake. Just like that."

"But why?"

His steps slowed. He sighed, shook his head. "I never knew."

"He didn't say anything?"

"He didn't know our language, as far as I could tell." Again, that shake of the head. "At first, we were afraid it was a trap. We were sure he was just releasing us so they'd have a good reason to shoot us while we were on the run, though the Germans never needed an excuse to kill their prisoners. They just killed them."

"But he let you go."

Red disengaged from Bertie's grasp, fumbled with the cane, and bent over and picked up a flat rock. He drew back with his right hand and skipped the rock across the smooth surface of the moving water. It skipped six times, if Bertie was counting right. His rock-skipping skills were getting awkward.

"I'm pretty sure that runty soldier saved all of us," Red said, bending over to pick up another flat rock. "I'd understood a few words that passed between the men the day before, though I'm so rusty with my German I only knew a little. From what words I caught, it sounded like they were planning to kill us soon."

"That's why you thought the release was a trick," Bertie said. "But why did he—"

"I don't know. Our team talked about it later, as we made our way back to camp. We couldn't come up with any reasons, 'ceptin' it was a miracle from God." He looked down at her. "Yes, there you go, I said it. I believe it was a miracle. Some answers to all those prayers you were prayin'. We were so glad to get out of there with our lives, we didn't hang around and ask questions." He paused and closed his eyes. "Didn't even take the time to thank him."

"Word never reached us back home that you were a prisoner of war," Bertie said.

"We weren't missing long enough. We went right back to

work when the next battle broke out." He tossed the rock into the water, not even trying to skip it this time—as if the act of sinking that rock into the river was satisfying enough.

She waited for him to continue. Yes, it would've been a horrible experience to go through, wondering if he was going to be killed by his captors at any moment, but he'd lived through three years of that kind of threat.

"Four days after we reached our company, fresh battle broke out," he said. "I think the Germans knew time was gettin' short, so they decided to kill all they could while they had a chance."

"That's when your leg was hit?"

He stopped, leaning heavily on the cane. Splashes from ripples along the river's edge filled the silence. "I got caught in a foxhole, separated from the rest of my team. Two men had been there before me, and didn't make it out. They were dead at the far end of the hole. I heard footsteps coming toward me, and I saw a German helmet peering over the edge of the hole." His eyes closed. He swallowed, as if words had suddenly caught in his throat. "I shot him. Got him straight-on in the chest, killed him just like that." Red snapped his fingers.

Bertie waited, holding her breath.

"He fell into the mud beside me without a single cry. Face-first into that thick mud." Red looked at her, his blue eyes filmed with moisture, his face filled with horror. "It was the kid who'd saved our lives."

She felt the shock of his words through her whole body, felt a shadow of the pain he must be feeling. Instinctively, she reached for him, but he backed away, as if he was afraid of her touch, her comfort.

But at the moment, she felt as if she was the one who

needed comforting. Just seeing what Red had gone through cut her deeply.

"When no one else followed him into the foxhole, I went to him and turned him over. There were those blue eyes, staring without life into the sky, looking like he could've been a brother of yours. I couldn't stay there, Bertie. Not facing what I'd done."

"Red, it was war. You did what you had to do, what you were taught to do."

He cast her a sharp glance.

"Sorry," she said, glimpsing the raw memory of that moment in his eyes. She knew she would always see it there. Nothing she could say or do would help him heal that wound. Only God could do that, and she'd promised not to preach.

"Anyway, you're right. That's when I got hit. There've been times I wished the shrapnel had found a more deadly place to lodge."

"But it didn't, and you can't go wishing your life away. Did you ever think, even though Fritz let you go, he would've shot you then?"

He gave her another sharp glance.

She couldn't hold his gaze, nor her tongue. "I said I wouldn't preach, and I won't, but I didn't promise to keep my mouth shut completely."

He continued to watch her. She grimaced.

"Don't know how I'm going to live with this," he said, looking away at last. "I for sure don't expect anybody else to put up with me while I try to find a way through it. I've heard stories of men in the first war who were shellshocked and never came out of it. I couldn't put anybody through what they put their families through. Especially not my Bertie."

Those words—my Bertie—felt to her like a physical caress.

"We've already had this fight," she said gently. "I'm not changing my mind."

"You don't have a choice." He turned from her then, and walked along the riverside, shoulders squared, back stiff.

"You're right," she called after him. "I don't have a choice. My heart already belongs to you." She didn't follow him, but watched him go. She wasn't finished with him, and whether he liked it or not, she'd developed a little more perseverance about waiting since he went off to war. She could be patient.

Chapter Thirty-Four

The last thing Red wanted to do was mingle with a bunch of people after reliving that harsh memory to Bertie, but after a long, silent talk with himself, he returned to the church grounds. He could talk to people while he ate his ma's ham and beans and Bertie's dishpan cookies, discussed the crops and the price of cattle and hogs with Herbert Morrow and Homer Jarvis.

Homer Jarvis, he discovered, thought Earl Krueger had been the culprit in the recent livestock rustling, because he'd needed the money the stock brought at the sale barn to make his yearly mortgage payment, which had been overdue for a month.

Furthermore, Herbert Morrow believed Joseph Moennig had tracked down Krueger and confronted him as the thief. Then, after killing Joseph, Krueger took off with his family. When Red asked Morrow who might have been behind the vandalism at Joseph's house on Thursday, Morrow thought maybe Krueger had slipped back into town when no one was looking. It seemed quite a few folks thought Krueger was a Nazi sympathizer, and they were glad to be rid of him.

John Martin's mother, Cora Lee, interrupted their discussion. "Red Meyer, you need to try a helping of my raspberry cobbler." She handed him a dish with red berries oozing from beneath a crispy crust, topped by ice cream. "John cranked the ice-cream freezer himself."

Already full as a tick, Red accepted the dessert and thanked her, excused himself from the group to walk around the churchyard.

He tried hard not to look at Bertie, but sight of her drew him like being pulled around by a mule on a thick lead rope. There was no missing the sadness in her eyes that he'd put there with his own confession.

He saw Arielle Potts working beside his mother at the serving line, and recalled what she'd told him about the Bald Knobbers. The real reason those rascals ran so many people off their farms in Taney County was because they knew the railroad was coming in.

It was only hearsay, of course, that the property of those farmers who were frightened into leaving their homes just happened to be on that line. He'd probably been gazing down at some of those very plots of land when he rode the train in on Monday.

There was no railroad going in now, but there were plans for a dam. Which would mean a lake. The Moennig and Krueger property might all be lakeshore in a few years. A fella might buy it cheap, and make a killin' on it in a few years when the dam went in at Branson, if he was willing to wait that long.

From what Red had heard, it seemed the Kruegers were about to lose their place. If the bank foreclosed on the loan, it could do pretty much anything it wanted to get that money back. Red wondered who might have profited from that.

He'd spent some time with Wyatt Brown in Italy last year,

before Wyatt got shot up and sent home. He'd heard Wyatt got a job over in Galena, the county seat, after he recovered. It was a wild guess, but could be someone had already made a move on the Krueger place. Maybe Wyatt could look up that information for him.

Definitely a crazy theory, but worth checking into.

Hideaway was already a resort town, with many wealthy folks from all over the country vacationing here. How much more popular would it become with a lake? The Moennig place would for sure be on that shore.

Could Joseph have lost his life because someone wanted his land?

Red took his dish back to the serving table and handed it to Cora Lee Martin. "Have you seen Bertie around anywhere?" he asked her.

"Sure did, Red. She took off walking down the road a while back. Poor thing. I know she's plumb worn out from all this."

"Did anyone go with her?"

"Not that I noticed." Cora Lee glanced at him skeptically. "She's a grown woman, Red, she can walk herself home, I expect."

He thanked her and went to find Ivan, who, predictably, was sitting on a blanket under a shady tree, talking to Edith, who was taking a brief rest from serving.

Red asked Edith if she knew where Bertie had gone.

"I'm sure she just got tired and went to your house," Edith said. "She probably needed a nap, since she barely slept last night."

"She didn't say anything about going to gather comfrey leaves, did she?" Red asked.

"I don't think she would go by herself," Edith said. "Not after our experience yesterday."

Red figured he knew Bertie a little better than her roommate of eight months knew her.

"Not to worry," Ivan said. "Even if she did go, Dad's gone to his favorite fishing hole, and that's just below the Moennig place. She'll be safe." He stretched his long legs and leaned back against the sycamore tree, looking relaxed and happy to be home.

Red turned away. He would check the house, and if Bertie wasn't there, he'd saddle Seymour and go—

He turned back, and looked down at Ivan's shoe…where there was a deep gash in the left heel.

"Ivan, are those your shoes?"

Ivan frowned at him, then looked down at his shoes. "They are now. Why?"

"Where'd you get 'em?"

"Dad gave them to me to wear today. He's breaking in some new ones."

"They're your *father's?*"

"Well, did you expect me to wear my combat boots to the funeral? All my others were too tight on me. These are Dad's old shoes. Not dressy, but for everyday."

Red realized the mistake he'd made, thinking the print he'd been tracking was from a work boot because the shoe was so wide and long. Extra width for a sturdy work boot. But the extra width on these shoes was because they were a larger size shoe, made to fit a man with a larger foot. Like Gerald Potts.

The very thought led Red to other thoughts that made him suddenly sick.

"I've got to get to Bertie."

"Why, Red?" Ivan asked. "I told you, Dad's going out that way."

"How do you know he's there yet? I don't feel safe leaving her alone. You know how much trouble Bertie can get herself into without thinkin' twice."

Ivan looked at Edith, and together they got to their feet. "We'll take my car," Ivan said.

Once upon a time, Bertie had been able to ride her bicycle anywhere she wanted, even out into the field to take water to Dad and Lloyd when they were planting or gathering—when she wasn't working alongside them. With a hundred and twenty acres of land—ninety of which were good for crops—it had taken the whole family and sometimes several of the boys from town to help gather the hay into their big barn.

This morning she walked, carrying a scratchy burlap bag from Seymour's stable over her arm. She would collect the comfrey she needed, then carry it back to the house and scrub herself down to remove any summer critters that might have hitched a ride on her clothing—Lilly said it had been a bad summer for ticks.

Then she would boil the comfrey for tea; the large leaves she would use as dressing. The leaves were a perfect size for that kind of a poultice.

The old cow trail was still a well-used path to the riverbank, with gooseberry bushes and blackberry brambles only a few steps from the trail. She would come back another day to pick berries. Today, she was gathering something much more important.

Red would most likely put up a fight, but now that Lilly was as determined as Bertie to help him heal, she thought between the two of them they'd convince him to at least try it.

Oh, Lord, touch his heart and heal him, she prayed as she

stepped over an old tree root that used to trip her when she was a kid. *He's been through so much.*

She couldn't imagine how she would have reacted to the horror Red had endured these past three years. She was surprised more men didn't come back from the war shell-shocked, unable to function. She hated war with a passion.

And yet she knew the alternative could have been a whole world under the evil reign of Nazi Germany—with Hitler the supreme commander. Red and Ivan and the men who had fought this war were heroes. Why couldn't Red realize how much his sacrifice meant to her? To everyone?

She found the comfrey plants exactly where they had always been, watered by a tiny spring on the hillside, just above the cliffs that dropped down to the largest of the caves at the foot of the hill. She was bending down to collect the first few huge leaves—which would work so well to wrap around Red's knee and thigh—when she heard voices below her.

She couldn't quite make out the words, but she did recognize Gerald's deep voice. That was nothing new. The riverbank below was a popular fishing spot for the locals, who knew where to catch the best striper on the river. She'd known he would be down there today.

But as she continued to collect the leaves, the tone of Gerald's voice changed. He sounded angry.

Frowning, she broke the final comfrey leaf from its stem, eased it gently into the bag on the ground, then, curious, she stepped over to the edge of the cliff and looked down. All she could see were the tops of two heads, two men in separate flat-bottomed boats, directly below her.

Gerald wore the old fishing hat he always wore. Gramercy Short was the other man, his balding head already turning pink in the sun.

"Look, we had an agreement," Gramercy snapped, his voice echoing along the water. "My silence for a price. You owe me."

As the words registered, Bertie took a step backward. This didn't feel like a place she wanted to be right now.

"We agreed this would be a long-term investment of our mutual time and silence," Gerald said.

"Don't give me your highfalutin words. I don't want no long-term nothing! I'm not waiting 'til the lake comes in. I could be dead by then. I want my share now."

"You should know I don't have that kind of money. Where would I get it?"

"Don't try to pull that one on me, Potts. Everybody knows your wife's family is loaded to the gills."

There was a silence, then came Gerald's voice, low and cold—so soft, Bertie wouldn't't've heard him, except their voices carried from the water up the side of the cliff like a natural amplifier.

"You leave my wife out of this."

There was a wicked chuckle. "But isn't that what this is all about? Me leaving everyone else out of our little discovery?"

"It was an accident!"

"Hideaway needs to have another accident. Or did you talk little Miss Moennig into selling?"

"I never said anything about the Moennig farm."

"You said you'd see to it that—"

The ground shifted beneath Bertie's feet. She gasped, scrambling backward. The voices hushed below as rocks and pebbles splashed and echoed.

She needed to grab her bag of leaves and get out of here before—

The ground beneath her gave way completely. There was a shout from below, and she screamed. Suddenly she was tumbling down amidst mud and gravel. Rocks dug into her legs and gouged her shoulders.

She hit the river with a splash of shocking cold. Water stung her nose and she gagged. Her feet touched the rocky bottom as more pebbles rained down on her from above.

When she broke surface the stones had stopped falling, but as she blinked her eyes and her vision cleared, she saw something more dangerous.

Gramercy Short was on his knees in the boat, and he had his paddle raised over his head, directly above her.

"Short!" Gerald called from behind him. "What are you doing? Are you crazy?"

The paddle started down. Bertie didn't wait. She dove beneath the surface again, clawing her way beneath Short's boat to avoid his weapon. She came out on the other side, gasping for breath, only to find Gramercy in the water with her, reaching for her, his face twisted with some kind of vicious determination.

He snagged her by the hem of her skirt as she tried to swim away. She went under, choked, fought her way back to the surface, coughing.

"No!" Gerald shouted behind her.

"Looks like trouble has decided to pay us a call," Short said. "Probably another one of those Nazis you're so eager to kill."

"Let her go, Short!" Gerald said. "Bertie isn't a part of this."

"Sure she is," Gramercy said, treading water, gripping his boat with one hand and more of Bertie's skirt with the other. "This little gal's up to her neck in it, 'specially if you're collecting lakeshore land. Her father's gone, and I've heard her brother has tuberculosis. With her out of the way, we'd have that much more stock in our company."

"There's no stock! No company!" Gerald snapped. "Let her go, Short. Now!"

Gramercy dragged Bertie under. She kicked and struggled against him, but here she couldn't touch bottom, couldn't reach the surface.

She was going to die.

Fingers dug cruelly into her arm. She kicked and shoved and tried to dive away.

She heard a shout that was loud enough to penetrate the water and her terror. "Short!"

She fought those hands, kicking, thrusting her body toward the surface, fighting with desperation for her life. He shoved her again, and as her body went down, he kicked her hard in the ribs. His fingers dug into her throat, squeezing. Darkness surrounded her. Blackness smothered her.

Then suddenly, it ended. He released her. She floated for a bare second or two, unable to find her bearings. Before she could force her arms and legs to move, her hair was caught in a painful grip, and she felt herself being jerked upward.

Air kissed her face, and she sucked it into her lungs in greedy gasps. Strong hands pulled her to the shore. She blinked, then looked up to see Gerald hovering over her, his face pale, wide, terrified eyes suddenly filling with relief.

"Bertie? I'm so sorry."

She looked back where she had been. Gramercy Short's thick body floated face down in the water, bumping against Gerald's boat as it tried to float downstream with the current. His arms were splayed out beside him, bald head shining in the sun, with a gash in the back of it that had stopped bleeding.

Gerald reached down and pulled the man over, pressed his fingers to his neck, then closed his eyes and shook his head.

Gramercy Short was dead.

Chapter Thirty-Five

In spite of the cane, the pain in his leg, the weakness, Red had no trouble leading Ivan, Edith and John through the brush and up the incline to the top of the cliffs, where he heard splashing, where he'd heard shouting just seconds before. Now, he heard someone gasping for breath.

"Bertie!" he shouted.

Red crested the cliff and nearly fell down the other side, where the earth had obviously given way, providing a long slide of rocks and dirt from the cliff top into the river twenty feet below.

What he saw froze him, and he held a hand up for the others to use caution as they joined him. He dropped to his knees. Bertie was lying on the riverbank, drenched, coughing.

Gerald stood half in half out of the water, staring down at Bertie, his face white. Gramercy Short lay in the water, and his lifeless body was bumping against Gerald's flat-bottomed boat.

Bertie turned to Gerald, still catching her breath.

"I killed him," he told her, his voice carrying upward. "I didn't know what else to do. He just about had you."

Gerald looked down at the oar, and at his own hands, and then back at Bertie. "He was killing you."

"Dad!" Ivan cried, and started down the cliff.

Red grabbed him. "Wait, Ivan. Something else is up."

Ivan tried to pull away, but Red held him firm. "We need to have a talk with your father."

Ivan turned to him. "Why? Isn't it obvious what happened? Short's been up to his old tricks. Looks like he tried to get to Bertie this time."

Red looked back down at his best friend's father, the man he and Bertie had known all their lives. "What was it, Gerald?"

Gerald didn't answer. He dropped to his knees beside Bertie.

"Dad?" Ivan pulled from Red's grip. "What's he talking about? What's going on here?"

Still on his knees, Red turned to his side and released his cane. Using his hands, ignoring the pain, he slid down the steep cliff side, using the dirt from the recent collapse to break his fall. He reached Bertie where she lay drenched and shivering, and pulled her into his arms.

"Dad?" Ivan said. "Tell me what's happening."

"I didn't mean to do it—"

"Gerald," Bertie said softly, "Gramercy said something about a deal you two had made. Why did he try to kill me? What's going on?"

"The sheriff's coming," Red told Gerald. "You'd better practice your story on us."

"I don't have a story, Red." Gerald sounded utterly beaten. "It was all a horrible mistake."

"You can tell that to the sheriff, too," Red said. "I don't suppose you'd believe that your own wife and son are the ones that helped give you away."

Gerald looked up at Ivan, and tears filled his eyes. "Oh, son, what have I done?"

"I don't know, Dad," Ivan called down. "Tell me. Please. Help me understand what's going on here."

"The shoes you were wearing when you laid all those limbs," Red said, "and turned our horse out and put your vile mark on our stable were the same shoes you let Ivan wear to the funeral today."

He felt Bertie's shoulders shake with sobs, and drew her to his chest.

"I didn't do those things, Red," Gerald's voice, already too soft, sounded as if it was losing strength. "I made some bad moves, did some wicked things, but I would never have hurt Joseph if I'd known it was him."

Red felt Bertie tense. She pulled away, dashing the tears from her face with the back of her hand. "You killed my father?"

Gerald covered his face with his hands. A moan came from his throat. "I never meant to kill him," he said, then looked over at Gramercy's body. "I never meant to kill anybody. With Short, I didn't know what else to do to save you, Bertie. I couldn't get to him in time to wrestle him away from you. There was no other way."

Bertie shivered again. "I can't be hearing this. Not you, Gerald."

"Dad." Ivan's voice thickened with pain. "You killed Joseph?"

Gerald closed his eyes and covered his face with his hands. "I didn't…I didn't know it was him, I swear it."

"Who did you think it was?" Red demanded.

Gerald reached a hand out as if to touch Bertie. She shrunk away from him.

He shook his head. "I thought it was Krueger, and I thought Krueger was a Nazi infiltrator. I still think that. I *knew* he was the cattle thief, because I caught him at it. I didn't even mean to kill him, just run him out of Hideaway."

"And get his land?" Bertie asked, remembering something else she'd overheard between the men when they were arguing.

Gerald winced. "I'm sorry. I didn't see that it would hurt anyone, with the cattle thief gone."

"And you hit my father instead of Krueger?" Bertie asked. "Why? What were you doing on our land?"

"It didn't happen on your land," Gerald said. "It was on Krueger's land. I'd just followed him from your place, where he'd tried to rustle another calf from your herd. I'd gotten tired of waiting for the sheriff to help us with our rustling problem and the vandalism, and I decided to take it on myself to find who was doing it."

"So it really was Krueger doing the rustling?" Red asked.

Gerald nodded. "I didn't realize Joseph had also been watching him. By the time I followed Krueger back to his place after his failed attempt to catch the calf, it was getting dark. I turned and saw a shadow of someone behind me, thought it was Krueger, and that he was coming after me. I grabbed the first thing I could find to hit him. It was a board. I didn't realize until afterward that it had nails in it. When I saw that it wasn't Krueger, but Joseph, I think I…I know I went a little crazy."

"But why did you try to hide it?" Bertie asked.

"I'm sorry, Bertie. I didn't mean to hurt you. I never meant to hurt your father, I was trying to help. But when I discovered what I'd done, and Krueger witnessed it, I threatened to tell the sheriff that Krueger was the one who killed Joseph. It would have been easy to convince Butch, especially since

Krueger was the rustler. I was also thinking of my wife and son. How could I let Ivan come home from that war to find his father had killed the father of one of his best friends?"

"But Dad, you lied to save yourself," Ivan said. "You let Bertie and Red and the rest of us wonder all this time who could have done this. You even encouraged Red to try to find the killer. Why?"

Gerald shook his head. "I thought Red would surely come to the same conclusion everyone else has. I told Krueger if he would pack up and leave immediately, I wouldn't tell the sheriff anything, but I wanted that land."

"For Ivan's future," Red said.

Gerald nodded. "Forgive me, I was thinking of my wife and son. The Exchange is doing okay financially, but we don't have land, nothing to leave for our son. Nothing from me. Only from Arielle's family. I'm a proud enough man I need to know I've passed a legacy on to my son and grandchildren."

"With the dam coming in a few years," Red said, "Krueger's property will be lakefront property."

Gerald nodded. "Like I said, I'd do anything for my son."

"What about the swastikas, the gassed cat in Bertie's house?" Red asked.

Gerald shook his head, gesturing to Gramercy's body. "I'm thinking he did it. There's no other reason he'd have been at Krueger's house the night of Joseph's death, because he never made a secret of the fact that he hated Krueger. He came to me later and told me he saw what I did, and he wanted a cut."

"He was blackmailing you?" Ivan asked.

Gerald nodded, then looked at Bertie, sorrow etched deeply into every line of a face that seemed to have aged far too much in the past few minutes. "That wasn't why I killed him, Bertie. You have to believe that. I couldn't let him hurt you. I'd rather go to prison for the rest of my life than be responsible for your death."

Red's arms automatically tightened around her as Ivan scrambled down the cliff side to his father.

This was just one more wound that would haunt the history of Hideaway.

Red and Bertie made it to the top of the cliff before Edith returned with a blanket and wrapped it around Bertie. Its warmth felt good, in spite of the heat of the day. Bertie wasn't sure she would ever recover from the chill that had settled deep inside her.

And yet, the healing touch of Red's concern, his obvious caring, his dedication to her safety was beginning to work its way through the icy feel of her skin.

Edith hugged her tightly. "Are you going to be okay, honey?" she whispered in Bertie's ear.

Bertie lied. "I'll be fine."

"Then I'll leave you in Red's capable care. The sheriff's loading Gerald in his car. John's with Ivan, and they're going to go tell Arielle what's happened."

Bertie nodded. "You go on. I'll be…okay."

Edith kissed her on the cheek, squeezed Red's arm, and turned to follow the trail back to the farmhouse.

Bertie felt battered as she walked beside Red up the cow trail behind Edith. She couldn't bear to think about Gerald. How could she ever face Ivan or Arielle again? How would *Gerald* ever be able to face his family?

"I kind of know how Gerald feels," Red said, his voice quiet, filled with the sadness that Bertie felt.

"You didn't kill a neighbor, then try to hide the truth for your own benefit."

Red looked down at her. "Who is my neighbor? Someone who lives down the road from me? Or is it someone who saved my life once?"

"Red, you were fighting a war. You did what you had to do."

"Gerald was trying to find the cattle rustler. Yes, he lost his way, and didn't own up to what he did. You may never forgive him for what he did to your father. I figure there'll always be someone in Germany who'll never forgive me for killing their son, their brother."

"But it's not the same thing."

He stopped and turned to her. Still leaning on his cane, with his free hand he reached up and cupped the side of her face. "I've been doing some thinking, and I've decided you're not gonna get any easier to handle."

"You make me sound like a plow mule."

A shadow of the old Red peeked from his eyes. "As long as you keep stepping into trouble, you're gonna need somebody to follow along behind and get you out."

"You have anybody in mind for that chore?" she asked.

He shrugged. "I figure there's nobody around who knows you better than I do, so I'll have to take the job to make sure it gets done right."

She gazed up into those beautiful blue eyes that reflected the color of the James River on a sunny day. "What are you saying?"

"I'm saying I'll have to do all I can to get this leg better if I'm gonna keep up with you. I think you came out here to gather comfrey."

She nodded.

"Then maybe we should get started on those treatments as soon as possible."

"You mean now? Today?"

He nodded.

She threw her arms around him. Finally, he realized it was possible to heal. Her Red was coming home at last.

"There was another death two thousand years ago that covers everything we've seen in this war," Red said, still holding her, his touch gentle, loving.

"He paid it all then," she said. "The Savior willingly laid down His life for me, for you, for Fritz."

"For Gerald."

She nodded.

"It helps me to think about that when I think about Fritz," Red said. "I don't know if Fritz or his family will ever forgive what I did to him, but I know now that I had no choice. It was war. I had to fight, or I could've died, and then you and Ma and a lot of other people would have been going through what his family must be going through now."

"You'll probably always have that ache in your chest when you think about Fritz, but living with the constant guilt isn't the best way to honor Fritz's death."

Red reached up and touched her cheek. "I think you're right."

"I'm sorry. I'm preaching," she said. "You told me not to do that."

He pulled her closer. "Do you know how much I've missed you? I didn't realize a feller could miss a gal so much, especially when she's right up on the next floor in the same house."

She let him draw her to his chest, so grateful to see signs of her old Red back in place, she wanted to sing in spite of the day's pain. Instead, she kissed him. And then she kissed him again, and very nearly swooned right over when he kissed her back with all the fervor of the old Red.

She let him wrap her in his strong arms, and she rested her head on his chest, and thanked God in her heart for the touch of the man she loved more than anyone else in the world.

"I don't suppose you'd ever given any thought to my question last year," he said, his voice rumbling deep in his chest.

"Which question?"

"The one where I asked if you'd be interested in never leaving Hideaway again, once we returned."

She leaned back to look up at him. "Why, Red Meyer, if that isn't a proposal, then I've not learned to read you as well as I thought I had."

He drew her close again, tangling his fingers in her hair. "Will you marry me, Roberta Moennig?"

"You'd better believe I will, Charles Frederick Meyer. I've been waiting to hear those words for far too long."

"How about these words," he said, brushing his fingers against her cheek and looking into her eyes, his gaze serious. "I'll love you 'til the day I die. That's a promise you can count on."

Epilogue

On August 15, 1945, the day after World War Two ended, Bertie grinned at Second Lieutenant Charles Frederick Meyer as she watched him walk to the front of the church, cane-free, with barely a limp.

He turned to wait for her, his attention completely on her, his blue eyes shining with the love he had shown her throughout the war in so many ways—through his letters, his constant thoughts of her, his determination to protect her at any cost, even if it meant denying his love for her.

There was no denial of that love in his expression now, a fact that no one in the packed church could miss.

Red wore his full dress uniform, his Bronze Star and his Purple Heart amidst several other medals across his chest. He wore them with pride.

Ivan joined him, to stand beside him as best man. In spite of all, their friendship had remained strong, and Bertie had grown to admire her good friend even more in the painful weeks since Gerald's arrest. His mother, Arielle, had stepped into the breach at the MFA Exchange, and was now running the place during her husband's absence. Ironically, what would ordinarily have been the family's disgrace had served to unite Arielle to the town of Hideaway as nothing else had done.

Bertie fumbled with her bouquet as she struggled to battle tears. How she loved this town. This church.

This was the church where, two months ago, her father's funeral had been conducted. The contrast between that day—the result of pain upon pain—and this day of joy and triumph could not be more dramatic.

Edith Frost, Bertie's dearest friend, walked ahead of her down the aisle, holding a small bouquet of yellow roses from Lilly's garden.

The past two months had been a battle, for sure, right here in Hideaway, as Bertie learned to forgive those who had hurt her and her family, and as Red learned to trust her to help him heal physically.

Yes, this day was a triumph, indeed.

Bertie took Lloyd's arm and followed slowly behind Edith. Bertie proudly wore the pale green dress of chiffon and lace her mother had worn at her wedding.

The church was full of people she loved. She winked at Louise Morrow, who stood smiling at her from the aisle, eyes filmed with tears. She squeezed Lloyd's arm as they passed by his wife, Mary, and his children, Steven and Joann. God had answered their prayers. Lloyd didn't have tuberculosis. He'd been able to return home to his family.

Recently, he and Mary had decided to move back to Hideaway. They had enough money saved for a down payment on the Kruegers' old place, and the Moennig property was now double the size it had been.

One of Bertie's most difficult decisions had been to forgive the man who had killed her father. She hadn't thought it would be so hard. After all, it had been an accident. At the time, Gerald had been trying to protect the town. It had turned out to be more painful than she'd expected, but the day she went to Gerald at the jail and told him to his face she forgave him, had been the day his whole family began to heal.

He would be home soon, and she knew she would have yet another battle to fight with herself as Gerald struggled to regain the trust he had broken with friends and family.

Bertie was distracted from thoughts of Gerald by the sight of young Pearl Cooper standing between her parents, eyes as wide and hopeful as any young girl's as she watched Bertie come down the aisle. Pearl was a beauty, and she had taken every chance to sit by Bertie at church on Sunday—when her parents allowed her to attend church at all. Bertie prayed as she walked that Pearl would be able to overcome tribulations in her own family history, and build a new legacy.

As Edith reached the front, she turned to stand beside Ivan. Those two lovebirds had a strong start. Edith had stood beside Ivan throughout his father's trial and jail sentencing, and had become good friends with Arielle, assisting her at the Exchange. If Edith ever left Hideaway, Bertie would be amazed.

Cecil Martin, proud Marine, stood watching the procession from near the front of the church. He, too, was home to stay, and was already preparing his high-school classroom for upcoming science projects.

Bertie reached the altar and released her brother's arm as she held her hands out to Red. Together they turned to face the minister.

Today was their triumph, a triumph for the town, a triumph of the heart. Red and Bertie Meyer would soon have a whole future to explore together.

When their union was sealed with a kiss, the whole congregation applauded their approval. The old Red was back. Red and Bertie Meyer would be a force for good in their beloved town of Hideaway.

* * * * *

Dear Reader,

It has been such a thrill to delve into the history of two of our favorite contemporary Hideaway characters, Red and Bertie Meyer, and discover their romance. This is especially true since we've heard from many readers who loved this couple in their old age in the first Hideaway novel.

We received a great deal of helpful input from Cheryl's mother, Lorene Cook, who, along with Cheryl's late father, Johnnie Cook, worked at Hughes Aircraft in Southern California during the Second World War. Lorene was also able to share her experiences as a machinist and give us valuable information about farm and small-town life during the early 1940s. It was a joy to be able to work with her on this project.

Mel's father and six of Cheryl's uncles served in the armed forces during WWII. Some of their experiences were incorporated in this story, as well, though no one but the soldiers themselves will ever know the true horrors they faced as they risked their lives for our freedom.

We hope you have enjoyed this realistic taste of days gone by, and the romance of a couple who will live in our hearts for a long time to come.

With Love,

Hannah Alexander

DISCUSSION QUESTIONS

1. What do you believe is Red's motivation for his decision to withdraw from Bertie's life? How much is love, and how much is pride? What other motivation might drive him?

2. Imagine how Bertie must feel as she faces not only her father's death, but the possibility of her brother's death, and the loss of Red's love, all within a few days. What would your response be in her situation?

3. When Bertie's life threatens to unravel, her friend Edith leaves everything to go with her. Why does she do this? Do you know anyone who has been this self-sacrificing in an emotionally healthy way?

4. Lilly Meyer loves her youngest son enough to confront him about the way he's behaving toward Bertie, but can you see aspects of her character that might have influenced his behavior? If Joseph had lived, what kind of a relationship do you believe might have developed between himself and Lilly?

5. Bertie risks her life and Edith's to return to the farmhouse where she grew up. Why do you believe she takes such a risk? Is it because she doesn't truly believe it's dangerous or because she believes herself to be indestructible?

6. Edith Frost feels guilty for being attracted to Ivan Potts, even though her husband has been dead since the beginning of the war. Why do you think she feels that way?

7. Gerald Potts has made a horrible error in judgment that affects his family and his standing in the community. How might things have been different if he had come forward with the truth to begin with?

8. What do you think would have happened if Bertie had obeyed Red's command for her to remain in California when she received news of her father's death?

9. Red and Bertie grew up together in Hideaway, were best friends and knew one another well. Do you think that kind of foundation promotes a deeper commitment, or do you feel that, since they already know one another so well, they might eventually become bored with their relationship?

10. Bertie takes a big risk when she becomes the pursuer in the relationship. Have you ever had this experience? What was the result?

Turn the page for a sneak preview
of Hidden Motive *by Hannah Alexander,*
available in April
from Love Inspired Suspense.

A flash of lightning illuminated the sprawling old home. The storm split the clouds with its violence, accentuating the lack of illumination in the house. Noah wasn't on the porch waiting for her, as he'd said he would be.

Dr. Sable Chamberlain unlatched the gate and pulled it open with a creak of rusty hinges, then stepped carefully along the flagstone path. She stopped as another flash of lightning illuminated the top step of the porch and the wide-open doorway.

In that instant, Sable felt a blast of shock at the sight of her elderly friend sprawled across the threshold. His body wedged open both the heavy oak and screen doors.

With a cry, Sable rushed up the porch steps and fell to her knees at her friend's side. "Noah! Oh, Lord, no!"

More lightning revealed a pool of blood from a hole in Noah's temple. His glazed eyes held the blank stare of death.

Anguished beyond thought, she felt for a pulse at his throat. Noah's head fell sideways, revealing a mass of blood at the back of his skull. The shooter had completed the job.

Sable felt the porch spin, her body numbing from the shock. She leaned against the doorframe as tears blinded her and icy wind whipped her hair across her face.

This was murder. She dashed the tears from her eyes and the hair from her face and cast a frantic look around the shadowed entryway and the living room beyond. Dark shapes lurked in every corner of the huge room. Lightning outlined the sofa and chairs and Noah's old desk in sharp relief.

The storm blocked any other sounds, and the wind scattered papers across the foyer. Those papers…were they the ones Noah had called her about? Terrified of lingering, yet desperate to find out why he had died, she grabbed as many as she could find and stuffed them into the deep left pocket of her coat.

The wind broke briefly, and Sable heard a footfall in the darkness near the kitchen door.

Movement! Lightning revealed a man lunging from the shadows. Sable screamed and stumbled backward, tripping over Noah's body. She fell on her side, then scrambled up and away.

The man grabbed her coat sleeve. She screamed again, yanking from his grip as she ran off the porch toward her car.

Footsteps came behind her, splashing mud. She'd never make the car. She broke and dove into a clump of bushes. Thorns scraped her exposed hands. She fought her way through the hedgerow, fighting brambles that clung to her clothes.

Sable fumbled in her pocket for her keys as she set her sights on her car, but her foot caught on a root and she fell. The man caught her. She swung around to claw at his face…there was no face.

Lightning revealed a ski mask.

A brilliant flash of headlights glared through the spiny

branches of the shrubs. Her attacker released her abruptly, swung away, stumbled, broke back through the hedgerow and disappeared into the darkness.

Sable froze, heart pounding in rhythm of the engine, breath coming in hard rasps. The vehicle passed. She turned and ran toward her car, but the SUV pulled in behind it, blocking her escape. She plunged into the blackness beyond the driveway.

"Hey!" a man shouted from the vehicle.

Sable staggered over the uneven ground. Again, she heard the sound of pursuing footsteps. She reached level ground and raced toward the tool shed. There might be a weapon of some sort among the garden tools, maybe a hoe, or—

Large, strong hands gripped her shoulders and spun her around, shoving her against the wall of the shed.

She screamed, jerking her knee upward until it hit something solid.

The man grunted, but held fast.

She raked her nails down the side of his neck, kicked at his legs. "Let go of me!"

Another grunt. "Dr. Chamberlain?" Shocked surprise.

"Get away from me!"

"Sable!" He grabbed her by the arms. "Doctor, stop it!"

The familiar voice registered. She froze, recognizing the light scent of aftershave, the breadth of his shoulders.

"Doctor, it's me. It's Murph." He groaned in pain.

Relief flooded her, gradually mingling with alarm at her behavior. "Murph?" She peered through the shadowy gloom at Paul Murphy's face—the paramedic who had been with the clinic for the past six weeks.

"Oh, Murph, I'm so—"

"What happened? Where's Noah?"

She swallowed hard as the first fat drops of rain splashed against her face. "He's on the porch. Oh, Murph, he's dead!"

There was a deep gasp.

"He's been murdered." She fought back her own horror. No time. "He called me no more than fifteen minutes ago with—"

Murph released her and turned toward the house, sucking in air as if he'd been kicked. "He called me, too."

Sable realized what he was going to do, and she grabbed his arm. "Murph, don't go up there. He was shot. That had to be his murderer you saw chasing me. That murderer is armed."

Murph looked back at her. "All I saw was you running."

"Your headlights startled him and he ran, but I don't know how far. He could be anywhere, and he has a gun. We've got to get away unless you're wearing a bullet-proof vest. I'm not."

There was another long crackle of chain-link thunder, and when the echo of it died away, it was replaced by a siren.

Sable caught Murph's arm. "That's got to be the police, and Noah warned me not to trust them. We've got to go now. Murph, come on." She released him and raced toward her car. "Get in!"

The sirens drew louder as Sable jumped into the car, slammed the door and turned on the key. The motor sprang to life with a rumble of power. As she put the car into gear, Murph slid in on the passenger side.

The wide tires of the Camaro tore up grass and slung mud as they gripped the earth. Sable held her breath and pressed the accelerator to the floorboard. They cleared the bushes at the far end of Noah's front yard just as red flashing lights stained the night sky. Sable didn't switch on her headlights.

She turned onto a straight stretch of road. "So you believe me?"

"Yes. Are you okay? Did that man hurt you?"

"He killed Noah!" She fought tears. No time.

Her ruse with the headlights worked. As the sirens receded, she relaxed her foot on the accelerator, but too soon. Lights hit her rearview mirror. No colors, no siren.

"Someone's following us," she told Murph.

"Just keep driving, and get your headlights on or we'll plunge into the canal."

Sable complied, downshifting for a burst of power, bracing herself for the dangerous turn at the edge of the deep, water-filled channel less than a quarter mile ahead.

Despite her speed, the car behind drew closer. She tightened her grip on the steering wheel.

Only a few hundred feet from the curve, the other car accelerated. Sable pressed her right foot to the floorboard and the Camaro responded with still another burst of speed.

High-beams swung around the curve ahead and into her face. Swerving, Sable realized too late how close she was to the canal curve. She yanked the steering wheel hard left. The road was too slick, even for the Camaro. The car slammed against a concrete abutment. Murph's door flew open. Sable screamed.

"We're going over!" Murph grabbed Sable's arm. "Jump!"

Sable dove across the seat toward the opening. The car bumped off the blacktop and plummeted toward the water.

Pushing themselves free from the car, Sable and Murph plunged into the icy wet blackness.

* * * * *

Love Inspired.
HISTORICAL

INSPIRATIONAL HISTORICAL ROMANCE

Amid the splendors of the Gilded Age, Neala Shaw suddenly found herself entirely alone. The penniless young heiress had no choice but to face her family's fatal legacy of secrets and lies. And as she fled from a ruthless killer, an honorable man unlike any she had ever known stood between her and certain death.

Look for

Legacy of Secrets

by
SARA MITCHELL

Available April wherever books are sold.

www.SteepleHill.com

Steeple Hill®

LIH82785

Love Inspired
SUSPENSE
RIVETING INSPIRATIONAL ROMANCE

REUNION REVELATIONS

**Secrets surface when old friends—
and foes—get together.**

Look for these six riveting Reunion Revelations stories!

Hidden in the Wall
by VALERIE HANSEN
January 2008

Missing Persons
by SHIRLEE McCOY
February 2008

Don't Look Back
by MARGARET DALEY
March 2008

In His Sights
by CAROL STEWARD
April 2008

A Face in the Shadows
by LENORA WORTH
May 2008

Final Justice
by MARTA PERRY
June 2008

Available wherever books are sold.

Steeple
Hill®

REQUEST YOUR FREE BOOKS!

2 FREE INSPIRATIONAL NOVELS

PLUS 2
FREE
MYSTERY GIFTS

Love Inspired
HISTORICAL
INSPIRATIONAL HISTORICAL ROMANCE

YES! Please send me 2 FREE Love Inspired® Historical novels and my 2 FREE mystery gifts (gifts are worth about $10). After receiving them, if I don't wish to receive any more books, I can return the shipping statement marked "cancel". If I don't cancel, I will receive 4 brand-new novels every other month and be billed just $4.24 per book in the U.S. or $4.74 per book in Canada, plus 25¢ shipping and handling per book and applicable taxes, if any*. That's a savings of over 20% off the cover price! I understand that accepting the 2 free books and gifts places me under no obligation to buy anything. I can always return a shipment and cancel at any time. Even if I never buy another book, the two free books and gifts are mine to keep forever. 102 IDN ERYA 302 IDN ERYM

Name _____ (PLEASE PRINT) _____

Address _____ Apt. # _____

City _____ State/Prov. _____ Zip/Postal Code _____

Signature (if under 18, a parent or guardian must sign)

Mail to Steeple Hill Reader Service:
IN U.S.A.: P.O. Box 1867, Buffalo, NY 14240-1867
IN CANADA: P.O. Box 609, Fort Erie, Ontario L2A 5X3

Not valid to current subscribers of Love Inspired Historical books.

Want to try two free books from another series?
Call 1-800-873-8635 or visit www.morefreebooks.com

* Terms and prices subject to change without notice. N.Y. residents add applicable sales tax. Canadian residents will be charged applicable provincial taxes and GST. This offer is limited to one order per household. All orders subject to approval. Credit or debit balances in a customer's account(s) may be offset by any other outstanding balance owed by or to the customer. Please allow 4 to 6 weeks for delivery. Offer available while quantities last.

LIH08

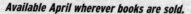

Love Inspired
HISTORICAL

INSPIRATIONAL HISTORICAL ROMANCE

The long journey across the West ended in sorrow for Dani Baxter, a hopeful mail-order bride. Upon arriving in Colorado, she learned that her intended had died suddenly, leaving three young daughters behind. Her late fiancé's brother Beau Morgan proposed they marry—in name only—for the children's sake. But she wondered if even this lost man could somehow find peace in her loving arms.

Look for

The Bounty
Hunter's Bride

by

VICTORIA BYLIN

Available May wherever books are sold.

www.SteepleHill.com

Steeple
Hill®

LIH82788

Love Inspired.
HISTORICAL

INSPIRATIONAL HISTORICAL ROMANCE

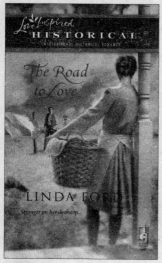

The Long Way Home

In the depths of the Depression, young widow Kate Bradshaw was struggling to hold on to the family farm and raise two small children. She had only her faith to sustain her—until the day drifter Hatcher Jones came walking up that long, lonely road. She longed to make him see that all his wandering had brought him home at last.

Look for

The Road to Love

by

LINDA FORD

Available May wherever books are sold.

Steeple Hill®

www.SteepleHill.com

LIH82787

Love Inspired. HISTORICAL

TITLES AVAILABLE NEXT MONTH

Don't miss these two stories in April

LEGACY OF SECRETS by Sara Mitchell
At the turn of the century, penniless Virginia heiress
Neala Shaw had never felt more alone. A killer was after her,
and former detective and bounty hunter Grayson Faulkner
was her only hope to survive. Together they sought to solve
the mystery of her family's past, so they could have a future.

HEARTS IN THE HIGHLANDS by Ruth Axtell Morren
Maddie Norton had long since resigned herself to her
spinster's lot—until she met Egyptologist Reid Gallagher
in his aunt's London home. His memory-haunted eyes
touched Maddie's heart. Could these two solitary souls
find new life—and love—as one?